SHADOW DUEL

PROF CROFT 9

BRAD MAGNARELLA

Copyright © 2021 by Brad Magnarella

All rights reserved.

No part of this book may be reproduced in any form or by any electronic or mechanical means, including information storage and retrieval systems, without written permission from the author, except for the use of brief quotations in a book review.

Cover design by Damonza.com

THE PROF CROFT SERIES

PREQUELS
Book of Souls
Siren Call

MAIN SERIES
Demon Moon
Blood Deal
Purge City
Death Mage
Black Luck
Power Game
Druid Bond
Night Rune
Shadow Duel
Shadow Deep
Godly Wars
Angel Doom

SPIN-OFFS
Croft & Tabby
Croft & Wesson

MORE COMING!

1

"Thanks again for the lift," I said, gathering my coat and cane.

"Any time." Using the hand controls, Bree-yark finished parking his giant Hummer. "No way was I gonna let you cab it all the way out here."

"My wallet and I appreciate that."

I got out and surveyed the scene. Bree-yark came around to join me, grunting with each step. "What in thunder are we doing here anyway?" he asked, one hand playing visor to his squinting goblin eyes.

"That's what I'd like to know."

A week ago, the citywide wards had picked up an energy discharge suggesting an arrival into our world. I rushed to the location, an alley in the Lower East Side, and found squat. Just the barest trace of dissipating energy. The conjured creature had flamed out, and the amateur caster had gathered his or her implements and scooted. Best case, the fool had been scared straight. Worst, he'd be fool enough to try again.

And here we were, just as the sun was rising over a lovely landfill in central Queens.

My cane tugged toward the valley of garbage, where earth-moving machines were already at work distributing the filth, and clouds of seagulls cried overhead. Minor conjurings typically led me to apartments, back alleys, and the occasional hobby shop, but there was a first time for everything.

And hopefully a last.

The wind shifted, scattering debris over the landfill. "You don't have to join me," I said, fishing a handkerchief from a coat pocket to breathe through. "I shouldn't be long."

"Forget it. We're going in together."

"You're still not a hundred percent."

"Hey, I'm not the one carrying a cane," he joked.

"Well, I wasn't demon-torched in a time catch and left for dead."

Bree-yark waved a hand as if I were referring to a minor bump. But it was a miracle he'd recovered, much less been able to fulfill his duties as my best man a few months later. Of course, we were talking about someone who'd spent nearly a century in the goblin army. He pulled off his collared shirt, his muscled torso a canvas of scars and faded tattoos, and draped it over his rearview mirror.

"Lead the way," he barked.

I donned my trench coat and cinched it tight around my waist, then stuffed the cuffs of my pantlegs into my socks. Stepping over the guardrail, I began picking my way across a slope of rankness. Though I'd never wanted a protective shield more, I couldn't risk it interfering with a hunting spell that was only tenuously locked onto its target. By the weakness of the signal, the target was probably sublimating, but I was still duty-bound to check it out. Plus, the city had been quiet in the last few months and I needed the practice.

Bree-yark powered his stocky four-foot frame in my wake, trying hard to conceal his limp. "What are we even looking for?"

"Shallow nether creature," I said through my handkerchief. "They're usually crablike or buggy. And they always show up hungry, so watch yourself." The thing would have plenty to pick over here, I thought grimly.

"Don't worry. I'm packing goblin steel."

My lead foot plunged from view, and I nearly face-planted into a plastic bag squirming with maggots. Swearing, I drew my muck-covered foot back out. I was going to have plenty to say to the idiot conjurer when we found him—not only for getting me out of bed in the predawn, but for ruining a perfectly good pair of shoes.

"You all right?" Bree-yark asked.

"Fine."

The hunting spell continued to pull us toward a nearby hill. Above, a garbage truck beeped into reverse and sent its cargo spilling down an embankment. We were headed for the fresh stuff, which made me wonder if the creature had climbed into a trash container that had been picked up that morning.

"How are things going with the move?" Bree-yark asked as I started forward again.

"Oh, you know, adjustments all around," I answered through my handkerchief. "Tabitha's not thrilled."

Since the wedding last month, my wife, Ricki, had remained in Brooklyn with her young son so he could finish out the school year. That done, and following some modifications to my West Village loft, they were moving in permanently.

"Aw, give Tabby time," Bree-yark said. "She's used to having you all to herself."

"I think it's more that she's used to having the loft all to herself."

Bree-yark chortled. How he was freely breathing this stuff, I had no idea.

"How are things with Mae?" I asked.

"Top notch. Thinking about popping the question."

I stopped to peer over a shoulder. "No kidding? That's great."

"Well, she's old fashioned, and I'm getting tired of just escorting her to her door at night. I'd like to be walking through it for a change. But, hey, this is just between us. I'm still working up the nerve."

"My lips are sealed," I said, the final word ending on a gag. "How is the smell not strangling you?" I demanded, adjusting my handkerchief.

He shrugged. "When you've lived in a goblin barracks, you've pretty much smelled it all."

As we neared the hill, my cane made small adjustments, guiding me toward a recent spill of garbage. Something skittered beneath the debris. *There you are.* My body hummed as I gathered ambient energy and funneled it toward my mental prism. A shrinking enclosure would do the trick, I decided. Nothing fancy.

"Entrapolarle."

The invocation vibrated down my cane, flashed from the opal end, and manifested as a glimmering sphere around the motion. Newspapers, empty packaging, and yard waste kicked inside the sphere, but I was already upping the power, closing the hardened air around the creature like a fist. In a moment or two, the pressure would pop the thing out of existence and I could go take a shower.

"Hey, Everson?" Bree-yark said.

I recognized the warning in his voice. The debris around us was shifting, and not from the wind.

"What the—?" I managed before the entire hill shot upward, lifting me from my feet.

My sphere burst into sparks, and I landed in a backpedal. Bree-yark caught me, and we craned our necks back, struggling to comprehend what had happened. But as the hillock took shape, so did the situation. What I'd mistaken for a nether creature was, in fact, a piece of something much larger.

"That doesn't look like a bug," Bree-yark said.

Above us, the pile was morphing into a massive humanoid shape.

"It's an animation," I groaned.

"Made of garbage?"

"Apparently so."

Another first, but where in the hell was the magic coming from?

I looked quickly around before refocusing on Stinky. The ends of its upper appendages had morphed into a pair of fists packed with discarded appliance parts and glinting with shards of broken glass.

Wonderful.

Moaning, the animation lurched toward us.

"Stay low," I told Bree-yark, manifesting a shield.

Stinky's descending fist landed against it, driving us a foot into the debris.

Half in anger, half in desperation, I shouted, *"Respingere!"*

Light and force pulsed from the shield, sending the animation back several paces and scattering loose bits of garbage from its body.

"What's the plan for this thing?" Bree-yark asked, climbing from his depression.

I'd managed to keep my handkerchief to my face, and I replied through it now in a muffled voice. "Often it's just a case of overwhelming the forces holding it together. Like so."

I thrust my cane forward and summoned a force bolt. It released with a boom and blew a hole through Stinky's middle. But the animation ignored the assault, garbage climbing up to fill the void again.

We were talking hefty magic.

"Got a plan B?" Bree-yark asked.

I stuffed my hanky into a pocket and drew my cane into sword and staff. As sunlight glinted along the blade's nine runes, I considered activating the second one, for fire. But while the elemental flames could burn through animating magic, the question was *when?* I didn't want to add fire to Stinky's arsenal before he succumbed. I slotted the blade home and dug inside a coat pocket.

"Plan B is to find whatever's animating this thing," I said.

I drew out a premade potion, my charged words igniting tiny gems to activate the potion's encumbering magic. As Stinky lumbered in for another strike, I hurled the open tube at him. It struck his chest in a burst of steam and spilled the potion down his front. Immediately, his motions turned sluggish.

"Think you can keep him occupied?" I asked.

"With pleasure," Bree-yark replied, stalking past me, a drawn blade in each fist.

He evaded Stinky's descending fist and scrambled between his legs. Using the blades like climbing spikes, he scaled the animation's back. Stinky moaned and rotated in a lumbering circle, arms flailing in slower and slower motion.

"Keep it up," I called to Bree-yark, who was hacking away now.

Freed from having to fend off the animation, I activated the hunting spell again. The wards hadn't led me to a creature, I decided, but an object. Stinky was acting as some sort of guardian.

As my cane rattled back to life, I stumbled after its weak pull. After several feet, it aimed straight down at a flattened box of detergent. I kicked the box aside, revealing a section of metal. Swirling energy distorted its dull glow.

Bingo.

I cleared the debris from around it until I was looking at the metallic lid of a box the size of a book. It was dark gray with ornate glyphs running around the border. A light, faint and green, pulsed along the lid's seam. I angled my head several ways, but I couldn't make sense of the symbols. Protections for what was inside, most likely. Just as strange was the magic they exuded. Not evil, and definitely not infernal, but something about it disturbed me. Like it didn't belong here.

I snapped a photo with my flip phone. Then, pulling out a vial of copper filings, I scattered them around the metal box.

"Any time!" Bree-yark shouted.

When I looked over, he was dangling from where Stinky had him by a leg, the animation's other fist drawn back. *Shit.* With no time to finish the protective circle, I aimed my cane down at the object.

"Disfare!" I shouted.

The sudden release of magic blew me onto my back. Off to my left, Stinky exploded, sending Bree-yark somersaulting through the air. He landed nearby, but now the tonnage of garbage that had comprised the animation was raining over us. Stunned, and with no time to invoke a shield, I covered my head in my arms until the final pieces pelted down. Fortunately, I was spared anything heavy.

"You all right?" I called, peering between my elbows.

"Never better," Bree-yark grumbled, shaking a small trash pile from his head.

I checked myself for any magical damage before crawling forward to where I'd last seen the small box. It was still there, the protective energy in the glyphs disorganized from the release. I hovered my cane over the box's lid, tempted to crack it open for a peek, but not while it was still active.

Instead, I retrieved a bag of gray salt from a pocket and placed the box carefully inside. I eyed the strange symbols again before shifting the bag around, burying the box inside the neutralizing medium.

Though its magic was stifled, the box continued to generate uneasy thoughts. What did it hold? How had it ended up in a New York City landfill? Why had the wards misinterpreted its energy? And most importantly, who had been using it? I may not have recognized its magic, but I'd felt its potential.

"Found it?" Bree-yark asked, wiping off his arms as he arrived beside me.

"Yeah." I placed the salt bag in a coat pocket, glanced over, and did a double take. "Whoa, hold still," I said, reaching for his head.

"What?" he barked, leaning away.

I pulled a hypodermic needle from his temple and showed it to him.

"Oh." He rubbed the spot.

Fortunately, goblins were immune to just about every disease known to man, including hepatitis. I tossed the needle aside and eyed our return route across the landfill. I'd lost my handkerchief, but I was more bothered by the item I'd found. Though it intrigued me, too many questions surrounded it.

Questions for a more experienced magic-user, I decided. Questions for the Order.

2

"Hold yer noses, everyone!" Bree-yark called as we entered my loft apartment.

Leaning my cane against the coat rack, I set a plastic shopping bag with my potions and spell implements beside it, hoping I hadn't left something in a coat pocket. I'd swapped my clothes for a spare set I kept in my interplanar cubbyhole and dropped my trench coat off at the cleaners. Bree-yark was wearing the shirt he'd stripped off, and he'd ditched his shoes, but his jeans and my hair still reeked of landfill.

"Morning, Tabitha," I said.

On the window-side divan, a pair of green eyes narrowed from a mound of orange hair.

"Hey, how's my second favorite lady doing?" Bree-yark called cheerfully. The two had worked together on a case the year before that had taken us through Epic Con, and they'd actually gotten along.

"This is *not* the week to ask me that," Tabitha replied testily.

She'd gotten used to me schlepping off to Brooklyn and having the loft mostly to herself. Now, not only was I back full time, but she was having to share what she'd come to consider *her* place with an additional two humans she could barely tolerate. She was about to say more, when our smell reached her. Her nose wrinkled savagely from her bared teeth, and she buried her head in her paws.

"Fucking *hell*," she exclaimed.

"Language," I reminded her. "We have an eight-year-old in the house."

"And a baby on the way," a woman's voice added. "Morning, Bree-yark."

Ricki Serrano Vega Croft appeared from the back bedroom, guiding a very squinty-eyed and bed-headed Tony out in front of her. She was wearing NYPD blues, the swollen belly above her tactical belt almost eight months along.

"Whoa," she said, bringing the back of a hand to her nose. "Tabitha has a point."

"And may I remind you that a feline's nose is forty times more sensitive than a dullard human's," Tabitha said. It was the closest to agreement I'd heard between my wife and cat all week.

Tony, who was still in his Avengers pajamas, seemed not to notice our stink. He managed a sleepy "Morning, Dad, morning, Bree-yark" and climbed onto a chair at the dining room table, head propped in his hands.

We returned the greeting, and I nodded toward the bathroom. "Why don't you go ahead," I told Bree-yark. "Fresh soap and towels are in the closet. Oh, and here." I brought around the hanger of clothes I'd picked up from the cleaners and tossed him a pair of slacks. "The waist should be about your size."

"Thanks, buddy," he said, catching them and padding away.

Ricki blew me a kiss. "I'll save the real thing for after *your* shower."

"Can't blame you," I chuckled. "Mind if Bree-yark joins us for breakfast?"

"Of course not. How'd the hunt go?" she asked, opening a window.

"Oh, it was an adventure. I'll tell you all about it after I drop something off in the lab."

I climbed the ladder to my library/lab, fished the salt-packed metal box from my pocket, and placed it inside a containing circle. As I pushed energy into it, the circle glowed amber. When the containment became self-sustaining, I looked over the box a final time, really curious to hear what the Order would have to say.

Back downstairs, I told Ricki about the landfill and animation. By the time I finished, Tony was staring up at me, wide awake.

"You fought a pile of living garbage?" he asked. "Sweet!"

"It was a lot less sweet than it sounds," I said. "In fact, it stunk."

To his credit, Tony smirked at the dad joke. Ricki tousled her son's hair and placed a bowl of raisin bran in front of him. She'd prepared three more bowls, and I carried mine to the far end of the table. Coffee and juice were usually my job, but she signaled for me to stay put while she took care of those as well.

In the bathroom, Bree-yark was crooning above the sound of the shower going full blast.

"I'm guessing he'll be a while," I said when Ricki returned. "We can go ahead and start."

She took a seat at the opposite head of the table. "So, all of that magic came out of a little box?"

"Yeah, one with engravings, about this size." I showed her with my hands. "Not sure where it came from, though." I chewed slowly, revisiting the angular glyphs, the green glow, the strange currents of magic ...

"All right, I know that look," Ricki said.

I emerged from my thoughts to find her making the let's-hear-it gesture. I glanced over at Tony, but he was engrossed in a puzzle on the back of the cereal box, his dripping spoonful suspended halfway to his mouth.

"It's just that it's magic I've never felt," I said in a lowered voice. "Powerful magic that the wards interpreted as having nether qualities, but I didn't sense that up close. It was completely foreign."

"Dangerous?" she asked, her eyebrows drawing together.

I understood her concern. The mystery box was now in an enclosed space with her son and our future little girl. That had been one of the main discussions about our living arrangements. I would be casting magic and bringing the occasional suspect item back to the loft. On the other hand, the loft featured some of the most powerful protective wards in the city, wards that had taken me years to infuse and strengthen. Unless we found something at a meeting of ley lines, few places in the city would be safer for our family.

"It's isolated in a powerful protective circle now," I assured her. "I called Claudius on the way home. He's arranging for a member of the Order to come get it."

"Claudius?" she said skeptically.

She'd seen him up close enough times to know that the absent-minded old man who conjured portals, undid complex bindings, and answered phones for the Order was hardly someone to be relied upon.

"I'll send him a reminder," I said.

"And you won't be poking at it in the meantime?"

"What, the box?"

My wife raised a stern eyebrow.

"All right, all right," I laughed. "I won't lie, strange magic is as sexy to me as that summer dress you wore in Spain last month, and I *am* tempted to take a peek inside." She cleared her throat at the innuendo and darted her eyes toward Tony, who was still absorbed in the cereal box. "*However,*" I continued, "after my shower, I've got to get to the college." It was the first day of the summer term, and I had two classes to teach.

"I'm going to hold you to that."

I nodded at her NYPD uniform. "What's with the blues?" As a homicide detective, she usually wore a black suit—which went really nicely with her midnight hair and Latin features, I had to say.

"I'm going light duty this week, remember?"

"Oh, that's right," I said, snapping my fingers. "I just didn't realize it involved a wardrobe change."

"I'm helping out another department. That reminds me," she said following a sip of coffee. "Camilla's out sick, so I arranged for another sitter."

"Aww," Tony said, picking up the last part.

"Who?" I asked.

A knock sounded at the door. I started to stand, but Ricki signaled for me to stay put. She answered the door and exchanged a warm greeting with someone. My wards recognized the visitor before I did, muting their defenses.

A moment later, Mae Johnson stepped into view. In the past, she had helped me in her capacity as "nether whisperer" and we'd become as close as a grandmother and grandson. I'd also played a modest role in getting her and Bree-yark together, for which I was proud. Even though it was already eighty degrees out, Mae wore a padded floral coat over her sizable figure. She smiled broadly over the collar.

"Well, hello there, Everson," she said. "Hi, Tony."

"Morning, Mae," I said. "I'd get up and give you a hug, but I don't want to knock you out. Thanks for coming."

"Anytime, hon. I'm just up Ninth."

While the Ninth Avenue part was true enough, she was all the way up in Harlem, which was no quick trip.

"You remember Mae," Ricki said to her son as she closed the door. "She's going to be watching you while your dad and I are at work."

Tony waved at her over the back of his chair, but his eyes were fixed on her pet carrier. Small tentacles writhed through the mesh door.

"Care for some breakfast?" I asked Mae.

"Oh, no, no. I eat breakfast at five, then only carrots and celery till lunchtime. Trying to manage my sugars." She set her carrier and a tote bag down and took two steps toward us before pulling up. "Whoo-eee!" she cried, fanning the air in front of her nose and large glasses. "What did you do, child? Go dumpster diving?"

"Close," I said. "Landfill diving."

"And he fought a garbage monster," Tony bragged.

"Well, it smells like the garbage monster got the best of him this time," Mae said with a laugh. "But you're okay?"

"Excuse me?" Tabitha called. "Some of us are trying to *lounge* over here."

At the sound of her voice, the creature inside the cage chirped excitedly. Mae stooped and opened the door.

"Go on, Buster," she said. "Just don't get into anything that isn't yours."

The lobster-like creature with tentacles for lips skittered out and bee-lined for the divan, where he snapped up at Tabitha playfully.

Groaning, Tabitha flopped onto her other side. "Kill me now."

Bree-yark emerged from the bathroom in a cloud of steam, humming the tune he'd been singing. His thin strands of hair were parted to one side, and he'd tucked his shirt inside the pants, but instead of rolling them up, which I thought was implied when I made the loan, he'd torn the cuffs clean away.

"Well, *this* is a pleasant surprise," Mae said.

Bree-yark stopped suddenly and stammered. "M-Mae. What are you doing here?"

"I'm helping out the Crofts." She walked over, kissed the top of his head, and shook one of his large ears. "How's my handsome gent doing?"

"Nice," he said. "I mean, you—I mean, it's nice to see you too."

He took one of her hands to kiss, then seemed to decide on the other, before grunting and going back to the first. Mae giggled appreciatively, while Ricki and I exchanged questioning looks. Neither of us had ever seen Bree-yark this uneasy around her. Then I remembered his proposal plans. When he'd said he was working up the nerve, he wasn't kidding. The poor guy was scared out of his mind.

"Come on over and have a seat, Bree-yark," I said, attempting to settle him down. "Grab some eats."

"Oh, I'd like that, Everson, but I, ah, I've gotta run."

"Run?" Mae said. "Where do you have to run to at this hour?"

"You're more than welcome to stay and hang out," Ricki said. "I'm sure Tony would like that."

"Yeah!" Tony exclaimed. "We can build a giant cushion fort and then body-bomb it!"

The goblin looked between the four of us, his squash-colored eyes turning bright with panic. When the front door flung open, he let out a sound between a bark and a scream.

My own heart leapt as I shot up. *Intruder?*

Recalling my cane from the stand with a force invocation, I pulled it into sword and staff. Ricki drew her sidearm and aimed it two-handed. Bree-yark took one look at the doorway and fell flat on his back.

3

Colorful lights shimmered over the threshold, silhouetting a large figure. I moved in front of Tony, ley energy storming toward me. Ricki sidestepped with her service weapon for a better angle. Mae knelt beside Bree-yark.

"Who's there?" I demanded, my mind going to the strange box I'd recovered.

In the next moment, the large figure was standing beside the coat rack, blinking around. The light show faded.

I released my breath. "Jesus, Gretchen. Ever heard of knocking?"

Ricki lowered her weapon with a perturbed expression. "Or better yet, calling ahead."

My teacher waved a hand as if such formalities were for lesser beings, released a low burp, and took in the scene. Tony returned her stare, though in curiosity rather than fear. Buster had stopped in his attempts to play with Tabitha, and both were peering back at her. Gretchen's gaze fell to Bree-yark. He had landed spread-eagle, the soles of his splayed feet facing her.

"What's with him?" she asked in the scornful way of an ex.

"You tell us," I growled.

For ten years Gretchen had strung Bree-yark along, manipulating his affections into chores and lonely stretches of house-sitting. I'd convinced him that he could do better about the same time Mae entered his life. I'd also been there during his breakup with Gretchen in her kitchen. She had not taken it well.

"What? You think *I* did that?" she said now.

"You once threatened him with a casserole dish," I reminded her.

"Well, he doesn't need my help to faint. For all their swagger, goblins aren't wired to handle emotional stress, especially in matters of the heart. It short circuits their puny brains."

Mae suspended her efforts to revive Bree-yark and rose. "What did you say about him?"

Gretchen's eyes narrowed over her hooked nose as she gave Mae a thorough up and down. "I merely made an observation. And who are you supposed to be?"

"I'm not *supposed* to be anyone. I'm Mae Johnson, his lady friend. Who are *you*?"

Gretchen thrust out her chin. "Only his former *lover*."

"Well let's keep the emphasis where it belongs," Mae said, stepping forward. "On *former*."

Tabitha's eyes brightened at the prospect of a cat fight, but I stepped between the two large women before things could get ugly. "Whoa, whoa. You're here for the box, right?" I said to Gretchen. "Just give me a sec and I'll grab it."

But Gretchen stared at me as if I were offering to retrieve a dead rat. "What in the world would I want with your box?"

"It's the one I found this morning. Claudius didn't tell you? Last week, the wards detected an energy signature that—"

She showed her palms, some magic in the motion cutting me off. "Enthralling, engrossing, fascinating—all those things, I'm sure. But I'm not here for your box. Good gods, what is that smell?"

"I found the box in a landfill," I said, then added in a mutter, "and if *you're* reacting, it has to be bad."

"Well, here." She waved a hand in annoyance.

A prickling wave broke over me, as if I were being scrubbed with a stiff brush. The sensation sent me into an involuntary jitter—and a full blown dance when it reached my delicate parts. Moments later, the scrubbing stopped, leaving behind a faint afterburn. I touched my hair, slick and parted now. When I sniffed my arm, it smelled like fresh lavender. Gretchen had cast a cleaning spell.

"Thanks," I said thinly.

"And while we're at it…"

With the snap of her fingers, Bree-yark jolted upright. He put one hand to his heart and the other to his head. With Mae's help, he pushed himself to his feet, eyes squinting as if from a bad hangover.

"What in thunder happened?" he grumbled.

"You went woozy, you poor thing." Mae said, guiding him to my reading chair.

"I tend to have that effect on him," Gretchen remarked, arching a provocative eyebrow.

With a head-clearing shake, the goblin looked between Mae and Gretchen. Brightness returned to his eyes, but it wasn't the full-blown look of panic from earlier. The fainting must have reset his nervous system.

"Got anything I can take a shot of, Everson?" he asked.

Ricki nodded that she'd get it and disappeared into the kitchen.

"If you didn't come for the box," I said to Gretchen, "to what do we owe the *pleasure* of your visit?"

"I'll be going away for a while."

I snorted. "Since when do you announce your departures? You usually just disappear."

"Someone has asked me on a trip," she continued, as if I hadn't spoken. "A wonderful man. But it's all very last minute. He's quite..." She circled a hand as she searched for the word. "*Adventurous*. And he can afford to be. He's done extremely well for himself. Anyway, I've told him yes."

I noticed something that had escaped me in the confusion of her arrival: Gretchen had undergone a makeover. Her unruly hair was now a trendy, shoulder-length bob with blond highlights. Gone too was the frumpy housedress. She was wearing a fashionable blazer over a blouse, and straight-leg jeans tucked into a pair of women's boots. Flashes of gold jewelry completed the stylish look. To impress this mystery man? Maybe, but I also noticed she was speaking loudly enough for Bree-yark to hear.

I shook my head. She wasn't doing me any courtesy by announcing her departure; she was trying to make her ex jealous.

"He mentioned a cliffside villa in the Cinque Terre with a *wonderful* ocean view," she was saying. "And then we'll be in Paris for the *Fete de la*—"

"All right, all right," I cut in. "When will you be back?"

Despite my very mixed feelings about Gretchen, the Order still felt she was the best teacher for my stage of development. And when she was around long enough to string a few training sessions together, I actually learned some things. She'd shown me a kickass potion the month before that I couldn't wait to use.

"I'll be back when I'm back," she snapped, annoyed I'd interrupted her itinerary. "But when it comes to someone as tall, strong, and spontaneous as Enzo, a girl never really knows."

"Enzo," Bree-yark repeated dismissively.

A smile spread over Gretchen's glossed lips. She'd gotten the reaction she wanted. "Well, wish me and my new beau the best," she called.

Tabitha made a sour face. "I think we all just wish you'd fu—"

A starburst of colors flashed, causing everyone to flinch back, and Gretchen was gone.

"Whoa. How'd she do that?" Tony asked, the lights lingering in his eyes.

"We're going to need to set some ground rules with her," Ricki said, returning with Bree-yark's shot of liquor.

"Yeah, no kidding," I agreed. "You all right, man?" I asked Bree-yark.

He tilted the shot back and wiped his lips with a leathery forearm of corded muscles.

"I'm fine, guys," he said, noticing we were all watching him. "That happens sometimes."

"Are you sure you're not coming down with something?" Mae reached over to feel his ridged brow. "I can fix you some soup."

He took her hand and folded his around it, in control once more. "I'm grand, Mae. But I really do have to be going. Call you later?" He kissed her cheek and made for the door. "I owe you a pair of pants, Everson."

"Consider them payment for the help," I said.

Mae's concerned gaze lingered as the door closed behind him. "Anything I should be worried about?"

I shook my head. "Nah, he and Gretchen are history."

"I don't care about that mess of a woman," she said, waving a hand. "I mean Bree-yark. I've never seen him behave like that. Even before she turned up he was acting like he couldn't get out of here fast enough."

"Can you blame him?" Tabitha grumbled.

"You spent the morning with him," Mae said to me. "Did he say anything?"

Besides that he's planning on proposing? I thought, but I'd pledged my silence.

"Say anything?" I repeated.

Buster returned and climbed onto Mae's shoulder. She stroked his head absently, making his mouth tentacles wriggle, as she awaited my response. Ricki crossed her arms, a questioning smile slanting her lips.

"Well, nothing stands out," I said. "But he did get into it with a garbage monster, and he was breathing all that foul air. I wouldn't doubt some combination of the two knocked him off his game."

"Maybe," Mae allowed, but her frown suggested she wasn't convinced.

I checked my watch. "Shoot, guys. I've gotta get to the college."

"I should be going too," Ricki said. She stepped into the halo of my sparkling clean scent, courtesy of Gretchen's spell, and kissed me. "You can tell me what's really going on later," she whispered.

Damn.

4

I couldn't help but smile as I strolled down the bustling main hall of Midtown College.

Having spent more than fifteen years here, first as a student, then an adjunct professor, and now fully tenured, it had become as much a part of me as my occult lab back home. Wizarding may have been in my blood, but academia competed hard for those corpuscles. When I was away for any length of time, such as the few weeks between the end of spring term and the start of summer, I felt incomplete. I missed the students and the outdated library and the tedious hours of research.

Hell, I even missed the departmental back-biting.

"Professor Croft?" someone called from behind me.

But if there was one thing I would never, ever miss, it was hearing that voice. For as long as I lived.

I turned to find Professor Snodgrass struggling against the current of student traffic. The diminutive head of my department was wearing a tweed suit, complete with one of his signature bow ties. Beneath his strenuously parted hair, his face was pink and exasperated. He arrived in front of me, out of breath.

"Might want to pace yourself there," I said. "It's only the first day."

"Yes, very amusing," he panted, "but you never submitted your lesson plans. They were due two weeks ago. They need to be approved."

"The course syllabus? I submitted it last month."

He shook his head emphatically. "No, no, the *lesson plans*."

"All right, calm down. Since when do we submit those?"

"Since I instituted the requirement. I have standards to uphold in our department and will be signing off on all plans henceforth. And they're to be *structured* plans. No more extemporaneous story-telling." His eyes narrowed up at me.

Great, we were back to this.

"So you want me to submit a plan for every class I'll be teaching for the next six weeks?" I asked, incredulous.

"That's the new requirement, yes."

"Well, I never got the memo." I resumed my stroll, refusing to let Snodgrass dampen my mood.

He adjusted his oval glasses as he struggled to keep up. "I posted it to our online forum as a priority announcement."

"Ah, there you go. I don't use computers, remember? My magic doesn't play well with anything more complex than a flip phone. Next time print it off and stick it in my mail slot. Problem solved."

"I can't make exceptions for you," he hissed. "Magic or not, you're no different than the other members of our faculty."

"Not even when your cable's out?" I asked innocently.

I was referring to the time he'd hired me to reroute a ley line from his cable box so he and his wife could watch their regency romance serial.

"Well, yes, but that was an isolated—"

"How is Miriam, by the way?" I asked, while he was still on his back heel.

His wife was a wealthy socialite who also happened to be a big fan of mine, even more so after I'd solved their cable issue. To say she wore the pants in the household was putting it mildly. On multiple occasions, I'd observed her using said pants to flog her husband's self-esteem into the turf. I felt a little guilty playing that card now, but if Snodgrass was going to go full dick on day one...

"She's fine," he replied thinly.

"Come to think of it, she mentioned getting together for dinner again. Should we schedule that now, or...?" I let the question linger.

"Have your lesson plans to me by the end of the week," Snodgrass said. "And I stand by what I said. I am not going to make exceptions for you. If you can't use a computer, hire a graduate assistant who can."

At the door to my classroom, I turned suddenly. "Graduate assistant?"

He must have caught something in my reaction because his lips pinched into a grin.

"That's not a suggestion," he decided. "It's a requirement."

Wonderful.

"Good morning," I said to my class of fifteen. "I'm Professor Croft, and this is Intro to Ancient Mythology and Lore. I can't fathom what you're doing here, but welcome anyway."

That always earned a nice ice-breaking chuckle.

"Over the course of this class, we're going to explore the roots of mythology. We're going to talk creation and destruction—fun stuff. We're going to do a comparative analysis of the gods, heroes, and monsters across cultures. We're going to grapple with fundamental questions of good and evil. And we're going to discuss how all of this is relevant today. Indeed, commit yourself to this class, and it *will* change the way you see the world." I paused the appropriate beat. "It could even save your life."

Though that aroused more laughter, I was being much more serious than they knew.

I clapped my hands. "Okay, let's begin with an overview of the next six weeks…"

I had taught the course so many times I could recite the first day material in my sleep. A good thing, because for the next two hours that was pretty much what I did. Sure, I paced and gestured and underscored, my wizard's voice holding the students rapt, but my mind was on Snodgrass's directives.

One of the perks of my position here had been the flexibility. When things got heavy in the wizarding dimensions of my life, I could schedule reading in lieu of a class or do my research at odd hours. As long as the student assessments remained glowing and the grants rolled in, the college board couldn't care less.

But Snodgrass's lesson-plan requirement coupled with having to take on a graduate assistant was going to put a serious crimp in my style. And right when I needed to be allotting more of myself to my home life.

Fortunately, the senior members of the Order were more available for supernatural issues, such as the box I'd recovered. Repairing tears around our world remained their priority, but Arianna could spare personnel now. I was really itching to learn what was inside the box. On the way to class, I'd called Claudius again, and he assured me that he himself would retrieve it later that morning.

"Professor Croft?"

I snapped to and focused on the raised hand. It belonged to a male student who looked way too young to be in college.

"Yes?" I said, afraid I'd spaced out.

"Question. You just mentioned Prometheus as an example of the archetypal trickster, but wouldn't a figure like Loki be more appropriate?"

So I hadn't spaced, but I found something about the young man jarring. And it wasn't just the smoothness of his dusky face or the directness of his question. While the others were still emerging from their mild trances, his eyes were alert, mouth set in a way that could best be described as defiant.

"Your name?" I asked.

"Sven Roe," he replied. "R-O-E."

My mind, which unconsciously went to origins, noted the interesting combo. Sven was Nordic for "young man," and the surname Roe was Celtic, signifying red hair. My student looked neither Nordic nor like a fiery Celt. His intense eyes were as dark as his hair—and they appeared ready for a brain brawl.

This should be interesting.

"All right, Young Man Roe," I said. "Let's hear your argument."

"Prometheus wasn't a pure trickster," he said. "Sure, he deceived Zeus into accepting the bones of sacrificial animals instead of the meat, and he stole fire, but he did both to benefit humans. He loved them more than he did the gods. That makes him a cultural hero. Tricksters are pranksters and rule-breakers, indifferent to humans. They have no concept of right or wrong. They're jerks, basically."

I nodded, duly impressed. "Solid point, but keep in mind that tricksters such as Loki did benefit humankind, even though they may not have intend—"

"And *because* they have no concept of right or wrong," Sven interrupted, "they can't be considered good or evil, much less heroes. They're amoral. That's their defining quality, on par with the pranking, I'd argue."

"Are you sure you should be in intro?" I asked.

The other students laughed, but my adversary wasn't ready to back down.

"It's just that if we're going to throw around terms like 'archetypal trickster,' we need to be clear on what they mean. Prometheus is an alloy at best. He has *way* too much hero in him to be archetypal anything, least of all a trickster."

The students looked between us nervously, but Sven's forwardness didn't bother me. I was thinking of something else.

"Do you happen to be doing work-study this term?" I asked.

Sven's brow furrowed at the sudden change in direction. "Yeah?"

"Have a professor yet?"

"No."

I grinned. "You *do* now."

5

I held Sven after class to discuss the position, and he remained sitting while the students filed out. I closed the door and took a seat on the corner of my desk, wanting to make this seem casual. I may have singled him out for his boldness, but I saw in him an opportunity to turn my problem into a solution.

"So, what's this going to involve?" he asked.

"First, how old are you?"

He rolled his eyes as if he got that question a lot. "I know, I know, I look fifteen, but I'm actually nineteen. Started college while I was still in high school and finished my major studies early. I can show you my ID if you want."

"No, that's fine." I smiled. "What did you study?"

"Dualed in psychology and philosophy."

I let out a low mental whistle. That explained his smarts and debating chops.

"Mythology is more of a hobby," he said. "My mom got me a kid's book of the Greek myths when I was six, and it took off from there. I wasn't trying to be rude earlier. I just think about this stuff a lot."

"No, no, I get it."

I looked him over just long enough for it not to be weird, but there was something about him I couldn't quite put a finger on. Something almost otherworldly, though nothing showed in his aura. I decided it was his youth and intensity and the way his dusky features seemed to blend with his gray hoodie and jeans.

"How are you with computers?" I asked.

He shrugged. "As competent as anyone, I guess."

"Good, I'm going to give you access to our departmental forum. I need you to scan it daily and print off anything that seems relevant."

"Shouldn't be hard."

"I also want you to go through the syllabus and come up with a lesson plan for each class. How you'd instruct it, in other words."

"Isn't that your job?"

"I'm assuming you'd like to teach at some point? This is one way to get experience, not to mention good references." I probably should have felt guiltier than I did about sloughing off my responsibilities to a student, not to mention throwing in a bribe, but the lesson plan requirement was horseshit. I would teach how I always taught. Short of Snodgrass auditing my course, he'd never know.

"Okay," Sven said. "What else?"

"That's it. Have the lesson plans to me by Friday, keep an eye on the forum, and I'll sign whatever you need me to sign for the rest of the term."

I waited for Sven to go on his stoked way—I was basically giving him free tuition money—but he remained seated, eyes narrowing as though weighing the proposal. "What about research assistance?"

I hadn't even considered that, but if he was willing, I could find some things for him to do. "All right, there are a couple papers I'm about to tackle. You could help me gather the source material."

"And two hours of your time a week," he said.

"What? Why?"

"Because I came to Midtown College specifically to learn from you."

Really? I thought. *Because for a second there, I thought you were intent on teaching me.* "Well, that's what my classes are for. But sure, anything else you want to discuss, my office hours are in the syllabus."

"I'd like an exclusive block."

Now I understood what had struck me about him. It wasn't just his intensity or dusky features, though that was part of it. He was a younger, more ambitious version of myself. I couldn't help but chuckle.

What had I gotten myself into?

"Look, Sven, there's really no point. Few students take advantage of my office hours. You could probably have all of them if you wanted. Anytime you want to talk mythology, just stop on in."

"I'm not referring to mythology."

"I'm sorry?"

"I'm not referring to *mythology.*" He looked meaningfully from me to my cane, which I'd leaned beside the desk.

I groaned inwardly. My second life as a magic-user was no secret, not after I'd been the public face of Mayor "Budge" Lowder's eradication program. But that had been two years ago, and the fanfare had died down. I was rarely recognized on the street anymore—thanks in part to an enchantment the Order had installed in the citywide wards. But I still got the occasional student who remembered and wanted more.

"I don't teach that here," I said.

"So where do you teach it?"

"I don't teach it, period."

"Why not?"

"I just don't," I said, pushing power into my wizard's voice.

"The work study requirement for a graduate assistantship is fifteen hours a week. I'm just asking for two."

My voice hadn't fazed him. And here I thought I was so clever selecting the loudest, most brazen student in the class.

"Look, maybe this was a bad idea," I said, standing.

He stood with me, his intense eyes turning earnest. "Professor Croft, I want to learn. I'm ready."

I took a calming breath. "I can't just teach the kind of magic I practice to anyone. Attempting to instruct you, even introducing you to the basic tenets, would be irresponsible and dangerous. Most of my work involves undoing the work of lay casters—and I don't always reach them in time. I've seen way more disembowelments than anyone should have to." Probably oversharing, but I needed to get my point across. He was exactly the kind of kid who would dabble in a powerful spell book. "My kind of magic requires a certain bloodline, understand? And it's not a bloodline you and I share."

Before he could reply, my flip phone rang. I checked the caller. Ricki.

"Hold on a sec," I told Sven, turning and opening the phone. "What's up?"

"You busy?" By her tone, she was asking in her capacity as an NYPD officer versus my wife.

"Not really. Do you need me for something?"

"There's a body we'd like you to take a look at."

"I thought you were on light duty in another department."

"This was Hoffman's call."

"Hoffman asked for me personally?" Though Ricki's partner in Homicide had come around to me and my magic in the last year or so, he'd never brought me in on a case. He usually pushed back.

"Right? Miracles and wonders," she deadpanned. "From what I can gather, the circumstances are unusual, and the vic is some sort of VIP. I'm guessing Hoffman's under pressure to deliver a suspect."

"Just text me the address, and I'll head over."

"How's your first day going?" she asked above the sound of tapping.

"Well, it hasn't been dull," I said, thinking of Snodgrass and then Sven. "Yours?"

"Wish I could say the same. I wasn't built for desk work."

"No, you weren't," I agreed. "But I'm sure the bad guys appreciate the break."

She snorted. "Address is sent."

My phone chimed. "Got it. I'll see you tonight."

As we ended the call, I turned back, surprised to find that Sven had left. A folded note sat on the corner of the desk. I strolled over and opened it.

"I'M READY," he'd written, and underlined for emphasis.

Below, he'd rendered a sigil-enhanced circle using what looked like a silver-flecked grease pencil.

Great, so the kid was already dabbling. Just what I needed.

With a sigh, I carried the note to the waste basket. As it fluttered down, blue light broke around the circle, and the entire note erupted into flames. I startled back, staring as the paper disintegrated into gray ash.

"What the *hell?*"

IT WAS A TRICK, I thought on the cab ride to the address Ricki had sent me. *Had to be.*

I'd raced after Sven, but he'd disappeared into the halls of Midtown College, and I didn't have time to go looking. Which left me searching for explanations. Something in the medium he'd used to draw the circle had clearly held a combustible component. But how in the hell had he ignited it? If he were a magic-user, he could have used a timing sigil, but he wasn't a damned magic-user. I'd checked.

Did he get his hands on a spell book?

It seemed he'd gotten his hands on something, but there was no use blowing a mental gasket trying to figure out what. I would agree to take him on as an "apprentice"—just long enough to learn what he knew and how he knew it.

I blew out my breath. Of all the things to have to deal with the first week of class.

The cab pulled over in front of one of the Upper East Side's palatial apartment buildings. An officer out front escorted me inside. The crime scene was a penthouse on the top level. I smelled the body the minute I stepped off the elevator, a sick, swampy odor you never quite got used to. At the far end of the corridor, beyond a barricade of police tape, Detective Hoffman was waiting for me.

I could tell by the set of his jaw that Ricki had been right. He was under extra pressure to deliver.

"Took you long enough," he growled, lifting the tape as I approached.

"I came as soon as I got the address." I ducked under and turned toward a table of personal protective equipment.

"Just mask and gloves," he said. "Don't bother with the rest. Forensics has already been here." I donned an N-95 mask, which helped blunt the dead-body odor, and pulled on a pair of latex gloves.

"What are we looking at?" I asked.

"A fucking puzzle," he replied, lifting his own mask back in place.

I usually took pleasure in riling him, but today wasn't the day. He was *really* in a mood. His brown polyester suit squeaked as he led the way past an officer stationed at the door. We entered a large penthouse that was surprisingly minimalist. A few pieces of modern furniture, a few potted plants.

Definitely a bachelor pad.

Framed photos lined one wall, all depicting whom I assumed to be the victim. The middle-aged man with copper hair—traversing an icy wall here, standing atop some jungle ruins there—looked like a wealthy adventurer.

"Watch your step," Hoffman said.

Avoiding an evidence marker on the floor, I followed him past a glass wall that looked over north Manhattan. We entered an office. The body was slumped over a desk, head atop forearms, as if the victim were merely taking a break from his open laptop. But the same copper hair I'd seen in the photos was now splayed over a pair of bloated blue hands, the fingernails the bone white of the dead.

"Bear Goldburn, forty-six years old. He was supposed to leave for a week-long conference on Sunday. His housekeeper turned up this morning and found him like this. She swears the alarm was set when she arrived. No signs of forced entry. A search of the body showed no outward signs of trauma."

"I'm guessing it wasn't natural causes?"

"Renal failure, according to the preliminary. His body filled up with piss, basically." Hoffman, who was sweating like a pig, sponged his balding head with a handkerchief.

"Okay... so what am I doing here?" I asked.

He stuffed the kerchief in a pocket and jerked his head. "Take a look."

I followed him around to the rear of the body. Reaching over the chair back, he peeled up the victim's shirt. I winced, expecting something horrible, but the distended skin across his back was intact.

"The examiner hasn't had her say yet, but the medic noticed something unusual. See these bruises?" He circled a finger above a pair of brown-black spots on either side of the victim's lower back.

"Yeah?"

"That's internal bleeding. The medic did a portable ultrasound, and guess what? The man's missing his kidneys."

"Both of them?"

"And without leaving a damned mark. Weren't taken through the front, either. So here's my question for you, Merlin. How could someone snatch two vital organs without making a single cut?"

6

I stood back, regarding the bruises where the man's kidneys had been as recently as Friday.

"Certain spells can accomplish that," I said. "Or a potion made to target organs. Or if we're talking manual removal, a translocation spell. That's where a magic-user creates a small portal, like this..." I signed into the air, opening my interplanar cubby hole. I removed a spell book, showed it to Hoffman, and put it back, signing the portal closed again. "That would eliminate the need for surgery."

"You can put a hole like that into someone's body?" he asked uncomfortably.

"Me, personally?" I shook my head. "Above my paygrade. And that would require two holes, one going into the interplanar space and a second going into the vic's body. We're talking advanced magic and, for organ removal, an absurd degree of precision. Anyone operating at that level would have alerted the senior members of my Order."

"And yet our boy's still dead. You sure it wasn't one of them?"

"I'm sure," I said thinly. "My point is we can probably rule out translocation as a mode of removal. Were there signs of anyone else in the apartment?"

"Nothing obvious. The techs collected a bunch of material for analysis, but that could take a few days. So, go ahead."

"I'm sorry?"

"Go ahead and do what you do." He motioned impatiently. "I need a name."

"I can't guarantee a *name,* but I'll find out what I can. First, let me take a look at this from another perspective."

"Sure," he muttered as I began centering myself. "Take as long as you need. We have all the freaking time in the world."

A roar like an incoming surf covered Hoffman's sarcasm as the astral realm bloomed into view. Colorful streaks crisscrossed the office, while a dull brown halo surrounded Hoffman's portly figure. At the desk, Bear's body appeared as a black void—a life recently lost. I focused where his kidneys had been.

Well, that's interesting...

I had expected to find some lingering sign of a spell or potion's effect. I moved closer, searching for faint symbols in the skin. Nothing. I moved around the body, prompting Hoffman to grunt and step back.

After another minute, more nothing.

I searched the large office, then embarked on a slow walk through the penthouse. I inspected every nuance of light and color. I was looking for anything at that point: a mini distortion, an odd field, some hint of a breach in the material fabric. But the astral layers acted as if life here had been as mundane as ever.

I clenched my jaw in frustration. Even remote spellwork left *some* trace of itself, dammit. Was it a case of me growing rusty, or was the perp just that good?

I recentered myself, this time tapping into my magic, which possessed its own intelligence. Gretchen took special pains to point out just how insignificant mine was in comparison. But the truly great magic-users, like my late father, knew this. They gave themselves over to it, even when the magic's counsel seemed counterintuitive or downright dangerous. Though I had my moments, I'd yet to achieve that level of surrender. And with everything going on in the last month, I'd fallen out of practice.

It took longer than usual, but I soon aligned with my magic's familiar weight and flow. It was shifting without a seeming purpose. I moved to different points of the main room as if that might improve the signal.

"Anything?" Hoffman asked loudly.

My focus evaporated, along with the astral plane, and the penthouse returned to form.

I was preparing to voice my irritation, but I was facing the wall of framed photos, and the one at eye level—"Arctic Expedition 2020"—arrested me. In it, Bear was standing beside a snow sled loaded with gear and posing with a small team.

"He did extreme shit in his free time," Hoffman remarked from behind me.

Bear was holding the pole of a flag planted in the snow, but I didn't recognize the banner. It featured three thick stripes, yellow and blue on each end, and a central white stripe with a line of esoteric symbols.

"What kind of flag is that?"

"The hell should I know?" Hoffman said. "What did you find?"

I took a picture of the photo with my flip phone. By the time Hoffman realized what I'd done, I was already slipping the phone back into a pocket. He looked like he wanted to make an issue of it, but returned to his question.

"What did you find?"

"Vega said he was some sort of VIP?" I asked. "No, listen, this is important."

Hoffman swore under his breath. "Yeah, CEO of Ramsa Inc., the big tech company."

"Weren't they planning to build a production center out in Brooklyn?"

"He and City Hall were thick as thieves on that thing. So guess who's been blowing up my phone?"

"Mayor Lowder?"

"Boy, you're good."

That explained his crankiness. "Did this Goldburn have any enemies?"

"Give me a fucking break, all right? I know how to conduct an investigation."

"If we're looking at a murder-for-hire, it would help me to know who might have done the hiring."

He rolled his eyes. "Enemies? Sure. Every big name in the business. Ramsa has been wiping the floor with them. Then there are the schmoes in his own company who probably wanted his seat. Murder, though?" He made a skeptical face. "The only real person of interest right now is his wife. They separated a couple months ago, that's how come he's living here. I don't know their legal arrangement, but if he had her on a prenup, she may have been looking at a giant goose egg when the divorce went through."

"So she has him killed before that happens," I said, finishing the scenario. "Gets a nice payout through his will, assuming he didn't alter it."

"Might also explain the alarm system. If the murder happened here and not through some *hole*"—he said the word as if he were referring to a human orifice—"then the perp would have needed the system's code to arm it before leaving. She might have known it. Anyway, we've got the security footage from the lobby. We're gonna ID everyone that came and went over the weekend."

"Just the lobby? What about the floor?"

"No cameras on the floors. Something about privacy. A lot of big shots live in the building, and they're not keen on having a record of their visitors. Especially the married ones."

"Has anyone talked to his wife yet?"

Hoffman released a sullen snort. "The second we reached out, she lawyered up. No telling when we'll get anything useful out of her."

"Okay, you asked what I found."

"Yeah?" He looked up expectantly.

"Nothing. But that doesn't mean a dead end," I added as he started into more grumbling. "There's still spellwork I can perform on the body that might give us some clues as to what happened."

"What kind of spellwork? Like bringing him back from the dead?"

It was something I'd actually considered. I'd performed the spell successfully on my first teacher, Lazlo, during my campaign against the Death Mage. But in his advanced decay, Lazlo suffered in ways I couldn't begin to imagine, ways I still felt guilty about. As a mortal, Bear would only fare worse.

"A scrying spell," I answered. "With a few hairs, I may be able to tap into the last moments of his life."

"How long's that going to take?"

"I have to teach an afternoon class, but I'll get started on it right after. I should have something for you by tonight."

Hoffman muttered a few choice words before nodding. "All right, go ahead."

Back in the victim's office, I pulled a small kit from a coat pocket and removed a pair of tweezers. Choosing several hairs at the center of his scalp, I plucked them one at a time, checking for follicles. The little cell clusters would make the spell more potent. When I finished, I searched my pockets for an empty vial.

"Here," Hoffman grunted, producing an evidence bag.

"Thanks." I placed the hairs inside and folded the bag over twice.

"Need anything else before the medical examiner takes over?"

"This should do it." I placed the bag in a pocket and patted it twice. "Let me know if you get anywhere with his wife," I said as we returned toward the front door. "And if you wouldn't mind sharing the results of the tox screen and whatever the examiner finds in his stomach, I'd appreciate it. Could help."

"All right, but I'm counting on you."

"I'm on it," I assured him. "I'll brief my Order too."

I was reaching for the door when Hoffman seized the back of my coat and pulled me around. His mask was down, his mouth in a tight grimace, but the eyes staring up at me had a panicked look. For a second I thought he was going to punch me. Glancing toward the door, he dropped his voice.

"Listen, this is the kind of case they sack detectives over. If I lose my job, I'll never work for the department again. That can't happen. I'm a New Yorker. My entire family's here. My *wife's* entire family's here." He sighed through his squat nose and looked away. "I've done things that probably should've gotten me thrown out. You remember the business with Mr. Moretti. But I don't do that shit anymore. And I know you and me have had our differences, but that's in the past too, far as I'm concerned."

I wasn't sure whether to back away from this sudden outpouring or give him a hug.

"I guess what I'm trying to say is that I've seen enough in this city to know I need you on this. You..." He gestured toward me, then dropped his hand in a kind of resignation. "You get things done."

Wow, that only took three years, I thought.

"Let's keep that streak going then, huh?" I said, clapping his shoulder.

For the first time since I arrived, Hoffman smiled. It wasn't a good look on him, but I'd take it over his constipated face any day.

"C'mon," he said, collecting himself. "I'll have a car take you back to the college."

Out in the corridor, I issued a departing nod that said, *We've got this*, but I wasn't feeling it. Not yet.

I'd never encountered magic that left no trace.

7

"Sorry I'm late," Ricki said.

I met her at the door of our apartment and took her bag. "Tony's already eaten, but I kept our dinner warm." We kissed, and I gave her tummy a hello pat. "I thought you were going on light duty."

"Don't get me started. The filing system I took over was a hot mess. Had to spend half the day organizing just so I could start my assignment. Welcome to the NYPD. Should go better from here."

"Just don't overdo it."

She shot me a look that said, *Appreciate the concern, but let's not revisit the issue.*

Her plan was to work up until the week before her due date, which meant roughly five more weeks. I'd tried to talk her down to two or three, but Dr. Greene took her side, assuring me that as long as my wife felt up to it, the schedule was perfectly normal. When I held fast to my concerns, the doctor assured me those were normal too.

"Well, at least let me draw you a bath after dinner."

"Now you're talking," she said. "And I wouldn't mind swapping shoulder massages before bed."

"Hey, tonight's is on the house."

She walked over to Tony, who was lying on the couch, an open book propped on his stomach. He'd recently discovered C.S. Lewis and was already on the fourth book in *The Chronicles of Narnia*.

"How'd your day go?" She kissed his forehead.

"Great," he answered, turning the page. "Can Mae come again?"

"She said she can cover for as long as Camilla's out," I called from the kitchen.

"Sounds like a yes, then," Ricki said.

"Is no one going to consult me?" Tabitha asked in a languid voice. "It's my domicile much more than *theirs*."

She was lying on her side, her stomach swollen from the extra bowl of goat's milk I'd allowed her. I figured if that was what it took to keep the peace, especially during the transition, I was willing to take on the extra litter work. But I'd underestimated my cat. She shifted her mound around to face me.

"I can't even *begin* to describe the torment they put me through today. Not a single moment's peace. And don't get me started on that horrid little *thing* Mae had running around here, clacking and squealing. It's like Satan himself gave him the perfect pitch to torment a feline's hearing. I spent half the day out on the ledge, I'll have you know."

"Good," I said. "You owed me surveillance hours. I'll credit you an extra two."

"It was more like four. I'll tell you right now, if that thing shows up here again, I'm not going to be so tolerant."

"Leave Buster alone," I said, setting a pair of steaming plates on the table. "He's harmless."

"Oh, I'll make certain of that. Next time he comes I'll have a tasty bisque waiting to boil him in."

Ricki only shook her head as she came over. She'd learned early on not to engage Tabitha when she was in one of her moods, which was most of the time. My wife was years beyond me in that regard.

"Is steak and pasta all right?" I asked, pulling her chair out.

"Mmm, it's like you read our minds," she said as I scooted her in. "How did your classes go?"

"Well, the students seem engaged, but that's pretty standard for day one. I'll let you know in a couple weeks when they're up to their eyeballs in reading. I have a graduate assistant this term."

"I thought you avoided those."

"Yeah, well, we'll see how it goes. He's going to help out with classes and basic research. His name's Sven."

I decided not to get into the exchange with Snodgrass. One, because it was only going to spike my blood pressure, and two, because my solution still felt morally ambiguous. But what about Sven's little magic stunt?

"Problem?" Ricki asked, gesturing with her fork at my furrowed brow.

"Possibly. I was meeting with Sven when you called. He said he had come to Midtown College specifically to learn from me, and he wasn't talking about mythology and lore. He meant my magic."

She raised an eyebrow.

"I discouraged him, of course," I said. "But here's the thing. By the time you and I finished our call, he'd dropped a note on my desk and left. On the note was a casting symbol. It incinerated the paper."

"What, like an attack?"

"No, no, it was harmless. More like he wanted to prove he was ready to be my apprentice."

"The sorcerer's apprentice, huh? Didn't go so well with Mickey. Have you told the Order?"

"Not yet," I said, smiling at the *Fantasia* reference. "I want to see if there's anything really there, first. Could've just been a trick."

"Between that and your landfill expedition, you've had quite a day," she said. "And I haven't even asked about your date with Hoffman."

I gave a dry laugh. "He was right to bring me in, he caught a strange one. A bigshot CEO had his kidneys removed without evidence of surgery or even magic. I'll be doing some spellwork after dinner, trying to figure out what the hell happened—I mean, the *heck* happened," I amended, glancing over at Tony.

"And you two got along?" Ricki asked carefully. She wasn't there to act as a buffer between me and her partner this time.

"Surprisingly, yes. I mean, as much as you can get along with someone like Hoffman. We even had a tender moment at the end. With the profile of the case, he's worried that failure could end his career."

"He's probably right."

"Would you miss him as a partner?"

"Like a bloated appendix, but I'd rather you solved the case."

"After all the crap he's given me over the years, it feels strangely empowering to be wielding the Sword of Damocles over him."

"Well, you won't be wielding it alone," she said with a sly look.

"Huh?"

"Hoffman got me assigned to the case on a part-time basis. From a desk," she added before I could voice my objection. "I'll also be acting as official liaison between the NYPD and one

Everson Croft, consultant. My job is to make sure case info reaches you in a timely manner and vice versa."

"So, what? You're going to be my babysitter?"

"More like your taskmaster." She grinned around her next bite of steak.

"That son of a ... *birch*," I said, shaking my head. "And after our tender moment. Well, welcome to the team."

She accepted my formal handshake, then aimed her knife at my food. "Eat."

My wife, who was dining for two, had already cleaned half her plate, while I'd only managed to twirl a wad of spaghetti onto my fork. The day's trifecta of puzzles—strange box, strange student, and stranger case—had me in full-blown cognitive mode, which tended to distract from my appetite. I began delivering food to mouth, if only so Ricki wouldn't worry about me. Could probably use the brain fuel too.

"You mentioned spellwork," she said as she was finishing up. "Anything I should be worried about?"

"It's just a scrying spell. I got everything set up." I lifted my eyes to indicate the lab. "I also reinforced the wards so no energy can escape the space."

She fell silent.

Sensing a familiar tension, I said, "It'll be fine."

"I know you'd never put us in danger. It's just that I don't entirely get spellwork, so my mind goes to all the things that could go wrong. And a lot of that worry is for you. You've had some close calls."

"You're right," I admitted. "When I was here by myself, flying solo, I took some risks I probably shouldn't have. I mean, if anything went wrong, I was the only one who got smoked, right?" I thought about the time I'd summoned a gatekeeper and nearly been pulled into the in-between realm. "That was my reasoning, anyway. My stupidity would equal my loss, and no one else's."

"What about my meals?" Tabitha called.

I ignored her. "But since you and I became *we,* it's been different. I've taken a lot more care. And now that it's *us,*" I gestured to include her pregnant belly and Tony, "I'm taking even more care. Like 'swaddled in bubble wrap and packaged in foam peanuts' care."

"And I appreciate that," she said, but I could see she still wasn't one-hundred percent assuaged. This was going to take time.

"Want seconds?" I asked, nodding at her plate.

"No, thanks. I think I've eaten enough for the next hour."

I stood and bussed the table. "If it's any consolation, the Order already has the box I found this morning, so that's one less worry in the household."

I'd been relieved to return home to an empty casting circle that afternoon. True to his word, Claudius, who had a direct line to my lab, had portaled in and out. Now, not only was there one less potential hazard in the household, but one less thing to puzzle over. The case and student were plenty.

I scraped the leftovers into Tupperware, rinsed everything off in the sink, and dropped them in the dishwasher.

"Is there anything I can be doing on the case?" Ricki called.

"No, no, you've had a long day, and I promised you a bath and shoulder rub. I'm not going to put you to work."

"Your dinner revived me. And since I'm technically your boss on this, I'm not really asking."

"Well, if you're going to put it that way…" I returned to the table, wiping my hands with a dish towel and slinging it over a shoulder. "Let me send you something." I pulled out my phone and texted her the shot I'd taken of Bear Goldburn's expedition photo. When she received it, she studied the image with a frown.

"Ookay..."

"When I was looking over the penthouse for anomalies, my magic directed me to this picture on his wall. I think I was specifically meant to see the flag. It's not a country flag—I already checked—and the symbols on the center stripe are odd. Not from any of the pictographic alphabets. While Hoffman's rounding up the usual suspects, I'd like to find out what the flag means, whether it's relevant."

"I can isolate it and do an image search."

"Excellent. I'll go ahead and get started on the spell, then. The *extra-safe* spell," I emphasized.

"Aren't you forgetting something? You were going to tell me what was up with Bree-yark."

"Oh, that." I scratched my neck. "Wellll... I sort of took a cone-of-silence vow."

"And you're married now, so that cone extends to your wife."

"Is that how it works?"

She cocked her head. "Do you really need me to explain that to you?"

"All right, all right." I peeked over at Tony and Tabitha, then crouched until I was level with her ear. "He's considering proposing."

She turned to me, eyes wide.

"Yeah, but just *considering*," I emphasized. "You saw what happened this morning. I think Gretchen's actually right about the whole 'emotional stress overwhelming a goblin's nervous system' thing."

"Well, try to work on him. They'd be so good for each other."

"Sure, but if he's going to lay out every time she turns up, maybe they're better off dating."

Tabitha cleared her throat. "And to *whom* are you referring?"

"*No one,*" Ricki and I said simultaneously.

8

I made a couple nervous adjustments to Bear's hair sample, then stood back and looked over the arrangement on my lab floor. Satisfied, I activated and downed a slick wizard potion in the unlikely event something tried to grab me. I did the same with a second potion, this one to strengthen the bond to my casting circle.

As I smacked on the bitter aftertastes, I thought of my promise to my wife.

The scrying spell would be as harmless as I'd sworn—but I'd omitted one detail. With deaths, particularly violent ones, memories stuck to cells. Seers projected those memories onto scrying objects, but since I wasn't a seer, I was left with absorbing the memories, essentially becoming a scrying object myself. More than just observing Bear's final moments, I would be experiencing them.

Safe, yes. Pleasant, not at all.

"Let's get this over with," I muttered.

As my skin turned slippery with the slick wizard potion, I lit a pair of silver candles and killed the light. The candles swelled on either side of a round mirror I'd placed on the floor. Beyond the mirror, three of Bear's hairs lay in a fresh casting circle, a sigil-enhanced line running back to the circle around my feet.

Tapping into my circle, I pushed energy until the symbols glowed the color of heated copper. The warm energy flowed out along the line, haloing the mirror and enclosing the smaller casting circle with the hairs.

A resonant hum took up in the lab. We were connected.

I drew a final potion from my coat, this one an Elixir of Seeing. It was the last of my potent '48 batch, and I choked it down, dregs and all. Almost immediately, I began to feel light and insubstantial.

As a growing pressure built above and between my eyes, I lowered myself to my knees until I was peering at my own reflection. As I began to incant, my mind made a note to do a better shave job along the groove of my neck. But a mist was drifting in from the sides now, occluding the dark swath of bristles.

And here comes the fun part...

I drew a hissing breath as the pressure in the center of my brow turned to a gouge—the opening of my third eye. The sharp pain relented. With it went the mist, and I was suddenly staring into a pair of blue eyes: Bear Goldburn's.

Then, in a terrifying inversion, I *was* him.

A hand clapped down on my shoulder.

I WAS HUNCHED OVER, forearms bracketing a glass of something on a shiny bar. Bourbon, maybe. Hard to tell. Everything in my vision was washed out and dim. Drink, bar, the shelves of bottles opposite me.

The hand that had clapped down squeezed now. It belonged to an arm across my back.

"We just need to give it some air," its owner said. The voice was male, friendly, and familiar to Bear. I wanted to turn, but I was merely an observer in his memories. I sipped my drink and shook my head.

"It's bullshit," I said, slurring the words. "The whole thing is bullshit."

Though drunkenness rolled through me, I was furious. And it was a kind of fury I'd never quite experienced as Everson Croft. I was in the head of someone who lived life at the extreme of extremes. This was a nuclear-rod level fury—contained for now, but hot and dangerous.

"Of course it's bullshit," the voice replied. "But it's too soon. Anything you do now is going to come off as desperate. Guilty, even. We need to assemble the right legal team. We need experts in data. We need a *strategy*."

"Speak for yourself," I said. "I'm ready to kill someone."

Though I was observing, I was also parsing through Bear's memories, trying to piece together what was happening. I couldn't go deep. All I had were his associations to what was happening in that present moment.

The location was a bar in Brooklyn, a place he liked to go when he wanted to drink incognito. It was Friday night. The referenced "bullshit" had to do with his position at Ramsa Inc. There had been an emergency board meeting that day, a vote. He'd been ousted as CEO over something on an email server. Evidence, or at least a strong suggestion, he'd leaked design secrets to a competitor.

The info must not have gone public yet, I thought. *It would have been massive news in the city.*

"Bear, baby," the man said, giving my shoulder another squeeze. "There are ways to come out of this even stronger. Trust me."

"But it's a fucking lie!" I roared.

Several heads turned, but Bear didn't care. He hadn't shared any trade secrets, intentionally or otherwise. Someone had set him up. He had a list of suspects, but it was long and scattered. I couldn't get a precise fix on any of them. Beneath the rage, I began to pick up other emotions now. Betrayal at being undermined by someone he'd apparently trusted. Sadness at being forced from a position he loved.

And fear, profound fear, that he'd lost his wife for good.

"I know," the man spoke softly. "But we need evidence. We need a strategy. That's what I'm trying to tell you."

I turned my head finally. The black man in a blazer and crisp shirt had one of those boyish middle-aged faces that was hard not to like. The edges of his pupils glinted strangely, but Bear's memory supplied a name: Vince Cole, his personal attorney and friend. Vince removed his arm from my back and jerked his thumb toward the door.

"C'mon," he said. "Let's take a drive."

My gaze fell to my unfinished drink, but Vince slid it out of reach.

"Forget about that," he said. "I've got better stuff in the car."

As Everson, red flags were unfurling. The events I was accessing could last seconds or minutes, but not much longer. Bear's death was fast approaching.

I was scared for him—hell, scared for *me*. But as a magic-user, I was also curious. Somehow, someway, Vince was either going to remove Bear's kidneys without making an incision or, more likely, deliver Bear to someone who could. It was like anticipating the secret to a magician's confounding trick.

Bear, of course, didn't have a clue.

I left my drink and staggered after Vince. A pair of guards with heavy armor and weapons flanked the entrance of the bar. Seemed like overkill. Out front, the valet delivered a tank of a car, and Vince helped me into the passenger seat. We talked as he drove, rehashing the events of the last twelve hours. As Everson, I only half listened. I was noting passing landmarks and blurry street signs. Several times, I searched Bear's memories, trying to find the odd flag from the photo, but it wasn't foremost in his thoughts.

"Where's the good stuff?" I asked.

Vince pointed. "Glove compartment."

I opened it and pulled out a small crystalline bottle that held a shot's worth of dark liquid. With the dim effect of the scrying spell, I couldn't see the color. "What is this?" I asked, giving it a clumsy shake.

"Go ahead, you'll thank me."

Though I resisted as Everson—imaginary brake pedal pressed firmly to floorboard—as Bear, I unstoppered the bottle and took an exploratory sip. An alcoholic sweetness washed over my tongue.

"I don't do girlie drinks," I said, replacing the stopper.

"Just wait."

In the next moment, a euphoria washed over me. The dark fury and fear in my head morphed into fluffy clouds bathed in brilliant sunshine. I felt more unburdened, more carefree than I ever had—as Bear *or* Everson.

"Holy shit," I murmured.

Vince grinned over at me. "What'd I tell you?"

I took the rest down in a single swallow. For the next minute, wave after wave of bliss pummeled me, each cycle stronger than the last. They carried away the events of the day, sent them drifting out to a dazzling sea, where they dissolved like salt. I slumped against the door, a mass of pleasure putty.

As the final wave receded, I tried to say something, but I couldn't talk. I tried to roll my head toward Vince, but I couldn't move. I didn't know what I'd drunk, but I didn't care. Ramsa Inc. felt a million miles away.

Did Vince slip him an enchanted roofie? I wondered from a distance.

As warehouses and a large sprawling junkyard zoomed past, I noted we were on the outer edges of Brooklyn. Vince turned into an old garage. WILSON'S BODY SHOP was written in faded paint over an office with broken windows. He drove through an open bay door beside it and past a single, dark pillar. Ahead, the headlights illuminated a clear space. Standing in the center was a gleaming mortician's table.

Oh, fuck no.

"Well, here we are," Vince said cheerfully as the car came to a stop.

I could feel the distant question in Bear's mind, but he still felt too good to care what they were doing at Wilson's Body Shop. As Everson, I considered shaping the Word that would return me to the casting circle.

But I didn't.

I had my perpetrator and crime scene, but if I hung around I could still get means and possibly motive.

My door opened. Lifting me out with surprising strength, Vince slung me over his shoulder. A moment later, he slammed me prone onto the metal table. It was the first shock to the drug's disarming effect, but soon the table was softening beneath me, whispering assurances that made me smile.

Someone began to whistle a tune. Vince? I couldn't tell anymore.

Further down the table, I caught the clinks of instruments being set beside me. A pair of surgical scissors bisected my shirt and jacket in back, and hands ripped them open, exposing bare skin.

"I'm sorry about this, buddy," Vince said. "I really am."

I felt Bear wanting to ask what he meant, but the question broke off in a mental scream.

A blade had punched into my low back, sending blood gushing down my side.

I JERKED UPRIGHT, the word *Retirare!* still ringing in my head. I was back in my lab, propped on my forearms, the reflection in the sweat-spattered mirror mine once more. Panting, I pushed myself back onto my heels.

"Are you all right?"

I blinked around until Ricki's concerned eyes were peering at me over the top rung of the ladder to my lab. I wasn't sure what I felt worse about, the worry I heard in her voice or that I'd caused her to race up a ladder eight months pregnant. But in my shock and confusion, I could only murmur, "I'm good."

"Did something happen to your back?"

I realized I was bracing the spot where the blade had gone in. I pulled my hand away and checked my palm. It was damp, but from the perspiration rolling down the inside of my shirt, not blood.

Ricki climbed up the rest of the way, turned on the light, and guided me to my desk chair.

Though I sat heavily, I was already feeling better. "I'm all right," I assured her. "The spell just takes a minute to wind down."

As I massaged the aching spot, her gaze shifted to the spent casting circles, where a faint haze lingered.

"How did it go?" she asked warily.

"We may have just saved Hoffman's job."

When her eyebrows went up, I nodded.

"I saw who did it and where."

9

"You sure this is the place?" Detective Hoffman asked from behind the wheel.

As his sedan's headlights grew over the body shop, I experienced a jarring sense of déjà vu. The same faded WILSON'S BODY SHOP I'd seen an hour earlier announced the business, only now in living color. The same line of broken windows stared back at us. The only change was that the bay door was now closed.

"One hundred percent," I said.

Hoffman spoke into a walkie-talkie, and a cluster of police vehicles accelerated past us, surrounding the building. As officers stacked and entered, Hoffman pulled to a stop, and he and I got out.

"Still doesn't explain the no cuts," he said. "Or how this Vince Cole placed the body in Goldburn's apartment without anyone seeing."

"On the ride here, Cole gave him a debilitating drink that may have contained a magical component," I said. "I'm betting he also had a potion that could heal wounds post mortem."

It wasn't something I'd considered in Bear's penthouse,

mainly because it didn't make sense. But a lawyer killing Bear for his kidneys didn't make a lot of sense, either—unless he'd been hired. Some spells saw potency boosts with fresh organ ingredients versus the dry stuff. But his own friend?

Could suggest enchantment. Or someone assuming his likeness.

And that was the problem. There were too many possibilities, and I hadn't remained in the spell long enough to narrow them down. I caught my fingers probing the spot where the blade had gone into my back.

"What about getting him back to the apartment?" Hoffman prompted.

"Your guess is as good as mine, though I wouldn't rule out some form of translocation."

Even as Hoffman made a dubious face, I could tell a weight had been lifted from his ponderous shoulders. He had a name now. "If we can establish a murder scene and place Cole in the thick of it," he said, "we should be able to get him to plead, info for lenience. He's a lawyer. He knows the game."

"All clear," an officer's voice crackled over Hoffman's walkie-talkie.

The bay door clattered up. Hoffman snapped on a flashlight and jerked his head for me to follow. "Show me where it happened."

"Straight ahead, in the back," I said.

We walked past the black pillar and around an automotive lift in the floor. But instead of an open area, the flashlight beam played over a pair of toppled filing cabinets and a scatter of old car parts. Hoffman motioned for me and the other officers to stay back as he panned his flashlight across the floor.

"It's covered in a half inch of dust," he growled.

"It's where it happened," I said defensively, replaying the sequence in my head. Car stopping, Cole lifting me out and carrying me over his shoulder, depositing me onto a metal table just past where Hoffman was standing. A table may not have been there now, but the exact same motor oil sign was hanging on the wall.

Hoffman wheeled on me. "Let's forget the fact there's no blood or signs of a clean-up. Where are the damned footprints?" He lashed the beam back toward the entrance. "Where are the fucking tire tracks?"

I opened my mouth to answer, but I couldn't. Unless...

"Rivelare!" I called, my voice echoing throughout the concrete enclosure.

The energy from the invocation rippled from my cane and spread over the floor. And revealed absolutely nothing.

Kneeling, I drew a finger through the dust and brought it to my nose. It wasn't a veiling spell or illusion. The damned stuff was real. As I rose, I caught several officers exchanging smug looks.

"All I can tell you is what his hair showed me," I said lamely.

"What his hair showed you," Hoffman muttered. "From where I'm standing, a turd would've worked just as well."

The officers to my left snickered, but my gaze remained on Hoffman. If my spell had bombed somehow, he came out of this looking a lot worse than me. And professionally, he had a lot more at stake.

Swearing, he paced a circle over what should have been the crime scene. When he arrived at one of the filing cabinets, he sent it clanging into the back wall with a foot. I couldn't help but notice the rectangle it left on the floor, where the cabinet had been lying for months, if not years. It definitely hadn't been there in Bear Goldburn's final moments. Favoring his kicking foot, Hoffman limped back toward me.

"Everyone out!" he shouted.

As the officers returned to their vehicles, he drew himself up in front of me.

"You told me it happened here," he said. "You goddamned *guaranteed* me it happened here."

"I know."

I took a moment to revisit the spell. I'd carefully selected each hair. The execution had been systematic and sound. I knew what I'd experienced. Had someone imbued the cells with false memories?

"Dammit, Croft," he growled. "You owe me more than 'I know.'"

"Look, I told you what I saw," I said, my own voice growing an edge. "That it was wrong suggests someone could be covering their tracks. If so, the same hairs I used for the scrying spell will contain evidence of that deception. It's another potential lead. I'll just need to cast a different spell."

"Are you fucking with me?"

"What are you talking about?"

"Are you trying to get me thrown off the force? Because I'll tell you right now—"

His phone rang, interrupting whatever he was going to say. He drew it from his pocket.

"Hoffman," he answered. "What?" Even in the ambient light of the flashlight hanging at his side, I could see the color drain from his face. "Yes, sir," he said in a stilted voice. "I'm on my way now, sir."

He ended the call and limped toward the door.

I hustled to catch up to him. "What's going on?"

"I ordered Cole taken into custody on your word, and guess what, asshole? He's suing the department for unlawful detention. Now I've got a meeting with the chief." As we neared his car, he scowled at me over a shoulder. "You know, I just thought of something. Find your own ride home."

10

"He really told you to find your own ride?" Ricki asked.

"Thankfully, you're a lot more popular than he is," I said. "After he left, one of the officers swung back to give me a lift."

She shook her head as she turned her sedan onto Sixth Avenue, sunlight glinting from her large shades. It was the next morning, and we were carpooling to the college before she had to start her shift at 1 Police Plaza. Not wanting to wake her when I'd returned home last night, or discuss the case in front of Tony at breakfast, I'd waited until we were in the car to share the perplexing events at Wilson's Body Shop.

"The thing is, he was right to be pissed," I said. "He acted on info I'd told him was high confidence."

"You're a consultant, babe, not God."

"Still, I steered him into a ditch. And that mess with Bear's lawyer...?"

"*Pfft.* That's on Hoffman. I can't think of anything more boneheaded than arresting a *lawyer* without cause, even if Hoffman did get his judge buddy to sign off."

"You think he still has a job?"

"Depends on the chief's mood. Either way, I can guarantee you he got chewed a new one. I'll find out today."

"Well, I can guarantee my services will no longer be needed," I muttered.

"I wouldn't bet on it. If the mayor was in Hoffman's ear, he's in the chief's too. And when it comes to magic, Budge thinks you walk on water. You restored his city to sanity; you kept Yankee Stadium from becoming a bloodbath." She was referring to my campaign against Lich and then my fight to stop the demon-vampire Arnaud from claiming the souls of 50,000 baseball fans for his master. "He's gonna want you on this," she finished.

"We'll see."

"Just watch."

"The thing is, I still can't figure out what happened," I said. "The scrying spell worked. I know what I saw, what I experienced. And when I got home last night, I ran tests on the hairs. There wasn't a scintilla of magic in those cells, meaning they hadn't been manipulated. And yet..." I replayed the moment when Hoffman and I entered the garage to find it hadn't been touched in at least three months, much less three days.

"How much sleep did you get last night?" she asked.

The truth was very little. After failing to find anything on the hairs, I'd remained in my library/lab pondering the puzzle. Kidneys taken, but no outer wounds. Messy crime, but no crime scene. Magic a factor, but no actual magic in evidence. I noodled some tenuous theories, each one slapped down by an authoritative tome on the subject. Around three in the morning, I balled up my final page of scribbled notes and just sat at my desk, trying to think like the killer. If anything had become clear by the time I finished it was that my opponent seemed superior to me in every way.

"Couple hours?" I said.

She looked over with an expression that was equal parts sympathy and dismay. "Have you talked to your Order yet?"

"Yeah," I sighed. "I left a message for Claudius."

"And bringing them in on this is a bad thing, why, exactly?"

"Arianna and the senior members entrusted the city to me. I'm responsible for New York. But in the last twenty-four hours, I've basically told them there are not one, but two cases here I can't handle. The box and now this. It's hard not to feel like I'm failing them, failing the city."

"Don't you think you're being a little hard on yourself? Last fall you stopped a demon apocalypse that involved going through, what, four different time periods, all about to collapse?"

"Five, if you count the Cretaceous Period," I said quietly.

She chuckled at my little joke, even though getting head-butted by a velociraptor had been no picnic. "My point is that I don't know too many people who could have managed that," she said.

"I appreciate the morale boost. Sadly, I don't even have a good lead. And my gut's telling me the perp's not done." My gut was also telling me that the perp had bigger plans for those kidneys.

"Well, I found some info on your mystery flag."

"Oh, yeah?"

"It matched with a few images online, all expeditions to extreme parts of the world. It's the banner for an explorer's club, the Discovery Society. In fact, the flag's symbols are just stylized versions of the two initials with a compass between them. They have a headquarters here in the city, Upper West Side. They also put on presentations for the public, basically anyone interested in that sort of thing."

"An explorer's club, huh?"

Was that what my magic had wanted me to learn about

Bear? I tuned into my magic now, but it was in one of its sullen, contemplative moods. Or maybe that was just me.

"Did you happen to—?"

"See when the next presentation was?" she finished for me. "There's one tonight. I printed off the schedule for the rest of the month."

"You're good. Will you marry me?"

She laughed, something I tried to make her do at least once a day. "Well, here you are, Professor Croft," she said, pulling up to the curb near the entrance closest to my office. "Midtown College."

"Thanks." I lingered a couple extra seconds on our goodbye kiss. I needed it this morning. "Have a great day."

"You too, babe. Try to get done early so you can come home and take a nap."

I didn't have a class until later that morning, but I had a good deal of organizing to accomplish in my office. Waving as Ricki pulled away, I turned in time to see my graduate assistant coming out of the side entrance.

"Sven!" I called.

I may have fumbled the murder and punted on the box, but I could definitely handle the stunt he pulled yesterday. He glanced over enough that I thought he'd seen me, but then he hiked up his dark pack and speed-walked the other way. I called his name again, at the exact moment a bus chose to blast its horn. It also looked as if Sven was wearing earbuds. As I hurried to catch him, my phone intoned in my pocket. I drew it out irritably, ready to silence the thing, but the caller was Claudius.

I flipped it open. "Hello?"

"Ah, yes, Everson? Is this Everson?"

"It's me, Claudius."

I was still trying to keep pace with Sven, or at least keep him in sight, but my satchel was swinging in a way that worked against my forward momentum, and the kid had fifteen years of youth on me.

"Good, good," Claudius breathed, as if he'd dialed a few wrong numbers before reaching me. "Well, I got your message about the murder and passed the information to the Order. They were concerned. Yes, very, *very* concerned." Papers shuffled in the background. "They're, ah, looking into it. Someone should be in touch shortly."

Ahead, Sven reached the street and got the perfect opening to make his way across four lanes of morning traffic. I pulled up beside a bus stop, swearing under my breath, and watched him disappear.

"Everson, you still there?" Claudius asked.

"Yeah, you said someone's going to be in touch." I headed back toward the campus. I'd catch Sven in class Thursday. "How about the box? Any updates?"

The line went quiet for a moment. "I'm sorry ... the box?"

"Yes, Claudius," I said as patiently as I could manage. "The one you picked up yesterday morning?"

"Ah, I was going to ask you about that."

"Sure, what do you want to know?"

"Well, for starters," he said, "what did you do with it?"

"Huh? I left it in the casting circle in my lab. You picked it up yesterday morning."

There were days when Claudius was as sharp as my blade, but this wasn't one of them.

"Yes, that's what I'm trying to tell you. When I arrived in your lab, it wasn't there."

How was that even possible? Already straightening the ID on my lanyard to show the security guard, I pulled open the door to the college. "Did you check all the places you might have set it?" I asked him as the guard nodded and waved me through. "Your desk, your bookshelves, the back of your toilet?"

"Everson," he said, "it wasn't there."

"Well, could you have taken two trips to my lab and, I don't know, neglected to remember the first?" As I accessed the stairs to the second floor, I had to remind myself it wasn't Claudius I was annoyed at, but the Order. How could they have entrusted him with something that important?

"Oh, most definitely not. If I take more than one round trip per day, my regularity goes right out the window."

"Your what?"

"It's one of the side effects of translocation they don't tell you about in the books, and no amount of laxative aid helps. Believe me, I've tried them all. Even Blast Root." He gave a little chuckle, as if I understood.

"All right, no need to paint me a picture."

"This morning, though?" he continued. "Everything dropped on schedule. So definitely just the one trip."

I winced at the visual. "And no one else from the Order would have picked it up?"

"No, no, the other members couldn't be spared. They're working on a stubborn tear that's scarred around the edges. All hands on deck, as they say. Have you considered whether someone in your household moved it? There was an awful lot of hullabaloo when I arrived."

It was a fair question, and I gave it its due. Mae wouldn't have touched it, much less gone up to my lab in the first place. Tony wouldn't have, either. If his being a good kid weren't enough, I'd warded the space against him at Ricki's request. Buster was out too. My magic didn't play nice with nether creatures.

That left Tabitha. I considered her vocal displeasure at having the loft taken over, but hiding the box? When Tabitha did something punitive, she usually let me know that a.) she'd done it, and b.) zero fucks were harmed in the act.

"I can check," I said, "but I doubt it."

"Well, what's the alternative? The box has to be somewhere."

As I approached my office, my thoughts spun a thread between the missing box, Bear's murder, and the question of translocation. A clammy heat spread over my face.

"Let me ask you a hypothetical question," I said. "You can translocate into my lab because we worked out a handshake, right?" I was referring to the pattern of sigils we'd installed so my magic would recognize his, allowing him to come and go. "Could you translocate there even if we hadn't?"

He made a sputtering sound with his lips as if considering different options. "Not without some very unpleasant consequences. But if the magic-user in question were powerful enough, I suppose it's possible."

"Someone came and took the box," I said. "Possibly the same person who murdered Bear Goldburn."

I was unlocking my office when Claudius responded, but I didn't hear him. A fireball erupted from the door, splintering it to pieces and swallowing me in a violent roar.

11

I slammed into the far side of the corridor, pieces of door clattering around me. In the instant before the detonation, I'd sensed a pressure change and invoked a shield. But the explosion arrived too fast. I only managed a flat barrier, and now fire surged around the edges, sending the arms of my coat up in flames.

Teeth grinding, I pushed back against the still-surging fire while struggling to shape the edges of the shield around me. Boosted by some sort of accelerant, the flames disintegrated my sleeves and ripped into skin.

Holy hell, that hurts!

My vision blurred with tears as I focused past the pain and fought for every last joule of energy I could gather. I channeled it all into my protection. A moment later, the shield snapped into place around me. I chased out the oxygen with a Word, withering the flames that wreathed both arms and had begun climbing my pant legs. They dwindled to smoke, but the world around me still looked like an inferno.

If I don't act, I thought, gasping, *it'll take down the entire college.*

Inside the thinning air of my confinement, I shouted, *"Respingere!"*

The pulse that detonated from the shield blew the flames back enough for me to stand and disperse my protection. Scorched air billowed around me. I seized a vial of ice crystals from a coat pocket.

"Ghiaccio!" I bellowed.

A cone of subzero frost shot from the tube and met the returning fire in a great plume of vapor. I forced the fire back further, directing the blast along the doorframe, where the flames were most intense. By the time I'd exhausted the tube, the fire was a paler version of itself.

A second tube finished the job.

Sagging against the wall, I waved the smoke from my face and inspected my throbbing arms. The burns were bad but appeared limited to second degree. Hovering the opal end of my cane over one arm and then the other, I spoke words of healing. Soothing light haloed the weeping areas like gauze.

With a long exhale, I peered around as fire alarms began sounding. Through the thinning smoke, icicles dripped from the splintered doorframe. Thick burn marks curled up the walls alongside patches of frost. In my office, it looked like a bomb had gone off. My desk was flat on its back and books lay everywhere. Shredded papers fluttered down, several on fire, while water dribbled from ceiling sprinklers.

"So much for organizing," I muttered, still half dazed.

I'd been hit by a concussive force, slammed into a wall, and half broiled, and it had all happened fast. Mere seconds from start to finish. Before I could get my bearings, doors opened along the corridor. Professors poked their heads out, some exclaiming over the explosion's aftermath, while others just peered from behind thick lenses like owls. A couple emerged to check on me.

"I don't need an ambulance," I assured them. "I'm okay."

"What's going on out here?" a new voice called above the alarms.

"*Was* okay," I amended.

Professor Snodgrass came bustling through the small congregation. He looked from the damage to me and back.

"What's this?" he demanded. "What did you do?"

"I was nearly cooked. Do you want an apology?"

"No, I want to know who's responsible for the destruction!"

I stared, not believing I'd ever felt sorry for this pathetic piece of—

"Ah, there you are, Everson!" someone called breathlessly. "Are you all right?"

I turned to see Claudius stumbling toward us as if he'd just been ejected from one of his portals. His presence was an immediate comfort. As he approached, he shook what looked like small slugs from his dyed-black hair, organisms from whatever realm he'd transited through. They dissolved as they struck the floor.

"I heard the explosion, and then your line went dead," he said.

He skipped back from something underfoot, then stooped to pick it up. He handed me my flip phone, which had been blown from my ear during the explosion. I opened it, surprised to find it still worked.

"Who are you?" Snodgrass asked Claudius.

The elder member of my order was dressed in a black silk robe that matched his socks and lanky curtains of hair. The fact he'd come straight here, not even sparing a few seconds to step into slippers, moved me. But as far as Snodgrass was concerned, Claudius wasn't faculty or staff, and he sure as hell wasn't a student.

"Oh, ah, I'm an associate of Everson's," he replied. "Well,

friend, I suppose. You'd consider us friends by now, right?" he asked to be sure.

"Of course," I said.

"How did you even get in here?" Snodgrass demanded, his voice verging on shrill.

Claudius adjusted his blue-tinted glasses as he peered down at him. Completing his assessment of the man, he brushed a couple stray slugs from his shoulder in Snodgrass's direction before returning his attention to me.

"So what happened?" he asked.

"Booby trap." Following his example, I sidestepped from Snodgrass. "The moment I turned the key, I felt something trigger, like a sigil. It sucked in the surrounding energy and released it as high-concentration incendiary magic. If I hadn't summoned a shield, you'd be sweeping me into a dust pan."

"Ooh."

He ran his gaze down the door frame, paused at the fractured bore space for the bolt, then squatted and searched along the floor. Realizing he was being ignored, Snodgrass scowled and paced off. The other professors peeled away to evacuate.

"Ah, here it is," Claudius said at last.

I took a knee beside him and squinted at the spot on the floor beside his trembling finger. The fire had burned most of it off, but an edge of the sigil remained, under where the door had been. The instant the door moved, it had triggered. But it was fading now as the magic that once sustained it bled away.

"Hmm, quite powerful," he remarked.

"Any idea where it came from?"

"Drat. I was about to ask you that very question."

I lowered my head for a better look. "Do you see this part?" I traced over the edge of the sigil with a fingernail. "It has the same sharp angle as the patterns on the lid of that box I found."

I pulled out my phone and snapped the fading markings. I

then accessed the photo I'd taken of the box the day before and held it beside the sigil on the floor for Claudius to compare. He frowned as his eyes bounced between the two.

"Yes, yes, I see what you mean."

Claudius's knees popped as he straightened. He cracked his back for good measure.

I considered the fading sigil. If it did match to the box, then it was a safe bet that the same person who translocated into my lab yesterday morning just tried to murder me. Was it the same person who murdered Bear Goldburn and returned his body to the secure penthouse?

"Well, let me take a gander inside the office," Claudius said, "see if there are any more traps."

I warned him to be careful, but he was already picking his way through the destruction. I remained in the corridor and called Ricki. It had only been a few minutes since she'd dropped me off, and she was still driving.

"Miss me already?" she teased.

"I'm going to preface this by saying I'm okay—"

"Why?" she cut in. "What happened?"

"The door to my office was booby-trapped with fire magic. The fire's out, and like I said, I'm fine." I glanced over a bare arm. Though it was still as red as a slapped ham, the wounds were closing. "The fire department is on the way, but I want the Sup Squad taking lead on the investigation." The last thing I needed was someone treating this like a mundane case, something my wife understood as well.

"I'll make the call as soon as we're done. Any idea who set the trap?"

"There might be a connection to the box I found. As well as to Bear Goldburn's murder."

I didn't share the very disturbing idea that someone other

than the Order had removed the box from my lab. The thought of an intruder breaching my protective wards while Tony was home made me sick to my stomach. I could only imagine what it would do to Ricki. I would tell her, just not now.

"Goldburn's murder?" she echoed. "Maybe you're closer to the truth than you thought."

"Maybe," I allowed. "In the meantime, I think it would be a good idea for Mae to take Tony up to her place until we can figure out what's going on."

"Wouldn't the apartment be safer?"

"I don't know who or what we're dealing with. If they came after me here, they could try the same there."

"All right. But you're sure you're okay?"

The *don't bullshit me* came through loud and clear.

"I might've caught on fire a little, but everything's healing. My coat didn't make it, though."

"Coats can be replaced. In fact, I was getting ready to burn that one myself."

"I thought that might cheer you up."

"I could never replace you, though," she said, turning serious again. "I know you're trying to live up to your responsibilities, but you're a target now. Ask for whatever you need, whether it's from the Order, the city, or me. I mean it."

"I hear you, and I will."

By the time police and fire arrived, Claudius had completed his inspection of my office. He padded over in wet socks to where I'd gathered the members of the Sup Squad. Clad in their formidable gear, they'd listened attentively to my account, their leader entering the info on a forearm tablet built into his suit.

"Well," Claudius said, dusting his hands off as he arrived among us. "No more sigils or traps."

"Any evidence of how the perp came or went?" I asked. Though Claudius had forgotten much of his magic over the years, he remained a pro in translocating. He was light years beyond me in that area.

"Some distortions," he replied, "but those probably resulted from the release of energy. I'll need to check back after things settle down."

"And tell the Order I need to talk to them ASAP."

"Of course, of course. Well, if that's all for now, I should probably get back to the phones."

Smiling, Claudius rapped a knuckle against a Sup Squad member's chest plate, then signed an opening into the wall beside him. A force sucked him through the portal and closed again. Though the Squad members looked at one another, they refrained from comment. Another reason I'd wanted them.

As a pair of explosives experts went into the office to begin evidence-collecting, I turned to the Squad leader, a thick-built guy named Trevor whom I'd helped train when he was a member of the Hundred.

"What do you need from me?" I asked.

He pointed out the hallway's cameras. "I arranged for campus security to pull the footage for the last twenty-four hours. Let's go take a look, see if anything stands out."

By the time Trevor and I arrived at the office of campus security, a young woman was awaiting us at a large monitor.

"No activity around the door until about an hour ago," she said.

"Let's see it," Trevor said.

As he and I took positions on either side of her, she started the recording from where it was paused. On the black-and-white feed, a figure entered from screen right. He stopped at my door, knocked, then appeared to try the knob. He brought a backpack around to his front, and for the next minute squatted with his back to the feed, arms working. As I watched, an ice floe grew in my stomach.

"Recognize him?" Trevor asked.

"He's a student here," I said. "His name's Sven Roe."

12

The security officer replayed the segment twice more. The feed was clear enough that there was no doubt. It was Sven's build, Sven's hair, Sven's manner of moving. And he was wearing the dark pack I'd seen over his shoulder that morning. The same pack he'd hiked up and sped away with when I called his name.

"Sven Roe," I repeated. "R-O-E."

I wrote his name in all caps in my notepad, ripped the page out, and handed it to Trevor.

While he called it in, a campus security officer left to pull Sven's registration info. I asked the young woman to fast-forward to the blast. She slowed to quarter speed as my recorded self neared the office, phone to my ear.

"Can you zoom in on the bottom half of the door?" I asked.

Just as the door started to move, I spotted a distortion in the space near my right foot, like a tiny jet of released gas. The sigil triggering. A moment later the fireball was erupting into the corridor.

I had her zoom out again as it enveloped me.

"How did you even survive that?" she asked.

"Magic," I said absently, prompting a surprised laugh.

For the next few seconds, my actions on screen were engulfed in fire and steam. I thought about the incendiary circle Sven had drawn and left on my desk the day before. A brazen act of foreshadowing?

"There's no Sven Roe in the system," the returning officer said. "Are you sure he's a student here?"

Still dazed by the events and revelations of the morning, it took me a moment to process what he'd said. "I guess not," I replied at last. "He showed up to my class, but I never checked to see if he was registered."

"Nothing on him in the city computers either," Trevor said, handing the torn-out page back to me. "Is that the right spelling?"

"That's what he told me," I said, looking over the name I'd written down. I stopped. "Wait a sec." Taking my pencil, I drew a mark through the first E in his name, then crossed out the V right before it. I continued, mouthing the remaining letters. At N, there were no more letters to strike out.

"Son of a bitch," I muttered.

"What is it?" Trevor asked.

Still shaking my head, I wrote another name beneath the one Sven had given me and held it up for Trevor to see.

"'Sven Roe' is just a rearrangement of the letters in my name: 'Everson.'"

So not only had the little shit just tried to burn me to a crisp, he'd been toying with me. I remembered too how he'd offered to show me his ID after class yesterday to prove his age. More toying.

As Trevor took the paper back, I pressed a knuckle to my bottom lip, vaguely aware of how absurd I looked in my sleeveless coat and singed pants. But I was too preoccupied with this latest piece of the puzzle to care.

What was *Sven* doing? How was he mixed up in this? Of course if the perp were assuming different forms—something I'd considered following the scrying spell—Sven wasn't mixed up in anything.

He *was* this.

Could explain why he targeted me.

But no, the timeline was off. He'd shown up in my class *before* the scrying spell—hell, before Hoffman had even brought me in on the case. Had he anticipated my involvement and wanted to keep tabs on me? If so, the incendiary circle may have been meant to pique my interest. Perhaps enough to take him on as an apprentice, even share details of the case I was working on. But with the scrying spell, maybe I'd gotten too close to something he hadn't wanted me to see. Hence the fireball.

Ricki may have been right about that.

"Do we have any leads to his real identity?" Trevor asked.

That was the key question, the one that would begin to unlock the others. But how to find him? With something of his, I could attempt a hunting spell. But the only tangible item I could come up with was the sigil he'd drawn under the door, which had conveniently disappeared right after the attack.

"I'll show you where he sat in my classroom yesterday," I said. "Also, if your explosives guys detect any unusual residue in the office, let me know. The composition could give us a clue." I turned to the young woman at the monitor. "In the meantime, can you follow his movements this morning?"

"Sure, just about everywhere but the classrooms." She was already pulling up an adjacent feed.

"It's a long shot, but look for anything he might have dropped or set down. Also, anyone he talked to."

"And grab a decent image with his face," Trevor put in. "We'll need it to canvas the campus and post for the public."

"Post what for the public?" a gruff voice asked.

Detective Hoffman entered the office in the same crumpled brown suit from the night before, his wreath of hair in disarray. He was also lurching to one side. When he rounded a desk, I saw why. A cumbersome orthopedic boot encased his right foot—the same foot he'd used to kick the filing cabinet at the body shop.

This was *not* going to be pleasant.

"There was an attempt on Everson's life," Trevor started to explain.

"Yeah, yeah." Hoffman waved an irritable hand. "Vega already told me, and I read the report from your team." He trained his bloodshot eyes on me, the fleshy bags underneath confirming the man was on no sleep. "You think this is related to the Goldburn case?"

"Are you still on it?" I asked to be sure.

"Yeah, no thanks to you. Anything I can use here?"

That was surprisingly tame for Hoffman, which suggested my wife was right again: Mayor Lowder wanted to keep me involved.

"Possibly," I hedged, having learned my lesson from the night before. "The sigil that triggered the explosion had markings that I saw on an enchanted box I recovered yesterday."

"So?"

"The same box was stolen from my lab later in the day."

"Whoop-dee-fucking-doo."

"Possibly through translocation," I continued. "And there are strong suggestions translocation was involved in Goldburn's murder."

"Yeah, we'll see about that," he muttered.

"Anyway, this guy who was posing as my student planted the explosive." I pointed to the monitor. "We don't have a name, so Trevor was talking about getting an image of his face to show the public."

I expected some kind of pushback, but Hoffman squinted at the footage for another moment before nodding. "Can you handle the campus canvassing?" he asked Trevor, who replied in the affirmative. "Good, get me two or three good images and send them to my office. They'll take care of the media outreach. Can I have a word, Croft?"

I followed him as he limped to a remote corner of the room.

"All right, look," he said. "For both our sakes, we're just gonna forget about last night. I don't know what kind of magic juice you were tripping on, or what you thought you saw, but here's the thing." He glanced around before lowering his voice. "You might've been onto something with that lawyer friend."

"Oh, yeah?"

"We've been going over the security footage from Goldburn's building. The doorman's helping us, a guy who's been on the job twenty-odd years. Has his own apartment on the ground floor and everything. Anyway, the medical examiner narrowed the time of death to an eight-hour window between Friday night and Saturday morning. All the traffic in and out around that time was other residents and their visitors—the doorman knows 'em by name. No one came for Goldburn, but the camera caught him leaving Friday night. Switch to the outdoor cam, and guess who's picking him up?"

"Vince Cole?" I asked.

"Vince fucking Cole," Hoffman confirmed. "And neither one came back. Based on the examiner's report and the footage, we secured a search warrant for Cole's home and office. A good one this time, one that frigging suit can't fight." Hoffman looked so smug, I hesitated to share what I was thinking.

"You need to be extra sure it was him."

Hoffman's face darkened. "What do you mean?"

"There's magic that can change someone's appearance, make them a dead ringer for someone else. Don't get mad, but a few years ago I used your likeness to enter the Financial District. All it took was a tuft of your hair."

"You did *what?*"

I'd been holding onto that nugget for a while now, and I would be lying if I said a part of me didn't relish his outrage. "My point is that the person you thought you saw on the camera may not have been him."

"Goddamned magic-users," he grumbled. "Well, we've got the warrant anyway. We'll see what turns up."

"What did the tox report say?"

Hoffman shook his head. "No poisons or drugs in his system at the time of death. Just alcohol. High levels, but nothing lethal."

"Stomach contents?"

"Normal dinner-type crap."

"Can you get me a sample?"

His swollen eyes narrowed. "Why?"

"I know you want to forget about the body shop, but what if my scrying spell didn't crap the bed? No, just hear me out. Cole, or someone who's assumed his form, picks up Bear from the apartment. They go to that bar and commiserate over Bear getting canned as CEO. All consistent with the evidence so far, right? When they leave, Cole has Bear drink something. Now what if it had a hallucinogenic effect, making Bear see and experience something that never happened? A scrying spell on a dead person isn't an objective record—it shows what that person *thought* happened. Clearly, Bear was never at the body shop. He ended up somewhere else, where someone took his kidneys and then transported him back to his apartment."

"What's that got to do with his stomach?"

"If I can isolate what he drank, I might be able to track it."

I watched the understanding dawn in Hoffman's spent eyes. "All right, I'll arrange for you to go over there and do your thing.

Might take a couple hours to set up. In the meantime, be looking for this guy."

"Who, Sven?"

"Might be a connection to the case, might not. Either way, we've got him on attempted murder. And if he's throwing around fireballs, I'd damned sure rather it be you chasing him than me. Use the Sup Squad. I've got plenty to follow up on with Cole. Plus, it means I don't have to deal with you."

"Thanks."

He paused to look over my battered, half-torched state. "You all right?"

"Yeah." I gestured to his orthopedic boot. "How about you?"

He lifted it up a couple inches. "Metatarsal fracture. Four to six weeks. But wanna know something funny? Seeing you like this makes me feel a whole lot better about myself." His lips bent into a grin as he set the boot down again.

I snorted. "Glad I could help."

"Now go find the bastard."

13

By the time I swapped for a fresh outfit, the explosives experts completed their analysis of my office. Trevor gave me the report. No conventional material, as expected, but they detected trace amounts of lurite.

"Mean anything to you?" he asked.

I'd helped develop the NYPD's protocols for supernatural investigations and apprehensions. I'd also advised on their particle detection systems and what to look for. To date, the Sup Squad had only needed me a couple times to interpret findings. Both times I had quick answers, but this one was going to take a little research.

"Mind stepping into my temporary office?" I asked, opening the door to the faculty restroom from which I'd just emerged.

Trevor frowned slightly before following. Double-checking to ensure we had it to ourselves, I locked the door and made a sign near the lockers. A small portal opened to my interplanar cubbyhole. I felt inside until my hand closed around an old alchemy book.

"Let's see..." I flipped open the gold-leaf pages of *Verum Alchimia*. "Lurite... Lurite...."

Trevor stood at attention beside the urinals, making a good show of accepting our meeting space as normal.

"Aha," I said, stopping and scanning a half page of dense text. "Lurite is a byproduct of a reaction between silver and red tanzanite." Meaning both had been components in the sigil that produced the fireball.

"What's tanzanite?" he asked.

"A rare mineral, which helps us a lot. The red variety is hard to score."

"Know any suppliers around here?"

"No, but I know someone who might." Out of habit, I reached for my coat, which I usually draped over a stall when I changed in the faculty restroom, but I'd stuffed the burnt thing in the trash can. I checked that I had my cane and plastic bag of spell implements before unlocking the door. "I'm going to take a trip to talk to him. Let me know if the footage or canvassing turns up anything on Sven."

I avoided Snodgrass and the bevy of administrators clucking away outside my office and exited through the front doors of the college. I was scanning the busy street for a cab when a Hummer pulled up, the passenger window sliding down. A familiar goblin's face leaned over the steering wheel.

"Everson!" Bree-yark called.

I hustled to the curb. "Hey, what are you doing here?"

"I tried calling earlier, but I hit your wife's number by mistake. She told me what happened. Thought you might need a little backup."

"I'm just about to run some errands in the city."

"Sounds good," he said. "Get your scrawny butt in here."

Despite the immense stress I was under, I smiled. Once Bree-yark got it into his head he had a friend in need, there was no discouraging him. Plus, he was good company. I climbed into the passenger seat.

"Where to?" he asked, lurching the large vehicle into traffic.

"I'm headed to Chinatown, but let's swing by the cleaners first. I need to pick up the coat I dropped off yesterday."

"You got it. So, a giant fireball, huh?"

"Yeah, helluva way to start the day." I filled him in on what had happened. The visor on my side was down, and as I talked, my gaze kept returning to the mirror. My right eyebrow had been singed to the roots, along with much of the hair on that side of my head. I pushed the visor back up as I finished.

"Just wait'll I get my hands on that little punk," Bree-yark scowled.

"We'll have to find him first. How are *you* doing, by the way?"

"Me? Fine." He glanced over. "Why?"

"We were worried about you yesterday."

"Oh, that." He let out an embarrassed laugh. "Just got a little light headed. My electrolytes have been out of whack. Keep meaning to buy some of that Pedialyte. In fact, I think I clipped a coupon the other day..." He reached across me, his short arm coming a foot shy of the glove compartment.

"Bree-yark, it's me," I said. "You can talk about it if you want."

Grunting, he withdrew his arm. "What's there to talk about?"

"Oh, I don't know. You and Mae?"

He gave me a panicked look. "You didn't tell her, did you?"

"Of course not," I said, relieved he didn't ask if I'd told *anyone*. I doubted he knew the rule about cones of silence extending to spouses. He sat back in his seat and squinted over the steering wheel for the next block.

"I don't know if I've got it in me, Everson," he said at last.

"What, popping the question?"

His arms went rigid as if he were on the verge of a seizure. I moved into position, ready to grab the wheel if he passed out again, but the alarm in his eyes dimmed after another moment, and he raised a hand to show me he was all right. He pounded his chest twice before returning his hand to the wheel.

"Yeah," he rasped. "Popping the question."

"Why, though? You're braver than anyone I've ever met."

"Not with this stuff. In my mind right now I'd rather challenge a wereboar to a pit fight than ask the most wonderful woman on Earth or Faerie to take me as her lawfully wedded. Is that messed up or what?"

"She's not going to say no."

"It's not that. It's the thought of asking. It builds and builds in my head. I start playing out all these scenarios, what could go wrong. My heart gets to racing, and next thing I know, I'm picking myself up off the floor."

"There are potions I could prepare, something to take the edge off."

"But then where would it end? Nah, if I'm going to do this, I need it to be clean, with a clear head. Not that I don't appreciate the offer."

"No, I understand."

"Did you get like this when you asked Ricki?"

"In the leadup I was anxious, yeah. But the moment itself was so spontaneous I forgot about all of that."

I went back to that moment seven months earlier. I had just returned from defeating Malphas, and Blade had just slain the demon-vampire Arnaud Thorne. Except for the fact I'd been in one of Claudius's silk gowns, or that the room smelled faintly of undead, the moment couldn't have been more perfect.

"Spontaneous, huh?" Bree-yark said. "Sort of like ripping a bandage from a dried axe gash?"

"Not the analogy I would have gone with, but ... sort of?"

"Hmm. That's not a bad idea, Everson. Not bad at all."

"The point is to try not to think about it, and when the moment presents itself—"

"Rip!" Bree-yark declared with a triumphant smile.
"Rip," I agreed.

We picked up my coat from the cleaners, then drove back along Central Park South. After almost two years, Mayor Lowder had finally secured the funding to complete his massive restoration project, and for the first time since its napalming, the park to our left was green with freshly planted trees, sod, and other growing things. The full park wouldn't be open for another year, but giant banners reminded everyone that the highly anticipated "Concert on the South Lawn" was scheduled for the following weekend.

Budge was determined to prove that New York City was back, baby.

In Chinatown, I called out the turns to Bree-yark, and before long we were pulling up in front of Mr. Han's Apothecary.

"Feel free to keep the engine running," I told him. "This shouldn't take long."

"Everson, there's a guy out there trying to incinerate you." He gave the emergency brake a decisive tug. "I'm going in too."

"All right, but, you know—"

"Control myself? I'm as calm as a clam."

A sharp *tring* sounded as I opened the door off the busy sidewalk. Bree-yark followed me into the maze-like shop of shelves packed with tonics, dried insects, and medicinal ingredients, much of it good for spell-casting. My gaze lingered on a bag of lizard tongues. *Could actually use some of those.*

"That Mr. Croft?" an accented voice asked.

I finished turning the corner until I was facing the store's socked-in register. Behind it, a late middle-aged man with jet-black hair was counting out money, his collarless shirt buttoned to the chin.

"Hey, Mr. Han," I said. "Been awhile. How are you?"

I'd been a little nervous about coming here. On my last visit, the year before, I'd triggered a smoke golem, and the ensuing battle had destroyed half his shop. I could still see burn marks along the ceiling.

But Mr. Han gave his standard response. "Oh, you know, just chilling out." He finished counting the money, tapped it into neat stacks, and placed the stacks in the register drawer. "How can help you? Have special on blue beetle dung today. Five dollar for five nugget. Vacuum packed. Very, very fresh."

"I might take a look at that. Oh, this is my friend, Bree-yark."

"I hope he is not here to rent room."

The last friend of mine to have rented the room above the shop was Jason, also known as the Blue Wolf, and it ended up trashed and bloodied. "No, Bree-yark's just keeping me company while I run errands."

Mr. Han glanced up, then did a double take. "Ahh. He is goblin, yes?"

"Born and bred," Bree-yark snarled. He turned from the blowfish sac he'd been prodding and pushed up his sleeves. "Got a problem with that?"

My hand met his heaving chest. "Calm as a clam, remember?"

"No problem," Mr. Han said. "Just want to know if you are selling *ears*."

"My ears?"

"I pay top dollar."

"Is that all my kind is to you?" he roared. "Something you can hack parts off of whenever it suits your bottom line?"

"You misunderstood him," I grunted, struggling to restrain his compact body. "He said *hairs*, not *ears*."

"Yes, yes, your *hears*," Mr. Han said, putting more emphasis on the *h* this time. "They are very good medicine for, how you say, the heartbreaking?"

"Oh." Bree-yark stopped. "So... how much we talking?" He smoothed the thin strands atop his head as if readying them for market.

As the two began negotiating, I took a basket and made a quick circuit of the shop, picking out ingredients I was low on as well as several for spells I might need. By the time I returned to the register, Mr. Han was placing Bree-yark's hairs in an envelope and Bree-yark was flipping through a sheaf of small bills.

"How come you never told me about this place?" he asked, smiling with his sharp teeth. "It's a frigging gold mine."

"Best prices in city too," Mr. Han put in.

As he began ringing up my items, I said, "Hey, you wouldn't happen to know where someone can get red tanzanite, do you?"

"Why want red tanzanite?"

I had to be careful. Though you wouldn't have known it to look at him, Mr. Han was connected to various illicit enterprises in the city. The Chinatown mafia, for one. Not only did Mr. Han pay the boss, Bashi, a protection tax, but his son had gotten involved with his White Hand enforcers. Mr. Han also dealt in specialty weapons and ammo, not all of them street legal. Meaning he was tied into at least one, but probably several, underground suppliers. That was all to say there were things Mr. Han couldn't disclose, whether for personal safety or his own personal code, probably both.

"I'm not looking to buy," I said. "I actually—"

"Ninety-two dollar, forty-eight cents," he declared.

"Oh, the bill." I paid him in cash. He took his time counting out the change and placing my items into a paper bag, which he folded over neatly. "So, about that tanzanite," I said. "There are certain spells that only red tanzanite can power, and I guess I'm looking for a place I can score some in an emergency."

"I don't understand you," he said.

"No?"

"Not with all that bullshit in your mouth."

Bree-yark laughed, prompting Mr. Han to slide him a smile.

"It is no problem, Mr. Croft," he said, releasing a hearty laugh himself now. "You want tanzanite, I get it for you. Four hundred dollar, one ounce."

Damn, he wasn't going to give up the supplier.

"Listen," Bree-yark cut in. "Someone tried to blow Everson to shit this morning, and the main ingredient was red tanzanite. We just want to know where the jerkoff got it so we can find and stomp him to a pulp. That's all. The supplier's not gonna be in any trouble, and neither are you. Our lips are sealed. Aren't they, Everson?"

I looked from him to Mr. Han in horror. The man's face had gone blank. What he was thinking, I couldn't begin to guess. I'd never been that blunt about his criminal connections. I braced for him to throw us out of his shop, maybe even order us to never come back.

"I tell you for goblin nails," he said suddenly.

"Bree-yark's fingernails?" I asked to be sure I'd heard right. "I don't know…"

"It's cool," Bree-yark said, then whispered to me, "I'm actually overdue a trim."

Mr. Han disappeared behind a curtain and reappeared with a pair of guillotine clippers. I watched to make sure he was only removing the ends of the spike-shaped talons and not the entire things.

"So what miracle cure are these used for?" Bree-yark asked proudly as Mr. Han placed each nail carefully into a bag.

"Very good for, how you say, the genital itching?"

Bree-yark's ears sagged. "Are they ground into a salve or something?"

"No, no. I glue them to stick."

Bree-yark's ears drooped further as he looked over his remaining nails. "Hear that, Everson? These are going to be scratching someone's junk."

When Mr. Han finished, he placed the clippers and bag of clippings into a fanny pack, then lowered his head. I instinctively did the same. Bree-yark shuffled forward until our brows were nearly touching.

"One place in city have red tanzanite," Mr. Han whispered. "Gowdie's."

"That's the *only* place?" I asked from our huddle. "Are you sure?"

"Yes, only place."

"Crap," I muttered.

14

"What's the problem?" Bree-yark asked as we returned outside.

"Gowdie's is an antique store owned by three sisters. Three *hag* sisters."

"Fae hags?" When I nodded, he said, "Crap is right, then."

Had we been dealing with a mortal supplier, there would have been ways to get the info from them, possibly nothing more than my wizard's voice. But the frigging Gowdies? I sighed. Besides being powerful, the three were nasty as all get out. They made the Gray Sisters from mythology look like the Golden Girls.

"In my novice years of magic-using," I said, "when I didn't know any better, I went to their place looking for a rare root. I still have nightmares."

"Did they threaten you or something?"

"Let's just leave it at 'or something.'" I didn't care to revisit the episode.

When Bree-yark fell silent, I looked over to find him eyeing the scattered bristles on his head in the Hummer's side mirror.

"This is actually a half decent cut," he remarked. "And to think it cures heartbreak."

"Between that and your nails, you've got relationships covered."

"Ha, ha," he deadpanned, stepping back from the mirror. "So, what's the plan?"

I was blowing out my breath when someone exclaimed, "Boys?"

Down the crowded sidewalk, a colorful parasol bobbed toward us. A familiar nose protruded from its shade.

"Speaking of hags," I muttered at the same time Bree-yark said, "What's she doing here?"

Gretchen arrived in front of us, fanning her face with a gloved hand. She was wearing a flowing kaftan dress, and her face looked way too cheerful. "There you are!"

"Aren't you supposed to be on your world tour?" I asked.

"Yes, well, it's been postponed."

"Really. What a shame."

As I'd suspected, there had never been any trip. The whole thing had been a ruse to stoke Bree-yark's jealousy. Having gotten a reaction yesterday, Gretchen was here to push her advantage, but I'd be damned if I was going to allow her another fainting goblin.

"Well, great seeing you," I said. "Now if you'll excuse us, we have work to do."

"Well, *duh*. Why do you think I tracked you down? The Order wants me to assist on your case."

I stopped and turned. "*You're* going to assist?"

She nodded agreeably.

"On my case?"

"Did a bird poop on my face? Why are you looking at me like that?"

"I don't know. Maybe because you've never willingly helped me on any of my cases ever."

"Oh, *pshaw*." She looked over at Bree-yark. "He's always exaggerating."

Bree-yark grunted noncommittally. I could only imagine his discomfort, but I was revisiting my conversation with Claudius from earlier. When he told me someone would be in touch had he meant Gretchen?

"So, how are you going to help?" I asked, testing her.

"For starters, I have some news on the box." She began digging inside her handbag, but it was too awkward with the parasol. "Here, make yourself useful," she snapped, handing me the frilly thing. As I took it, she produced a smartphone and began thumbing the screen clumsily. I'd never seen her use one and suspected she'd bought it as a trendy accessory. Confirming my hunch, she scowled and threw the phone back in her bag.

"The markings on the lid are from an ancient cult in Attica," she said impatiently. "They were devoted to the worship of Hermes."

"The Greek god?"

"Well, I don't mean the little fellow who turns tricks on Forty-second. And you were right—some of the glyphs were designed to animate available material into a guardian. So there's your garbage monster."

"Any clues as to what was inside?"

"Hold your crackers. I have my suspicions, but it could be any number of scripts or old relics. It would've helped if you'd been able to hold onto the thing. I'm still trying to figure out how you let someone snatch it from under your nose." She was becoming the Gretchen I knew and dreaded, but I turned hopeful.

"Any leads?"

"Well, I took a trip to your lab this morning."

"Funny, I didn't get a call that you were coming."

"Don't worry, no one was home." That wasn't the point, but I let it pass. "Well, except for your cat. Moody thing. Anyway, your defenses could use some work, but those don't appear to have been the problem."

"No?" I asked, confused.

"There were no breaches."

"How is that possible?"

She shrugged. "Beats the stuffing out of me. When we find who took it, we can ask them. *I'd* sure like to know."

"Well, you're in luck," I said. "We have a lead, but it takes us through Gowdie's Antiques. I could use your help with them."

"Oh, I'd love to, but..." She peered around and cried, "Yoo-hoo!"

I followed her fluttering fingers to a large man across the street. He was dressed in an Italian suit tailored to show off his broad shoulders and trim waist. A fedora hat shaded his face. When Gretchen waved for him to come over, he lifted the half dozen shopping bags in each hand to indicate his load.

She giggled. "Enzo *insisted* on buying me gifts while we were down here."

"That's Enzo?" I asked.

"Well, I better get going. We have a reservation for lunch. At *Le Bernardin,*" she added, glancing down at Bree-yark. "I'll be in touch."

She reclaimed her parasol, air-kissed my cheeks and then Bree-yark's, and pranced across the street, nearly getting leveled by a taxi. Seeming to remember something, she returned, barely avoiding death a second time.

"Arianna was sorry she couldn't come herself," she said, "but she wanted me to remind you to listen to your magic. She has a lot more faith in you than I do."

She peered over at Bree-yark as if to gauge his reaction a

second time before hustling off. Safely across the street, she took her man's arm, and they disappeared into the crowd beneath the bobbing parasol.

Bree-yark squinted after them.

"Well, that wasn't weird or anything," I said, trying to chuckle it off.

But Bree-yark didn't appear to want to talk about it. He gave his haircut a final critical look in the mirror and turned to me.

"So, what's the call?" he asked.

What choice did we have?

"Gowdie's," I muttered.

15

The sisters' antique store was located in the tidal wetlands on Long Island. Bree-yark pulled into a gravel lot facing a collection of ramshackle buildings on wooden stilts and connected by boardwalks.

"Place reeks," he remarked.

"Probably as much from the sisters as the marsh," I said. "They *are* swamp hags."

"Reminds me of the time my battalion was on a night march through the Ungling Bog. Our lead was this goblin named Cuirk. Strange kid, but had a nose like you wouldn't believe. Anyway, it was coming on midnight when we heard him shout, 'Hag!' The rest of us scattered. Never did see Cuirk again, though a salamander turned up at camp that night and wouldn't leave. Might've been coincidence, but who knows? We kept the thing just in case."

I finished activating a pair of pre-made potions, popped the tops off, and handed one to Bree-yark.

His nostrils wrinkled from the steam. "What's this?"

"Neutralizing potion," I said. "So we don't end up like Cuirk."

He shrugged and drank it down. I grabbed the empty tube

before he could chuck it out the window, then drank mine. As the potion tingled through my system, I checked my coat pockets to ensure my casting implements were at hand before grabbing my cane.

"Ready?"

"Yeah," he grunted, tightening the buckle of a blade strapped to his lower leg.

We made our way down the warped boardwalk toward the main building. Bree-yark was right about the stench. It was rank, and the midday sun on the stagnant water wasn't helping. Farther back in the reeds, I spotted three squat houses. In addition to their antiques business, the sisters also called the swamp home.

At the door to the main building, I stopped between a pair of potted shrubs and turned to Bree-yark. Though he hadn't brought it up on the ride here, I could tell the encounter with Gretchen and her boyfriend had bothered him. And there was no telling how that might manifest under stress.

"Listen, there can't be any outbursts," I said. "Not with these three. I'm going to have my hands full as it is."

"No, no, I get it."

We'd discussed the plan on the way here. It basically amounted to me taking the brunt of their viciousness until they wearied and told me what they wanted in exchange for the info on the tanzanite. That they would want *something* was guaranteed. And it wouldn't be hair and fingernail clippings.

"With any luck, two are out sick today," I muttered.

"No, they're all here," someone said. "Unfortunately."

Bree-yark and I looked around, but we were the only ones on the boardwalk.

"A little lower."

"Holy thunder!" Bree-yark exclaimed, jumping back.

The voice was coming from the scraggly two-foot-tall shrub

to the right of the door. Except for appearing in need of water, it looked commonplace. I couldn't even see where a mouth would go.

I followed Bree-yark's gaze to the other shrub.

"That one doesn't talk," the first shrub said. "Just me."

"Must be some sort of enchanted growth," I told Bree-yark. "Probably for security."

"I wish," the shrub said. "No, a few months back I tried to haggle the sisters down on a rocking chair. They didn't react very well."

"They turned you into this for trying to haggle?" Bree-yark asked, incredulous.

"Well, I was being sort of an ass about it."

"Do you have a name?" I asked.

"Yeah, but I forget it now. Plant memory isn't the same as human. Doug, I think. Anyway, I overheard you talking about the sisters, and I wanted to warn you that they're in a *really* weird mood today. Might want to come back another time."

"Sounds like a good idea," Bree-yark said, jerking his eyes back toward the lot.

"Unfortunately, we need something from them," I said. "And it's time sensitive."

Doug blew out his breath.

"Any advice?" Bree-yark asked.

"You want advice from a shrub? I mean, what can I say? Don't be me?"

I lowered my voice. "Listen, I have friends in the magical community who might be able to restore you."

"Don't bother."

"Are you sure?"

"I may not remember my old life, but I know I'm a lot less stressed. And my buddy over there isn't bad company." Bree-yark and I followed his subtle twist to the other shrub. It was half dead and listing to one side.

"Can we at least get you some water?" Bree-yark asked.

"A Diet Coke would be nice, actually. Haven't had one of those in ages. There's a machine in the store."

"You've got it," I said. "Well... good meeting you, Doug."

"Yeah," Bree-yark put in. "Thanks for the heads-up."

"Be careful," he called.

We entered the main building. The large space was filled from floor to ceiling with furniture, framed paintings, vintage collectibles, and memorabilia—everything well organized and in excellent condition. Thanks to hag magic, it was also illusory. Within a year of the purchase of a Gowdie *rarity*, the varnish would start to thin, the paint to flake, and rot to set in. Just enough time that the buyer would question their own care for the now-worthless item rather than blame the sisters.

The hags also dealt in hard-to-find ingredients, but those they didn't dare sully. Most magic types would spot the fraud and peg the blame where it actually belonged. The sisters hadn't remained in business for more than a century by pissing off customers they couldn't turn into shrubs.

"Place is kinda cool," Bree-yark said. "I mean, enchantments aside."

A door opened in back, and ominous footsteps approached. The elderly sisters had been wearing Victorian-era funeral dresses the last time I was here, so I expected something similar. Definitely not the prep school diva who stepped into view.

She was wearing knee high socks with a pleated green skirt and matching jacket. Blond hair fell neatly past her shoulders. But it was the face that nailed it. Besides the teenage smoothness, she'd mastered the snobbishness. Her two sisters fell in behind her, both similarly glamoured, though with brunette and auburn hair to accent their own bitch-faces.

"Weird is right," Bree-yark muttered, recalling what Doug had said.

The lead hag looked me up and down critically. "Can I *help* you?" she demanded in a Valley Girl voice.

"It's Everson," I said.

She squinted before the angles of her face softened, and she broke into a brilliant smile. "Everson Croft? Where have you been, babe? It's been, like, forevs."

"Grizela," I said in greeting, then nodded at the other two. "Elspeth. Minna." I recognized the hags by their auras, each a slightly different shade of bile. While Grizela continued with her charade of false friendliness, the two sisters rolled their eyes and smacked gum. I didn't know if they'd binged on the rack of VHS teen flicks I'd seen on the way in, but they'd mastered the mannerisms.

"And who's your friend?" Grizela asked.

"I'm Bree-yark," he grunted from behind me.

"A goblin, huh?" Grizela's smile hardened. "If we could boil the wrinkles out, he'd make a killer handbag."

I braced for Bree-yark's return shot, but he wisely stayed back and kept his mouth shut. I was guessing that if the salamander story hadn't sufficiently spooked him, Doug's life as a poorly watered plant had. Grizela's piercing gaze remained on him as if gauging the impact of her arrow before returning to me.

"So," she said. "Where were we?"

"Oh!" Elspeth chimed in. "The last time we were talking about his—"

"Listen," I interrupted, pushing power into my wizard's voice. "I'm looking for someone who may have purchased red tanzanite from you."

The sisters broke into a bout of mocking laughter I hadn't heard since high school.

"Name your price for the info," I pressed. "I'll consider anything within reason."

"You're such a killjoy," Grizela said when she'd gotten control of herself. "Can't we have a *little* fun first?"

"Fine," I said. "Get it out of your systems."

Though she continued to smile, her sparkling eyes narrowed as if I'd just thrown down a challenge.

"Let's rehash, then, shall we?"

"Do your worst," I muttered.

"Heidi Shih," she said. "Poor, poor Heidi. Bloodied her nose, didn't you?"

Heat warmed my cheeks as the sisters broke into laughter. Swamp hags had the ability to dig into someone's psyche and haul out their gravest humiliations. In my case, that was the realm of women. Much like wizarding, I'd bumbled around a lot before finding my stride.

My girlfriend in the eighth grade, Heidi Shih was the first girl I'd ever kissed—or tried to. Buzzing with nerves, I'd ducked in too fast and bumped her nose. Grizela was exaggerating about the bloodied part, but the collision *had* made Heidi's nose swell, effectively ending our three-week relationship.

Elspeth moved onto Sydney Rivera, and then Minna followed with Emily Schultz. The sisters were circling like vipers now, each lashing another episode off her tongue. Some were minor, others downright mortifying. After high school came college: Ally Palmer, Jennifer DeFazio, and Cassidy Cook.

Sinister enchantments accompanied the sisters' words, visuals of my humiliations, but my neutralizing potion blunted them.

"Oh, and then there was Claire Tarbert," Grizela said, forcing the taunt through her growing frustration. "She threw a basket of *potpourri* at you."

This time I laughed along with them. That had been kind of funny.

Regardless, all of this was old material, episodes they'd dug up during my first visit, when I was struggling to balance wizarding with my love life. Convinced I was destined for a lonely future, I'd been vulnerable. Now, not at all. I was married to a solid woman with a child on the way and surrounded by friends.

"Well, if we're done strolling down memory lane," I said, "can we get to business?"

The sisters had begun to withdraw in quasi-defeat when Grizela's eyes lit up. I realized my mistake too late. I'd relaxed my defenses just enough for her to snag the corner of something, dammit. As I struggled to pull it back, Elspeth and Minna joined in, and the three of them dragged it into full view.

"Married?" Elspeth exclaimed.

"Expecting?" Minna added.

"Oh, and that's just the tip," Grizela said. "Poor little Everson is terrified he won't be able to protect them."

"Is that right?" Minna asked, pouting out her lower lip. "The powerful magic-user can't defend his wife and baby girl?"

"There's more!" Elspeth shouted delightedly.

"He's afraid he's going to *hurt* them," Grizela announced.

The sisters broke into a triumphant bout of laughter. Past humiliations I could talk down; present fears and protective instincts were another matter. When my cheeks warmed this time, it wasn't from embarrassment, but rage.

"Oh, don't be upset," Grizela said. "I know how difficult it can be to live up to your parents' *example.*"

A blade of light glinted in her eyes as her enchantment cut through my defenses. Images of my mother placing me in my grandparents' care before falling to the Death Mage. My father plummeting into the nightmare portal created by the Whisperer. And finally, my deepest fear: returning home to an apartment engulfed in flames, with my wife, stepson, and newborn daughter trapped inside.

"Enough!" I boomed.

A blinding light burst from my hand, blasting through the image of my burning apartment and into the shrieking sisters.

16

"Stop!" the sisters screamed beyond the blinding light. "Spare us!"

Furniture crashed, portraits fell, and glass shattered. At one point, piano keys clashed. But I didn't relent. The all-consuming wrath that stormed through my invocation felt good. Really good. I wanted these hags to know the fear and pain they'd inflicted on me.

I upped the power.

"Everson!" Bree-yark called.

When he shouted a second time, I glanced over. The goblin was stalking toward me, head bowed, forearm to his eyes. He began pushing his other hand toward the floor in a "tamp it down" motion. But I was too steeped in my rage lust to listen. The sisters continued to scream. More items broke.

"Still laughing?" I shouted.

Bree-yark seized my arm. "Enough!"

I tensed to shake him off, but stopped myself. Because for a brief, flaring second, I felt something I'd never felt toward Bree-yark before. Anger. I considered the source of light in my outstretched hand. That was wrong too. Nodding, I cycled down my breaths and pulled power back into the object.

"I'm good," I said softly.

The light shrank back inside the glass orb. When the shop returned to view, it looked as if a tornado had visited. The sisters, returned to their true forms, were sprawled among the wreckage. They stared from wart-riddled faces and gray nests of hair, their gnarled fingers in conjuring postures, but I didn't back from them. A shield coupled with the neutralizing potion would negate anything they tried to cast. During their circling and taunting, I'd realized something. While my powers had grown considerably in the last ten years, theirs had stagnated, like the swamp they lived in.

I wasn't afraid of them.

"What *is* that?" Grizela demanded in a piercing voice more befitting a hag.

I looked at the orb in my hand. "It's called an emo ball. It was a gift from my mother."

The purest expression of love, an emo ball was foreign to vile creatures like the hag sisters—and painful. It hadn't even emitted a force. The wreckage was the result of the sisters trying to flee its intense benevolence. Still, I should never have used it in anger. It felt like a desecration of my mother's memory.

"Well, get it away from us!" Minna cried, shaking stained-glass shards from her hair.

Elspeth snarled in agreement as she crawled from under a toppled china cabinet.

I started to pocket the ball before realizing it offered a negotiating advantage. "I'll mute it completely in exchange for the info I came for."

The sisters scowled and attempted a few warding spells, but my protection broke the foul energies apart. Before long, the sisters were stooped and panting. Grizela, the oldest, waved a bone-thin arm.

"Fine," she spat.

I waited for her sisters to consent before drawing the power all the way down. "I'm looking for someone," I said, placing the ball carefully back into a coat pocket. "The person who purchased red tanzanite from here recently."

"Well, that's easy," Grizela said.

"His name was..." Elspeth took up.

"...*no one*," Minna finished.

Still fatigued, the hags could only celebrate my disappointment with rotten-toothed grins. I studied the eyes buried deep inside their shriveled sockets for any signs of deception.

"Are you sure? Who else sells red tanzanite?"

"We're the lone dealer in the Northeast," Minna, the youngest, boasted before Grizela could shush her.

I considered that information. Given the gem's storage requirements, it seemed unlikely Sven would have gotten it from hundreds of miles away. But if he could translocate locally, even into protected spaces, there was another explanation.

"Is any missing?" I asked.

Minna started to answer, but Grizela quieted her this time. "That wasn't the barter," she said. "If you want more, it's going to require more from *you*."

"How about I won't leave your business a one-star review?" I snapped.

"You'll leave us a *five*-star review," Grizela said, "and the praise will be lavish."

"Four stars," I countered. "And the praise will be modest."

The sisters fussed and scowled before nodding that the terms were acceptable.

"I just finished checking our precious stores when you

arrived," Grizela said. "And everything was all there. You lose again."

"You haven't distributed to any other sellers recently?" I asked, needing to cover all bases.

"No." Grizela said. "And that one was free, but oh so worth it for the look on your stupid face."

Sensing they'd clawed back the upper hand, the sisters broke into a gleeful bout of giggling that shook their ragged robes. I sighed. If there was a silver lining, it was that I'd gotten the info I'd come for with very little skin off my back. Though I wasn't relishing having to write them a review.

"Well, thanks," I said, turning.

"We also offer readings," Grizela called.

I was prepared to ignore her, but I paused. Swamp hags possessed powers of seeing, made more potent by their sisterhood. Though they most often used that information to torment, it could also be useful. Especially in a case like mine, where I had no leads on a conjurer who could enter my home at will.

"Oh, yeah?" I said casually. "What kind of reading?"

Shadows gathered over Grizela's face, and her voice turned ominous. "A reading to tell you what you face..."

"...what you fear..." Elspeth took up.

"...what is coming..." Minna said.

"...and how to protect the ones you love," Grizela finished.

They might have been weaker than I'd remembered, but that was a hell of a sales pitch. Worse, they could sense my interest.

"Your price?" I asked.

"A year of your youth," Grizela said.

"Oh, that's all? What a bargain," I said dryly.

Though every instinct of self-preservation in me recoiled, I wanted to test how low they were willing to go. The sisters held firm to one year. I then checked for loopholes. Though not as cunning as pure fae, hags were still plenty cunning.

"Not a year for each of you," I said. "One year *total,* correct?"

"Of course," Grizela replied, but I could sense her disappointment.

"And you mean the vitality of one year, not all of the memories and acquired experiences that go with it."

"Yes," Grizela agreed irritably, "the *vitality* of a single year."

How much was my family's safety worth? I consulted my magic. It shifted around aimlessly for several moments before seeming to issue a subtle nod. But was I just reading into it what I wanted?

"All right," I agreed.

Grizela broke into a crooked smile as the bargain took hold. "This way, then."

She and her sisters shuffled toward the door they'd entered through. They waved their hands en route, sending out smoky green tendrils that circled the shop. Bree-yark barked in surprise as the mess began to straighten up, everything returning to its place and in apparently collectible condition once more.

"Want me to come too?" he whispered. "I brought my iron blade."

"I'll be fine." I fished into a pocket for some change and nodded at the vintage vending machine. "Why don't you get that Diet Coke for Doug?"

"You sure about this reading, Everson?"

"No," I admitted. "But I need info, and the sooner, the better."

His eyes remained on mine, the skin around them lined with worry. The flash of anger I'd felt toward him earlier was now a stone of guilt. I squeezed his shoulder. "I really appreciate your concern, Bree-yark, but I can handle this."

"All right, buddy. Just remember who you're dealing with."

I followed his distrustful gaze back toward the hags. Grizela, who was holding the door open, beckoned me with a wicked finger.

"How can I not?"

A SHORT TIME LATER, I was perched on a wobbly stool, a foul-smelling sack over my head. Grizela claimed that the spell recipe was a family secret, hence the need for the sack. But above the sound of fire crackling in the hags' crowded back kitchen, they were arguing openly over the spell's ingredients.

"No, no, no, it's *cry* of newt," Grizela insisted. "Not *eye* of newt."

And then a few minutes later, "You idiot—you mixed them up! *Toe* of frog and *tongue* of dog!"

Splashes sounded, as if something were being ladled out of the large iron pot and replaced. A rancid smell filled the kitchen.

"Yes, yes," Grizela purred. "Now to color it with a bit of baboon's blood."

If my wife could see me now, I thought dryly. *Blindfolded before a hags' cauldron.*

Other than the sack, I was unbound, cane in hand and pockets heavy with spell items. Even so, I hoped this wasn't a mistake. If the sisters could tell me who I was up against and how to protect my family, the year of youth would be well spent in my mind. Just couldn't make these kinds of bargains on a regular basis.

A greedy hand yanked my hair.

"Hey!" I shouted as the rip of a dull blade released it.

The sisters giggled. "Relax, Everson. We just need a wee bit for the spell."

"That felt like a lot more than a 'wee bit,'" I said, patting the small crater atop my head.

"There we are," Grizela purred. I pictured my hair being scattered into the brew. "Just needs to simmer for another minute now."

The humidity in the kitchen thickened along with the rancid smell, and I started to feel woozy. The sisters took up a cackling chant, which didn't help. I pictured the three huddled around the steaming cauldron. As it became harder to breathe, I began to feel steam-like myself, hovering above their brew.

"Speak!" Grizela shrieked.

The sisters' chant fell lower and then combined into a single voice that sounded like none of theirs. An ancestral spirit known as a Doideag was talking through them. And she didn't seem pleased with the summoning.

"Wretched hags," she muttered. *"Curse of my blood. Why have you called me?"*

"The young man desires a reading," Grizela said. "What he faces..."

"...what he fears..." Elspeth took up.

"...and what is coming," Minna finished.

They'd left out the most important part, how to protect my loved ones. But when I tried to point that out, I couldn't speak.

"What price?" the Doideag spat.

This time, the sisters fell silent.

"Oh, I see. You get his life blood while offering me poison hemlock and filthy wool of bat. Well done, wenches." A flush of pride seemed to enter her scornful voice. *"Let's get this done, then. Villages need plaguing."*

My steam-like form shifted, as if someone were stirring it with a long fingernail.

When the Doideag spoke again, it was in halting verse:

> *The cauldron speaks with foreign tongue*
> *Of ancient wars and songs unsung.*
>
> *Can a children's love restore lost time?*
> *Can the fleet of foot avert the crime?*
>
> *Beware the shadow of many faces,*
> *But fear the master of many places.*
>
> *If ye should fail and war should come,*
> *If seas should boil and lands should run,*
>
> *Allies gather, eleven and one,*
> *And be not afraid of thine own blood.*

There was a finality in the last verse, but she'd yet to address the question that was most important to me.

"How do I protect the ones I love?" I managed.

The Doideag snarled, but then as if compelled by the bargain, she wailed:

> *Wage, young mage, till your final breath,*
> *And come night's fall, accept your death.*

17

The Doideag's voice broke apart into cackling nonsense, and the stool hardened beneath me. The steam in the room thinned, replaced by thick smoke. Coughing, I tugged the sack from my head. The fire had gone out under the cauldron, and the sisters remained huddled in the gushing smoke, their arms linked, humped backs swaying back and forth. I scribbled down the Doideag's words in my notepad before they could escape me.

After another moment, the sisters hacked and came to. They shook their bony arms free from one another.

"What happened?" Minna asked.

Elspeth looked from the cauldron to me and back. "Is it done?"

They had been so entranced, they didn't remember the Doideag speaking through them, much less the reading.

"I trust we fulfilled our end?" Grizela said.

"You did." I waved at the smoke with my notepad before replacing it in my coat pocket. "Now, how do we get my year of youth ... into you three?" I was picturing a very unpleasant ritual, but the sisters laughed.

"It's already done, stupid," Elspeth said.

"Yeah, stupid," Minna cackled, returning with three stone bowls.

"Your hair did a little extra work in here," Grizela said, plunging a ladle into the cauldron.

She filled the bowls, and the three sisters drank greedily, the brew's lumpy brownness running down the sides of their faces. The sight was almost as horrible as the smell. It was time to go. As I stood, I noticed my legs were less robust than when I'd entered the kitchen: my spent year of youth.

"I'll, ah, show myself out," I said.

As if competing to claim more than their four-month share, the sisters ignored me and continued to guzzle noisily. Leaving the kitchen, I backtracked along the crooked corridor toward the main room.

"Don't forget to leave a review!" Grizela called.

"How'd it go?" Bree-yark asked as I returned to the lot.

"About as well as can be expected, I think. Scored some info, but it was in hag speak. Just a matter of making sense of it."

He'd been standing behind the open trunk door with his AK-47. Seeing I wasn't in danger, he returned the weapon to its safe. "Hag speak," he echoed, shaking his head. "Back to the city?"

"Yeah, we're done here."

As he pulled from the lot, I turned on my phone and found a message from Trevor of the Sup Squad.

"Hey, Everson. Just wanted to give an update on the search. Campus security backtracked Sven across a few cameras, but he disappeared in the cafeteria. We've been canvassing the college, but no actionable info yet. Did manage to lift a couple prints from his desk

and we're running them through the databases. We'll also do a facial recognition search on his photo, see what turns up. The news stations will start broadcasting it this afternoon. That's everything from here. I'll keep you posted."

I looked over my notes on the reading, trying to decipher what part of it pertained to Sven. But my gaze kept bouncing to the end. I sat back and massaged my closed eyes.

"Hey, uh, the hags said some things in there," Bree-yark ventured.

"Oh, you mean about my failed relationships?" I gave a dismal laugh. "All true, sadly."

"I mean the part about your wife and daughter. You know, about being worried you couldn't protect them? Afraid you might hurt them? You're always letting me get stuff off my chest. Can I return the favor?"

"I think they're concerns any expecting father has."

"And what was that thing about living up to your parents' example?"

Once again, the horrors of my parents' final moments jagged through me. My mother succumbing to the Death Mage's fire. My father plunging into the abyss. Both acts had been sacrifices meant in part to protect me.

Wage, young mage, till your final breath,
And come night's fall, accept your death.

"Hag speak," I repeated.

"Everson, you gave me a look back there…"

"Yeah," I sighed, revisiting the blistering flash when he'd seized my arm. "I'm sorry. I don't know what got into me, but you're probably right. The hags dragged out some pretty raw stuff."

"Well, if you ever want to talk, the offer stands."

"I know, man." I clapped his thick upper arm. "And I appreciate it."

"What's the wifey gonna say about your bargain back there?"

"Only one way to find out." I opened my phone and called her.

"Hey," she answered. "How's the hunt going?"

"Not great, I'm afraid." I took a few minutes telling her about our visit to Mr. Han's and then the hag sisters'. "And don't get mad, but I kind of, sort of bargained away a year of my youth in exchange for a reading."

"A year of your what?"

I winced. "It wasn't a bad deal, actually, and I think I got some good stuff."

"We'll talk more about that later," she said sternly. "I was just about to call you. There's some case info Hoffman wanted me to share. First, the lawyer has moved to the top of the suspect list. Vince Cole."

"No kidding?"

"The electronic warrant turned up a history of exchanges with Goldburn's wife—arrangements to meet, that sort of thing. Possibly an affair. Given that the victim was last seen alive with Cole, it's pretty damning."

"Is he talking?"

"He admits to meeting with Mrs. Goldburn, but he says they weren't romantic. He was friends with her before the separation, and he claims they were discussing Bear's welfare. He wouldn't get more specific. He also says he picked up Bear that night. They went to the Brooklyn bar you saw in your spell."

I'd been wrong about the body shop, but one for two as far as locations wasn't terrible. And it lined up with my theory that the disabling drink Bear had taken down also contained a hallucinogenic component. That was the dividing line between what Bear actually experienced and what he thought he experienced.

"But Goldburn wasn't sacked as CEO," she said.

"What? Are you sure? Maybe Ramsa Inc. just didn't want that info getting out."

"Cole knew nothing about it, and the board members deny it to the last. There wasn't even a meeting that afternoon."

I revisited Bear's memories. He'd been drunk while replaying the emergency meeting, but I could see it clearly. The accusations and his shouted counteraccusations; the stoic faces of the board members; his fury and betrayal and pain. As far as he knew, he had been sacked. What in the hell was going on?

"Anyway, Cole claims to have dropped him back at the apartment at one a.m. He said Goldburn had a key to a personnel entrance off the alleyway. He'd use it when he'd come home blitzed and didn't want to be observed, given his high profile and everything."

I refocused. "And the entrance checked out?"

"It leads to a service elevator. Goldburn could have made the entire trip back to his penthouse without being seen. Earlier footage shows a similar pattern—him leaving at night and not reappearing on the security cams until he left again the next day. Cole denies accompanying him up to the penthouse, says he went straight home. Cell tower data will establish that one way or the other."

There seemed to go my translocation theory, which didn't make me feel better or worse. Just more confused. Had Vince Cole or a lookalike done the deed in his apartment?

"Is he in custody?" I asked.

"No, nothing connects him to the actual murder. Hoffman made an appointment for you to check out the stomach contents."

"What time?"

"Can you be at the medical examiner's in thirty? Hoffman's freaking out. He needs something to stick on Cole."

"Sure, just one more thing." Confessing my bargain with the hag sisters wasn't the only reason I'd called. My thoughts turned now to what Gretchen had told me about the breach in my lab, or lack thereof. "I was thinking it might be safest if you and Tony stay at your brother's, at least for tonight."

"Carlos's?"

I didn't like it any more than she did, especially since Carlos still considered me a terrible choice for his sister and her son. His main issue was and remained the extra danger I introduced to their lives. And now here I was, suggesting he look after them because of the extra danger I'd introduced to their lives.

"That box I brought home yesterday?" I said. "Gretchen thinks it's connected to some sort of cult worship for the Greek god Hermes. Someone took it from my lab, and it wasn't Claudius."

"Someone got into the apartment?"

"I can't think of another explanation."

"You don't think Claudius took it and just forgot?"

"I already asked him, and he has this ... biological system for working out how many times he translocates. He says he only came for it the one time and the box wasn't there. No one else would have touched it."

My wife fell silent. "I'll arrange for Tony to spend the week with his cousins," she said at last, meaning her other brothers, who lived in the Bronx. That was some relief; those three had no problems with me.

"But I'm not leaving," she finished.

"Ricki, if someone got into my lab, the apartment isn't safe."

"Which is why I'm not leaving you there alone. We'll do whatever we need to do, but it's going to be together. This marriage thing isn't a one-way street, buddy. I took the same vows as you."

"And I thank God for that every day, but we need to—"

"But nothing. That's it. If you're staying, I'm staying."

What could I say? "Then I should probably solve this case."

"You will," she said, her voice relaxing a little. "You always do. Let me know what you need from the NYPD. More importantly, tell me what you need from me."

Amid the wreckage of my fallen theories, I thought about Gretchen's reminder that I listen to my magic. It had already shown me the flag in Bear Goldburn's photo, which Ricki learned belonged to an explorer's club in the city.

"What time is that presentation at the Discovery Society?" I asked her.

18

The medical examiner's was located in the Kips Bay neighborhood. Bree-yark dropped me off and went in search of a late lunch. He offered to bring me back something, and I agreed, not considering what my appetite would be like when I finished.

By the time I arrived in the cold lab, portions of Bear's stomach contents had been separated into two metal bowls—one holding solids, the other a dark liquid. Even though I was double-masked, the smell hit me in the throat.

Hoffman must have told the examiner I needed to work in private because after confirming I had everything I needed, she disappeared from sight.

I pushed the bowl of solids aside and stared at the liquid for several moments. I was much less confident than when I'd last talked to Hoffman. At the time, I believed that whatever Bear had chugged in Cole's car contained a magical hallucinogen. But after Ricki's updates, I didn't know what to believe. The entire timeline of Bear's final day seemed a mad patchwork of fact and fantasy.

Maybe this'll clear things up somehow.

Signing into the air, I conjured my cubbyhole and pulled out an alchemy kit. I then went to work, titrating the stomach liquid into a row of glass tubes and adding solutions from various dropper bottles.

On the fourth tube, the liquid began to smoke.

"Well, hello there, lovely," I whispered, lifting the tube to eye level.

The particular solution was meant to react with rose oil, a base ingredient in certain potions. A small nugget was taking shape at the tube's bottom. Enough to cast on?

I replaced the tube in its holder and quickly built a casting circle. Using surgical tweezers, I retrieved the crumbly pink nugget and set it at the circle's center. A couple incantations later, and my cane was inhaling the oil's essence.

The ingredient may have been common, but once rendered in a potion, it held the caster's signature. If there was any more potion in the city, my hunting spell would locate it. We'd have our perp.

My cane wiggled toward the stomach liquid. I crossed the room away from the work station, oriented the spell to the outside, and waited for a direction. My cane responded by going still.

Frowning, I rechecked it. The essence was there, but it was too weak, dammit. The hunting spell wasn't going to give me a direction. Like a transponder, it would only tell me if the potion were close. I tested to see how close by pacing slowly back toward the work station. When my cane wiggled again, I eyed the distance.

In a city of roughly three hundred square miles, I only had to come within fifteen feet of the potion for a hit.

Hoffman was going to love that.

"So what now?" Bree-yark asked as we pulled in front of my apartment.

I peered toward my fourth floor loft and sighed. "I start building golems."

The thought alone exhausted me. My plan was to shape and animate four lumps of clay—about all I could manage—infuse them with the hunting spell, and deploy them throughout the city. It was a long shot, but I'd promised Hoffman. Maybe one would get lucky, I told him. Which was about as likely as one getting a Broadway audition.

"Need any help?" Bree-yark asked.

"It's nice of you to offer, but besides being a one-wizard job, it's super tedious. And you've helped me a ton already."

"Well, call if you head out again."

"What are you going to be doing?"

"Me?" He made a popping sound with his lips. "Dunno, might go catch a movie."

"You know, Tony is at Mae's... I'm sure he'd love to see you."

"They're up there, huh?" By the way he said it, I could tell he was buying time to think up an excuse.

"What is it?"

"I might've told Mae I was gonna be busy all day. She called this morning and asked if I wanted to join her at your place," he explained. "I was about to say yes, but I got the shakes. It's the damned proposal thing."

"Is that why you came looking for me?" I asked, remembering how he'd intercepted me at the college. "To give yourself an excuse to be doing something else?"

He peered at me sidelong. "Maybe."

"What about Operation Rip?" I said. "You can't propose to her out of the blue if you keep avoiding her."

"I know. I've just got more to think about now."

When he glanced at me guiltily, I said, "No. Not Gretchen."

"She looked good, right?"

"Bree-yark, listen to me. This is your panic talking. It's casting around for any excuse to bail you out, and right now it's seized on your ex. Sure, she looked ... better, but it's like lipstick on a rhino. She's horrible. The only reason she's making any effort right now is because she knows if you marry Mae, she'll never control you again. I hate to be that blunt, but it's the truth, and I know you know that."

"Yeah," he allowed. "But if she and that guy get serious..."

"Let them! You're way too good for her. Promise me you won't talk to her, even if she comes looking for you."

He sighed. "I'll promise if you promise to eat that." He nodded at my wrapped hoagie. "It wasn't cheap."

"Then you have my word," I said, saluting him with the foot-long sandwich.

He laughed as I got out, but it sounded too shaky to be trusted.

"No Gretchen," I stressed.

As I arrived at my door, I checked my watch. Mid-afternoon, which gave me three hours to build the golems and still have enough time to make it to the presentation at the Discovery Society, where Ricki had reserved me a seat. To her credit, she wasn't questioning my decision to pursue something apparently unrelated to Bear Goldburn's murder, much less Sven's attempt on my life. Like me, she was learning to trust my magic.

I tuned into it now, asking if there were any intruders or danger. Its motion changed, giving me a hard no.

"Wow. Clarity."

After the day I'd had, I could have used those kinds of responses more often, but magic operated in its own dimension and on its own terms, beyond logic and intellect. A mage had to go to it, not vice versa. Despite my magic's assurance, I scanned the frame before unlocking and opening the door. The lights were out and the curtains drawn, telling me Tabitha was having another one of her migraines.

"You're in luck," I said, feeling for the dimmer switch. "I just stocked up on..."

But where the switch should have been, my hand encountered crumbling drywall. As my eyes adjusted, the shapes that emerged from the darkness didn't line up at all with my furniture arrangement.

"Illuminare," I called, sending up a ball of light.

As the ball crackled and grew, I jerked my cane into sword and staff. My apartment was a flophouse. A pair of soiled mattresses lay among old couches and chairs that looked like they'd been carried up from the street. Holes and graffiti competed for wall space while garbage littered the floor. And the smell—sweet Moses!

For a moment, my shocked brain tried to convince me I was in the wrong unit, but I'd just unlocked the door. I peered over a shoulder. Instead of the three bolts I'd installed a decade earlier, there was only one now, as well as a thick barrel bolt that was drawn. I shouldn't have been able to open it from the outside.

Okay, stop for a moment, I told myself. *Think.*

Gretchen had been here earlier. Was this her idea of a joke?

I activated and drank a neutralizing potion, then waited. As the magic took tingling effect, I expected the glamour to thin and my own apartment, with the framed photos Ricki had hung that weekend, to return to form. Instead, I remained staring around a wasted, decrepit space that even the junkies appeared to have deserted. My invoked light, normally clean white, shone gritty overhead.

"Hello?" I called. "Tabitha?"

A whimper sounded from the back bedroom. Dropping the hoagie, I summoned a shield and strode behind my hovering ball of light. One way or another, I was going to get some damned answers.

At my bedroom door, I peered over a king-sized mattress strewn with blankets. "Who's here?"

When another whimper sounded, I couldn't tell whether it was human, animal, or other. But I pinpointed its source. Across the room stood my closet—only in this version, the folding doors were missing.

Stepping to the right for a better angle, I sent my light forward. In the closet's far corner, the light glimmered from two sets of eyes. They belonged to a young boy and girl. A dirty hand covered each of their mouths. In another step, I saw the woman huddled behind them, hugging them close. Her haggard eyes looked just as scared as theirs.

Holy crap, a family lives here.

In as soothing a voice as I could muster, I said, "It's all right. I'm not here to hurt you. I just have a couple questions."

The children shrank, whimpering, against their mother. Her gaze darted to my right. I looked over as a figure rose. The man had been crouched behind a dresser. He was aiming a shotgun at my face.

I spun from the room as the weapon discharged.

"What in the actual *fuck?*" someone cried.

When I stumbled to a stop, sunlight was slanting through the west-facing windows, and I was back in my apartment. Tabitha had risen on her divan, large eyes peering between me and the front door.

"What happened?" I stammered, my heart still slamming in my chest.

"You tell me," she said, her hair puffed out. "I heard the bolts unlock, and the next thing I knew you were stumbling from your room like a drunken ogre. You frightened the hell out of me—and when I was in the middle of digesting my afternoon milk." She rubbed her stomach. "Please don't do that again, darling."

"I didn't *do* anything." I looked around, even craning my neck into the bedroom, to ensure I was really back. "I walked through the door, and the apartment, or at least this version of it, was gone. There were people here, and—"

"More people?" Tabitha moaned.

"Not here. At least not *here* here."

"I can't pretend to understand or stay interested," she said, lying back down. "As long as it's just you and me, I'm content."

"And your contentment is all that matters," I said thinly.

"Thank you," she sighed. "There's hope for us yet, darling."

I returned to the outside hallway and repeated my earlier actions—unlocking the door, stepping through my defenses—but the apartment didn't change. I looked down at where I'd dropped the hoagie, which would have been beside the coat rack. The sandwich wasn't there. My thoughts immediately went to the box that had been in my casting circle.

Holy crap.

I ran across the room and clambered up the ladder to my library/lab, my mind going a mile a second. What if the perp wasn't translocating, but using a parallel reality to travel in and out of this one? How I'd ended up in that reality was another question, but the golems would have to wait.

I had research to do.

19

My phone's ringtone broke my concentration. I looked up from my book-heaped desk and hunted for the phone, finding it in the pocket of my coat, which I'd slung over the back of the chair. The caller was Ricki.

"Hi, hon," I answered.

"Are you on your way?"

"On my way where? Oh, crap." I drew the phone back to check the time. The lecture at the Discovery Society started in twenty minutes. "Ah, not quite. I'm going to put you on speaker while I get ready."

I grabbed my notes and scrambled down the ladder.

"I'm at my brothers' place," she said, making me think for a second. That's right—Tony was going to spend the week there. "I'm staying for dinner. Call me when the presentation ends, and I'll pick you up on my way home. Hoffman said you found something in the stomach contents?"

Tabitha's ears flattened at the sound of Ricki's broadcast voice. "God, she's here even when she isn't," she complained.

I entered my bedroom and closed the door. "Sort of," I said, telling Ricki about the weakness of the hunting spell and how it would need to come within fifteen feet of the potion to get any kind of reaction.

"Maybe your golems will get lucky," she said, echoing what I'd told Hoffman.

"Well, I sort of got sidetracked and never made them. When I came home earlier, I stepped into a shadow present."

"A shadow what?"

Tossing the phone onto the bed, I started pulling clean clothes from the closet. I checked both corners to make sure no one was hiding inside.

"The idea is basically this," I said. "Our reality unfolds in a linear sequence. Point A to B to C and so on. But in fact, reality is a sequence of *probabilities*—what's most likely to happen in any given moment. The probabilities that don't become our reality don't just fail to appear, though. They live on as alternate realities, shadows of the one we know. Less real, but still there. Are you with me so far?"

"I think so."

"Well, I first read about shadow presents in a book on soothsaying. The reason good diviners are as rare as hen's teeth is because they have to distinguish between reality and probable realities, often over a span of years or decades. One wrong turn, and they're chasing events through a shadow realm that will never manifest."

That was why I was trying not to dwell too much on the Doideag's prophecy about my death or even the war she'd mentioned.

"I'll take your word for it," Ricki said.

"The thing is, I didn't know these realms could be visited outside of soothsaying, but that's exactly what happened to me this afternoon. I opened our door and, bam, I was in a shadow present. Physically. The apartment was here, but another family was squatting in it. They were hiding in our bedroom, in fact—a man, woman, and a couple kids. Anyway, when the episode ended, I was in our actual bedroom. Tabitha confirmed I never entered the apartment. I manifested from a probable reality back to our present one." Even though I'd experienced it myself just a few hours earlier, the idea still seemed impossible.

"But ... how?" she asked.

"That's what I've been looking into. Turns out there's one recorded case of shadow travel, and it goes back to an ancient Greek cult. The Atticans."

"The one whose markings were on the box?"

"Yup, the Hermes devotees. The info on them is scant, but they were connected to a thieves' guild. Hermes was a patron of thieves among other things—including border crossings. Through worship of the Hermes essence, and with the help of powerful magic, the cult may have developed the ability to cross in and out of the shadow present."

"Must've been one hell of a thieves' guild."

"Right? A disappearing hoagie taught me that objects can be moved between the realities. Meaning that whatever the thieves stole could be shifted undetected through a shadow reality. I'm betting that's how the perp got my box. He entered the apartment through the shadow present, manifested in my lab long enough to seize it, and then left the way he'd entered. I couldn't find much more on the cult except that they were executed en masse, probably for their crimes. But they must have endowed their magic in an object for it to still exist. Dollars to donuts, that's what was in the box."

"Do you still see a connection to the Goldburn murder?"

"In my gut, yeah. I just haven't worked out the hows yet."

"Well, I'll run interference on Hoffman until you do. But I still don't understand how *you* entered this shadow present."

"I haven't quite figured that part out yet either. The perp's passage into my lab may have left a weakness in the boundary, one my wards preserved somehow. I haven't had time to check it out."

"So anyone could accidentally step through it?" she asked, concerned.

"Or maybe it takes a magical bloodline to trigger. I honestly don't know. What I do know is that I've found the answer to not only protecting our apartment, but catching the perp."

"Oh yeah?"

"I'll set a trap in the shadow present."

"You mean go back to that other apartment?"

"If the perp wants me, that's the route they'll have to take to get past my wards." Dressed now, I slipped the phone into my shirt pocket, checked myself in the mirror, and left the bedroom.

"But how would you even get there again?" she asked.

"If my theory about the weakness in the boundary is right, there are a couple things I can try when I get back tonight." I waved goodbye to Tabitha, who responded by closing her eyes. Grabbing my coat and cane, I stepped carefully over the threshold, locked the door behind me, and hurried downstairs.

"And you still think the perp is Sven?" she asked.

"He did try to kill me using a sigil from the Attican cult."

"But if he can travel through this shadow present, why didn't he plant the sigil from inside your office? Why do the deed in the hallway where anyone could see?"

It was a great question, but as I stepped outside, our connection started to go staticky.

"You're breaking up," I said, flagging an approaching cab. "I'll call you after the lecture."

Trevor of the Sup Squad phoned me on the way to the club with an update on the Sven Roe investigation.

"No match to the prints we lifted from his desk," he said. "Just means he's not in any of the crime databases. His picture went out this afternoon, and we've been getting some calls. Nothing solid yet. The facial recognition search is probably our best bet. If he's active online, we'll find him. A tech's working on it."

I'd left him a message earlier about my dead-end search for the tanzanite, and I filled in the details before ending the call. The cab was pulling up to a line of five-story townhouses on the Upper West Side. We stopped in front of a handsome stone mansion, a metal plaque beside the door reading *The Discovery Society*.

I paid the driver and hurried up the steps with about a minute to spare. A proper doorman who was long in years and short in stature confirmed my reservation number on a tablet, then ushered me down a wainscoted corridor lined with portraits. A large Discovery Society flag, like the one in Bear's photo, presided over them.

"The public should *always* arrive fifteen minutes before the start of a lecture," the doorman tutted, a purple mole bobbing beside his nose.

But distracted by the passing portraits of club luminaries, I only half heard him. I glimpsed one of Sir Edmund Hillary of Mount Everest fame and another of pilot Amelia Earhart. At a portrait of a man with copper-blond hair, I stopped.

Bear Goldburn, the plaque read, followed by a list of expeditions.

The doorman snapped his fingers and hissed, "Come! It's about to start."

Opening a door, he motioned me inside. I stepped past him and into an antiquated library adorned with old maps and several taxidermy mounts, including a massive Bengal tiger and polar bear. Rows of chairs faced a wooden lectern where a thin man was organizing some notes, his mustache a perfectly inverted V. The audience consisted mostly of older gentlemen in sweaters and tweed, and it looked as if every chair was taken.

"*Psst!*" someone called. "Over here."

A man with blond hair to his shoulders who looked to be about my age was motioning me over to an empty chair beside him. The doorman issued a final frown from the doorway before sealing it.

"Don't mind Eldred," the blond-haired man said in an accent that sounded Scandinavian. "He is like that with everyone. The authority of letting people in and out of the club for so many years has gone to his head. He is drunk with power."

"I know a few people like that," I muttered. "Thanks for the seat. I'm Everson."

"Ludvig," he replied. His bright blue eyes crossed slightly above a broad smile of crooked teeth. The features conspired to give him a semi-crazed look. "So, what is your interest in asteroid families?"

"Asteroid families?" The lecture topic, I realized. In the madness of the afternoon, I hadn't taken a good look at it. I hadn't even had time to consider a cover story. "I'm more interested in the club, really." Not a lie, but it was about as much as I wanted to share on the subject. "What about you?"

He released a high giggle that turned a few heads. "You are interested in membership?"

"Oh, well, not right away or anything," I stammered.

"No, this is excellent! I will introduce you to some people after the lecture."

Wonderful.

My plan had been to look around a little without drawing attention to myself. But if my magic had led me here, it may also have intended for me to meet Ludvig, an apparent insider. I nodded my thanks as the man with the inverted mustache tapped his notes into a pile and began speaking in a monotone.

I WAS AWAKENED by my head being nudged. I opened my eyes, startled to find I was still in the library at the Discovery Society. The lecture had apparently ended, and the audience was standing now, murmuring conversationally.

I jerked my head from Ludvig's shoulder. "Oh, man, I am so sorry. It's been a long day."

He giggled. "It is all right. When you come here as long as I have, you learn little tricks for staying awake. You did much better than I did my first time."

I wiped my mouth with a handkerchief. "Are you an explorer?"

"A statistician, but exploration is in my blood. My great grandfather was Jesper Lassgard. He was on both expeditions that were first to the North and South Poles. In fact, he was one of the club's founders. I'm just an associate. One of the fellows is sponsoring me for full membership, but this can take time. I have to prove myself, and nowadays it is not enough to cross an ocean or trek to the poles. You must advance knowledge in some way."

Given the stuffy crowd, I couldn't help but wonder if Ludvig's odd mannerisms were as much a hindrance to his membership as anything.

"The fellows?" I asked.

"Yes, four sit on the Council. Well, three now."

"I was sorry to hear about Bear Goldburn," I said, testing whether he was the subtracted fellow in question.

Ludvig nodded. "He brought a lot of energy and standing to the Society."

I was trying to come up with a follow-up question when someone caught Ludvig's eye. His chest convulsed with another giggle.

"Wait here!" he said and darted into the dispersing crowd.

Odd guy, but he seemed to know everyone. I used his absence to open my wizard's senses and peer around. But like at Bear Goldburn's penthouse apartment, there were no supernatural auras and nothing stood out on the astral level.

All right, magic, I thought. *Show me what I'm here for.*

I waded deeper until I felt the familiar shifting of tidal energies, but they were directionless and without guidance. My instinct was to be frustrated, but more and more I suspected that the seemingly random movement was my magic arranging things, ensuring I was in the right place at the right time.

"Everson!" Ludvig called.

The library returned to focus as he came rushing toward me, his face flush with excitement. "I've arranged for you to attend the private meeting of members and fellows. I'm going to find you a sponsor."

I stepped back. "What? Why?"

"Because you're the next frontier."

"Huh?"

"The club's original purpose was to further the exploration of land, sea, and air. It was later expanded to include space—but we've never explored the esoteric, not with any scientific rigor. You could change that. I recognized you the moment you walked in. You are Everson Croft, the great wizard!"

His eyes seemed to cross further as he spoke. I clutched my cane, muscles tensing with suspicion.

"Yes, yes, I remember you from the mayor's eradication campaign!"

"Let's not broadcast it," I said in a lowered voice. "I just came out of curiosity."

He seized my arm and whispered, "There they are! The fellows of the Council!"

I looked over at the three people walking toward us. One was the thin man with the V mustache who had just concluded his presentation. He was accompanied by a middle-aged woman in a red sari and a large gray-haired man, who looked vaguely familiar. When Ludvig waved, the large man returned an indifferent nod, suggesting I'd been right about the club's view of him.

My new friend was clutching me with both hands now and bouncing on his toes. The fellows continued past, toward the back of the library.

"Yeah, that's great," I whispered, trying to wrest myself from his grip.

I stopped suddenly and looked down at my cane. It was wiggling. When the fellows reached a doorway, the wiggling stopped. My hunting spell had just gotten a hit. One of the fellows was carrying the potion that had been in Bear Goldburn's stomach.

"Come," Ludvig said. "The meeting's about to start."

I let him seize my hand and pull me after him.

20

The meeting was held in a conference room that featured a massive pair of elephant tusks protruding from the far wall. By the time Ludvig and I entered, the fellows were taking their seats at an official-looking table on a dais. The remaining attendees congregated at a long table that bisected the room. I walked toward it with the aim of getting as close to the fellows as possible, but Ludvig grabbed my arm.

"That's for members," he explained.

He pulled me to a row of red-leather chairs along the side of the room. It took some tugging back on my part to get us into the two seats closest to the front, beside a large globe. My vibrating cane told me we were on the very edge of the spell's range. I focused on the fellows, my gaze going from the two men's jackets to the woman's shoulder bag. The potion could be on any of them.

"Who are they?" I whispered.

"The big one is Robert Strock," he said. "He is the club's fifty-second president."

No wonder he looked familiar. "The real estate developer?"

"Yes, but he also spends millions on research, especially

deep sea. He's a submarine enthusiast like his father, Harold Strock. Harold created one of the first comprehensive maps of the ocean floor. Robert has gone on many expeditions himself. His last one, to the Mariana Trench, discovered two new species of marine life."

It was hard to imagine someone Robert Strock's size spending any length of time in a deep-sea submersible, but my mind was too busy working out scenarios in which he would become involved with the occult or want Bear dead.

"The woman is Sunita Sharma," Ludvig continued, playing eager guide. "Her name is not as recognizable to lay people, but she is one of the top bioengineering researchers in the world. She and her team won the Nobel Prize three years ago for their work on gene splicing. I think she is very pretty, don't you?"

"Sure," I said absently, searching Sunita's green eyes for signs of magic or malice.

"And finally, Walter Mims. You heard his lecture. Or at least the beginning." He giggled loudly enough for heads to turn at the members' table. "Walter is an astronomer and the youngest son of astronaut Gene Mims, one of the first ever in space. Walter is also my sponsor. He was the one who gave me permission to bring you to the meeting. We'll find you a sponsor among the members."

As Ludvig was saying this, Walter's smallish eyes met mine and pinched critically.

"You didn't mention the wizard part to him, did you?" I asked in a lowered voice.

"Not yet." Ludvig's next giggle sounded like anticipation. "I just told him you were a foremost expert in your field."

"Let's keep that to ourselves for now," I said as Walter Mims looked away. He was probably upset I'd dozed off during his lecture.

Ludvig had run down the fellows in a line, and I couldn't

help but notice the empty chair at the far end. A flag, like the one in Bear Goldburn's photo and hanging in the hall of portraits, was folded into a triangle and set on the table in his place.

"How did the others get along with Bear?"

"Well, it wasn't all sunshine and rainbows." Before Ludvig could elaborate, Strock brought the room to order.

"Welcome to the one thousand two hundred and forty-third meeting of the Discovery Society," he said in a husky voice that commanded attention. "First, I have a tragic announcement." He motioned toward the empty chair. "As most of you know, Bear Goldburn lost his life this weekend. Besides being a dear friend, he epitomized the three d's of the Discovery Society: devotion, diligence, and, of course, discovery."

Light glistened from the dark hair of Sunita Sharma's bowed head, while Walter Mims compulsively smoothed his mustache with a finger and thumb.

"During his four years on the Council," Strock continued, "Bear led nine expeditions and published his findings in journals too numerous to mention. He was always pushing the boundaries of the known. And all while serving as CEO in one of the highest pressure industries there is. Second to real estate, of course," he added, which drew some laughs from the somber room.

"It's no secret that Bear and I were competitive. We shouted, we fought—hell, I even threw a punch at him at the Founder's Banquet last year. But I'd like to think I drove him, just as he drove me, and that those repeated collisions of our—let's face it, our egos—hoisted the club's flag that much higher."

As he patted the folded flag in Bear's place, I whispered, "Competitive over what?"

"Everything," Ludvig answered. "Bear used to go around saying Strock's contributions to exploration were shit, mostly because he didn't write his own research. Bear didn't think he should be the club's president."

Power struggle, I noted.

Strock started into a story about an expedition he and Bear co-funded.

"Was it the same way with Sunita?" I asked.

"Not quite," Ludvig whispered back. "They were ... very friendly."

I looked over in surprise. He nodded, his crossed eyes bright over his crooked teeth. "Oh, yes. Worst-kept secret in the club. Bear ended it after his wife separated from him."

Spurned lover? I noted, this one with a question mark.

"How did Bear get along with your sponsor?" I asked.

"They were as different as two people could be. Bear was very loud and outspoken. He enjoyed an audience. Walter prefers the quiet of an observatory or his office. As far as I know, they barely talked."

Strock concluded his eulogy with a minute of silence. The meeting then proceeded to announcements and votes. All the while, I made small adjustments to my cane, trying to draw a precise bead on the potion, but no dice. I would need to wait for the end of the meeting to get closer to the fellows.

"Is anyone here applying for membership?" Sunita asked the room.

I was almost too slow to grab Ludvig's hand as it went up. A few heads turned toward our ensuing scuffle, but when no one spoke, Sunita nodded.

"That concludes our meeting, then."

"Why did you do that?" Ludvig asked with a wounded expression.

I stood, releasing his hand. "I just think I should get a feel for the club first. You know, walk around, talk to some people."

"Yes, yes, of course," he said, then called, "Walter!"

The thin man, who was consulting with the other two fellows, looked over irritably. When Ludvig continued to wave, he came over.

"What is it?" he asked as he arrived in front of us, sounding more like Ludvig's babysitter than his sponsor.

"This is Everson Croft. The prospective member I told you about."

"Indeed." Walter Mims gave me a critical up and down. "And what is your expertise, Mr. Croft?"

"Mythology and lore. I'm a professor at Midtown College."

"Mythology and lore." He sniffed. "Well, perhaps you'll be interested in our community program. It comes with a discount on lectures and a Discovery Society pin. Now if you'll both excuse me..."

Ludvig looked disappointed as his mentor walked away, but I'd gotten what I'd wanted from the exchange. Walter wasn't the potion carrier. That left Strock and Sunita. The first had waded onto the main floor, where members thronged him. Sunita was still at the fellows' table, stowing meeting materials into her bag.

"Wait here," I told Ludvig and approached her.

Sunita was younger than she'd appeared from a distance. Her jet black hair was brushed to a sheen that hung neatly over one shoulder of her red, gold-beaded sari. She also possessed a mystical quality I couldn't quite pinpoint. She glanced up and caught me staring.

"Can I help you?" she asked, her green eyes narrowing slightly.

I was scrambling for something to say when I noticed a gold pin on the shoulder of her sari. It depicted a thick hand with a pointed object pinched between its first finger and thumb. "The right hand of Ganesh?" I asked.

She touched the pin, a curious smile playing across her lips. "How do you know about the right hand?"

"Years ago I did a study on protective symbols across cultures. I won't bore you with the details. I just wanted to say it's beautiful."

"Thanks," she said, the touch becoming a caress. "It was handed down through my family."

That was where the mystical quality was coming from. The right hand of the elephant god, Ganesh, exuded a subtle protective energy. The pointed object between his finger and thumb was the broken end of his tusk.

"Dr. Sharma?" someone asked.

I turned to find a member waiting to talk to her. I motioned for him to go ahead and said goodbye to Sunita. Though her pin was interesting, she wasn't the potion-carrier either. That left Strock.

Beware the shadow of many faces, the Doideag had said. *But fear the master of many places.*

Strock's role as president of an explorer's club seemed to fit the bill for the second. I turned, but there was a void where he'd been standing. I looked around. He was no longer in the meeting room. I rushed to Ludvig, who remained parked beside the globe, smiling over the room as if he were among his dearest friends—despite that no one had approached him or appeared ready to now.

"What happened to Strock?" I asked.

"The club has a lounge upstairs with a bar. Some of the members go there after the meeting. Often before the meeting too," he added with a conspiratorial smile. As I hurried away to the corridor of portraits in search of a staircase, I heard Ludvig exclaim, "Wait! It is only for members!"

I needed to confirm the potion was on Strock. Then it would be a matter of staying close, determining how and why he'd killed Bear. I was fully aware I was on my own here. Hoffman and the NYPD weren't going to touch someone of Robert

Strock's stature, not without irrefutable proof. And even then they might not.

But there was also the Doideag's prophecy about failure—wars coming, seas boiling, lands running.

I'd take him down myself if I had to.

I found a set of stairs leading up and took them two at a time. I'd gone halfway when someone called my name: "Everson Croft!"

Ricki?

Last we spoke she was going to wait for my call before driving from her brothers' to pick me up, but it looked like she'd come anyway. And she didn't sound happy. Her approaching shadow grew in the corridor beneath me. As I descended, I noticed the lights along the stairwell had dimmed from golden to a grayish yellow.

I arrived at the bottom of the stairs a few steps ahead of Ricki. She stopped and trained her service pistol at my head.

"Hey, it's me," I said, raising my free hand. I noticed she'd changed from her blues to her detective blacks. Had new evidence on the Goldburn case brought her? But what would she even be doing in the field?

"Drop your cane," she ordered, eyes cold and dark. "Lock your fingers behind your head and face the wall."

"Seriously?"

"Do it!"

It was my wife's voice, my wife's aura—but when my gaze traced her belly, my own stomach lurched.

She wasn't pregnant.

Four backup officers were approaching from farther down the corridor. I squinted, trying to see if I recognized them, but the corridor was much dimmer than only a few moments before, and the runner had changed.

The shadow present?

I'd theorized that I'd crossed over in my apartment because my wards had preserved the weakness the perp had introduced to the boundary. So how could it be happening here, at the Discovery Society?

"This is the last time I'm going to tell you," the shadow Vega said.

"Fine, but I have a right to know why you're detaining me at gunpoint."

"You're under arrest for the murder of Bear Goldburn."

21

"*What?*"

My stomach clenched with shock, but my mind was still working, struggling to make sense of what was happening. This version of Vega looked hard-bitten, the skin around her eyes heavy and stress-lined. She wore a dull band on her left ring finger, different than the one I'd given her. My heart staggered. Not only was this version of my wife not pregnant with our child, she was married to someone else.

And she's arresting me for Bear's murder?

I had a hundred questions, but I wasn't going to get any answers from her. That would be the judge and public defender's job—assuming I let her arrest me. And that was a *hell no*. Between the alt versions of my apartment and Vega, I was getting a good picture of the city in this shadow present, and it made the problems in the actual present look quaint in comparison. Prison would be a murder hole.

"*Protezione,*" I uttered.

Light burst from the opal end of my cane and gathered around me into a shield of hardened air. Shadow Vega responded by compressing her lips and firing. I grunted into a backpedal as the impacts flashed from my shield. I shouldn't have felt them this much, but the energy in the shadow present was just that—shadowy. No matter how much I channeled into my protection, the energy lacked the same solidity.

At both ends of the corridor, Vega's officers had taken blocking positions. They shouted a cacophony of surrender commands. Vega's next shot fractured my protection, the bullet searing my cheek.

"Respingere!" I bellowed.

Force and light burst from the shield, causing officers to throw forearms to faces and knocking Vega onto her back. I fled up the stairs. A minute earlier, I'd been intent on finding Strock. Now I just wanted to get the hell out of the Discovery Society and find refuge.

At the top of the stairs, I drew my sword and spoke into the second rune. Activated by an efreet, it held the power of elemental fire.

"Fuoco!"

The rune glowed like an ember and fire crackled down the blade. I wasted no time bathing the stairwell in flames. Beyond the storm, recovering officers arrived at the bottom of the steps. Vega stood among them, the fire's fury reflected in eyes that bore into mine. She shouted orders, and the officers split.

They're surrounding the building.

As sprinklers activated, I turned and accessed the second-story corridor. Knowing the front of the building would be covered from the street, I ran toward the back, passing various rooms.

My body might have been in flight mode, but my mind was still working furiously. Individuals in the actual and shadow realities were supposed to operate independently of one another, meaning the shadow Bear had been murdered too. And the shadow me had either committed the murder or been framed for it.

But how had Vega known to find me in the Discovery Society? Had someone tipped off the police and ensured I'd be in the shadow present when they arrived? And what about Strock? He'd been carrying the potion I found in Bear's system. How was he involved? Not to mention Sven Roe and the Hermes cult?

The corridor ended at a closed door. I hit it with a force blast and shouldered through the splintered wood into an office. A window overlooked an alley that ran between the back of the row of townhouses and the one behind it.

I stepped back and shouted another invocation. The force shattered the window but failed to blow out the security bars. Extending my staff between two of them, I summoned a shield and strained to grow it out and force the bars apart.

C'mon, dammit.

The aged bars yielded with a pair of surprising snaps and clanged down into the alley. I squeezed through the tight space until I was standing on a window ledge.

As fire alarms began to sound in the club behind me, I peered both ways. No police lights yet, but I knew how Vega and the NYPD operated. After surrounding the building, they would set up a perimeter. We'd be talking roughly twenty-five square blocks, since the suspect—i.e. me—was on foot.

The solution was to take to the air.

Angling my sword at the ledge, I shouted, *"Forza dura!"*

The force launched me across the alley. There was a four-story difference between the window ledge and my rooftop destination, and though I'd compensated for the flimsier energy here, I still came up short.

I braced against the incoming brick wall until pain exploded through my right shoulder. I'd had the presence to shape a platform of hardened air, only falling a few feet before it caught me. Pushing myself up, I summoned more platforms to act as steps until I was climbing over a retaining wall and onto the rooftop.

An instant later, police cruisers squealed into the alleyway from both ends.

I sagged with my back to the wall. I'd managed to escape the building without being seen, but that was just a start.

Touching the opal end of my staff to my throbbing shoulder, I panted words of healing. As a tepid warmth took hold, I considered my next move. Back in my apartment, I'd returned from the shadow present spontaneously, but that wasn't happening here. I searched a night sky thick with clouds and industrial smoke.

Vega will be calling a search chopper, I thought, *if she hasn't already.*

Meaning I needed to escape the perimeter before the chopper arrived. But escape where?

I crossed the roof of the townhouse until I was looking south. Past the spires of Midtown stretched the relative plains of the Villages. In the distance, a mass of skyscrapers marked Downtown. Sirens blanketed the length of the city, the forlorn sounds interspersed with cries and distant cracks of gunfire.

Who controlled this version of New York, I wondered? More importantly, did I have any allies?

I felt a stab of longing for my real wife as well as Bree-yark and Mae and our other friends, but right now, I needed to get somewhere safe. As I considered my options, I patted my pockets to ensure nothing had fallen out. When my keychain jangled, I narrowed my gaze at where Midtown College would be.

If the keys work here, I can take refuge inside the college.

With a running start, I shouted the Word for force and sent myself skyward, arcing over the street. A second invocation slowed my descent, and I landed at a run across the gravel rooftop of the next building.

I continued in this manner for six more blocks, arriving on the final roof as a distant chugging sounded. A chopper was coming in from the southeast, its powerful beam bathing entire city blocks, but I was outside its search radius. Good thing, because my throbbing right knee told me I was done roof-hopping.

I peered over the back of the building in search of a fire escape.

"What the fuck do you think you're doing?" a man's voice growled behind me.

Jerking around, I saw that the five men had been concealed in the shadow of the building's stair tower. Their silhouettes rose from camp chairs and upturned buckets, all of them armed.

Of course, I thought dismally.

I stepped back, a shield hardening around me, whatever good it would do. My encounter with shadow Vega had shown that my protection here wouldn't stop a full-blown assault. I would need to take the offensive, hit them hard. I had force, fire, and ice, and the right bottom pocket of my coat bulged with lightning grenades.

But as the men stepped out into the ambient light, they weren't the homicidal thugs I'd been expecting. They were clean-cut. A couple wore office clothes: slacks and tucked-in shirts with the sleeves rolled up. I instantly pieced it together. This was a resident watch group for the apartment building.

Taking a huge chance, I slid my cane through my coat's belt loop and showed my hands.

"I wasn't trying to break in," I said. "Someone's chasing me, and I was looking for a way down."

"Did we see you jump here?" one of them asked.

"Yeah," I said, still breathing hard from the exertion and adrenaline. "I was over there."

I indicated the rooftop across the alley. Fortunately, it was just high enough and the distance just narrow enough that someone desperate enough could have made the leap. The men must have done the same calculation because they didn't question my claim. A couple of them covered the neighboring rooftop with rifles. The rest returned their gazes to me as if searching for a chink in my own clean-cut look. After another moment, the oldest man nodded, and they lowered their weapons.

"Knife wound?" he asked, squinting behind a pair of glasses.

I touched my cheek, encountering the burning line of dried blood left by Vega's round. "Gunshot wound, actually."

The men grunted knowingly.

"What the hell are you even doing out this time of night?" the spokesman asked.

The fifty-something-year-old looked like he could have managed a regional bank, but he also possessed a certain hardness. They all did. These were men who had families to provide for and protect, but who also knew that one careless moment in this version of the city and they could lose everything.

"It's a long story," I breathed. "I'm not from here."

"I could have told you that." The man cracked a smile for the first time. "Where are you trying to get to?"

"Midtown College."

"Why do you want to go there?" he asked, an angle of suspicion returning to his voice.

"I know someone who used to work night security," I lied. "It was the safest place I could think of."

"Well, 'used to' would be the operative term. Midtown College went under years ago. It's all abandoned buildings now —but that's not to say devoid of life. Be glad you met us. A trip there, especially at this hour, would have ended really badly for you."

I wondered if this version of the city had also suffered a major economic crash, but instead of recovering from it, as ours was, theirs had fallen into deeper misfortune. In any case, I could strike Midtown College from my choices.

"Thanks for the warning. Would you guys mind if I stayed up here? I'm still pretty rattled, and I need to figure out my next move."

And up here felt a lot safer than down in the streets. But maybe my trip to the shadow present was a blessing in disguise. If I was still here come morning, I could venture to the rundown version of my apartment and install the wards to prevent the perp from using it to circumvent my protections in the actual present.

"Got a name?" the man asked.

"Yeah, sorry—Ethan," I said.

There was a manhunt on for me, and *Everson* was too uncommon to be throwing around.

"Gil," he said, shaking my hand. He introduced me to the others, but with everything happening, I only half heard their names.

I followed them back to where they'd been sitting. The arrangement of seats gave them angles on every part of the rooftop. Gil pushed out an upturned tar bucket with a foot and nodded that it was mine. I sat beside him.

"Had much trouble here?" I asked.

"Nothing like the massacre two summers ago."

The rest of the men murmured somberly.

"Massacre?"

"A werewolf got into the building and ravaged the fifth floor," he said. "Wasn't till Jerry from 212 arrived with a shotgun full of silver buckshot that we were able to drive it out. They found its body the next day in Riverside, but the damage was done. Six dead from the attack. Nine mauled. The Sup Squad took them away for treatment, but you know what that means. So, basically fifteen dead."

"The Sup Squad," I echoed.

"They come armed to the teeth, but we learned the hard way they only show up after the fact. At least for shmoes like us. The trick is to never need them in the first place."

"What else do you have running around here?"

Gil gave a hollow snort. "You name it. If it eats human flesh, blood, or soul, it's got a home in the city."

I shook my head. No wonder poor Ricki had looked so beaten down. I'd been considering whether it would be wise to try to locate my shadow self for help, but with all the supernatural threats here, there was no way he'd believe I was who I claimed to be. It had been hard enough in the time catch when the city was largely functional. I switched mental gears and decided to take a shot in the dark.

"Hey, did I read that Bear Goldburn was murdered?"

"Tech guy?" Gil nodded. "They found his body at a collision shop out in Brooklyn."

I stiffened. "A collision shop?"

"Yeah, someone did a real job on him. Didn't look like a sup attack either. Knifed out his kidneys and left him for dead."

"And on the same day he was canned as CEO," one of the men added.

I was too shocked to even nod. My scrying spell hadn't misled me. It *had* captured Bear's final moments—only it had been his shadow.

But why had the spell jumped tracks like that? And how had the actual Bear Goldburn turned up dead in his penthouse with his kidneys missing? The two Bears were independent entities.

What happened to the shadow Bear shouldn't have had any effect on the actual Bear. And yet, clearly, it had.

"Any suspects?" I ventured.

"Code red," one of the men said in a lowered voice.

We all turned to where he was rising from his seat and aiming his rifle. Something large had climbed onto the rooftop and was stalking toward us.

22

The men spread apart and covered the incoming figure. It was dark and hulking, as if the night itself had taken form. Beneath a ridged back, multiple legs stalked forward, like a muscular version of a giant spider.

"Stay back," Gil told me.

But I'd already drawn my cane into sword and staff. *"Entrapolare,"* I whispered.

Dull light glimmered, and the air around the creature hardened into an enclosure. The creature stopped and raised its front three legs. Except they weren't legs, but canine heads that had been sniffing the rooftop. Three sets of eyes smoldered red.

"Holy fuck," one of the men murmured.

Cerberus?

The heads erupted into a thunderous fit of barking. As the watch group opened fire, I reshaped my invocation to brace the creature from the sides. His giant paws raked up gravel and sheaves of tar paper while silver rounds tore through his body, sending out bursts of smoke. The Cerberus wasn't flesh.

He also wasn't succumbing to the attack.

Errant shots struck my magical restraint, making it wobble.

With the next volley, the Cerberus wrenched free and sprang at us. A man shrieked as one of the heads jerked him from his feet, thrashed him savagely, and flung him from the rooftop. The fading scream was almost as bad as the thump and sudden silence. The remaining men backpedaled, one fumbling his reload, sending shells clattering over the rooftop.

The Cerberus sighted on him and leapt.

"Not this time," I grunted, as he collided with a fresh shield. "Everyone inside!" I shouted.

The Cerberus scrambled to his feet among the spilled sparks. Whatever this being was, he was beyond the watch group's means to put down. For the first time, they seemed to notice I was wielding a glowing sword and staff.

Gil squinted at me. "Ethan?"

"Inside!" I repeated.

The youngest-looking man didn't need to be told again. He ran to the steel door of the stair tower, opened it, and waved anxiously for the others to follow. Three others backed toward him. I watched the Cerberus, expecting him to target them, but the eyes above his flaring nostrils remained fixed on me.

"C'mon, Gil!" one of the men called.

I looked over to find him standing beside me.

"I don't know who you are," he said, "but I'm not leaving you out here alone."

"I appreciate that, but I sort of do this for a living. I'd rather you get yourself to safety."

He didn't budge. Both of us were watching the creature now. He was stalking back and forth beyond the wall of shielding I'd erected, growls rumbling from his thickly muscled throats.

"Is that Cerberus?" Gil asked shakily.

"A version of him, anyway."

"What's he doing here?"

It couldn't be a coincidence that a creature from Greek

mythology was menacing me only a day after I'd found a box with inscriptions from a Hermes cult. Regardless, I didn't want to put Gil or any more of the men in his path, even if they were probabilities, shadows of their actual selves.

"Not sure," I replied. "But I really need you to get inside."

I moved away from Gil. The heads of the Cerberus followed me, confirming I was their target. I motioned for Gil to go. He hesitated before sidestepping toward the door his men held open.

I faced the creature, sword in one hand, staff in the other, cycling through everything I knew about my opponent. Cerberus was the formidable three-headed dog that guarded the entrance to Hades. Only a few major mythological figures had managed to get past him. Orpheus charmed him with his lyre, and Hercules beat the starch out of him with his superior strength—neither one of which I possessed. But Aeneas drugged him with a loaf of bread. I may not have had any baked goods on me, but I had a sleeping potion.

The activated tube was already bubbling as I pulled it from my coat and spiked it against the roof. The glass shattered around the Cerberus's front paws, releasing a plume of pink mist. Nostrils wrinkling, the Cerberus stalked back, but instead of stumbling or going woozy, his muscles contracted and he launched himself against the shield. I staggered from the impact, quickly reinforcing the barrier.

Okay, so the potion was a no-go, but he had to have a weakness.

I put my wizardry aside for a moment and went into full professor mode. There were parallels between the Greek and Abrahamic versions of the underworld. If the Cerberus held enough demon essence, he could be susceptible to banishment.

And what better time to test that theory.

The creature's six eyes canted down as the first rune on my

sword began to glow white. Growling, he backed off again. With a Word, I shaped a second wall of hardened air behind him, halting his retreat. Trapped, he lunged. I thrust my blade. The Cerberus's heads slammed into the shield, and my blade plunged into his chest with a faint scrape. I pulled in the realm's ambient energy.

"*Disfare!*" I shouted, releasing it through the rune.

Bright banishment light swelled from the sword and swallowed the creature. His barking climbed in pitch. I brought a shoulder to my right ear and kept pushing, expecting the headsplitting sound to break apart along with the Cerberus's form. But as the light receded, the damned mutt was still standing.

I withdrew the sword with a grunt and backed away. Thoroughly pissed now, the Cerberus threw his body against the shield, sending sparks rolling down the sides. His next charge brought it down.

You're not demonic enough for banishment, I thought, digging into a coat pocket. *But maybe you're spectral enough for this!*

My hand emerged with a fistful of gray salt. I shouted at the same moment the Cerberus leapt, sending the salt blasting into his barking faces. Flames flashed on impact. I dove away as the Cerberus landed awkwardly and slammed into the retaining wall.

He gained his feet and wheeled, smoke rising from the growling heads. A second dose of salt was already en route. This one met his chest, sending up a dark plume of fire.

Disperse, dammit!

The forces that held the creature together were too strong, and I was almost out of salt. I needed more—a lot more. Then it hit me. The Hudson River was only a few blocks away. If I could lead the Cerberus there, cast him in, the combo of salt and moving water would break him apart before he could dog-paddle to shore.

Holding out the remaining handful of salt in warning, I backed from the Cerberus.

He stalked after me, drool spilling from his muzzles and landing on the rooftop in hisses of steam. The men had all gone inside except for Gil, who was standing in the doorway, not ready to leave me.

"I'll be all right," I called, not at all sure as I climbed onto the retaining wall. "I'm taking him to the Hudson."

Returning the salt to my pocket, I glanced down and stepped from the roof. A series of force invocations slowed my descent, but the landing was jarring enough to send a spike through my throbbing right knee. I kept my feet and limp-ran west, my destination a pier off Seventieth Street, about four blocks away.

The Cerberus's three heads lunged over the side of the rooftop. They peered around before finding me and exploded into furious barking. The sound paralleled me until I reached the end of the block.

Take your time coming down, I thought at him.

The heads disappeared. But only because the creature was taking a running start. He landed in the intersection behind me, causing a muscle car roaring down Tenth Avenue to squall into a U-turn. Loud swears sounded from the kids packed inside. The Cerberus head-butted the vehicle, knocking it off its tires and into a series of rolls. That bought me a half block, but he was coming again.

"Attivare!" I shouted, lobbing a lightning grenade behind me.

Branching bolts of electricity seared from the sky and hit the street in deafening whipcracks. Windows blew from parked cars. The Cerberus stumbled to his knees amid several smoking craters.

Good, I thought. *The grenades pack a punch here.*

I pulled ahead as the Cerberus's momentum sent him into a roll.

A police cruiser sped past the intersection ahead of me, slammed its brakes, and shot into reverse. A second and a third cruiser appeared, the three vehicles skidding to stops to form an impromptu roadblock.

Behind me, the Cerberus gained his feet and shook his heads.

Shit. I'd started to slow before deciding I preferred my odds with the NYPD.

Magic hardened the air around me as I approached the roadblock. Officers jumped from their vehicles and took positions behind opened doors, weapons aimed. I was relieved to see Vega wasn't among them. I refused to harm even a shadow version of her, even if my life depended on it.

Shots sounded, and a bullet snapped past my head. I couldn't tell if the officers were shooting at me or the Cerberus.

I pulled another lightning grenade from a coat pocket, chucking this one forward. It bounced toward the roadblock. The bolts that arrived from the dark mass of clouds overhead reached the grenade at the same moment it rolled under the centermost cruiser. The vehicle's roof collapsed in a hammer-smash of blue and red lights, and then the entire vehicle detonated in a geyser of fire. The officers fell away.

Debris rained over my shielded body as I ran past them.

I cut left, taking the short block to Seventieth Street, then right again. I was on the final stretch. I passed a package store, Morton's, that also existed in the actual present. The elevated West Side Highway loomed ahead. But it was the longest stretch, and I wasn't sure I could make it ahead of the NYPD, much less the Cerberus. For the moment, though, I had the road to myself.

"C'mon, man," I gasped, urging myself onward.

As my shoes pounded asphalt, I tried to ignore the spike in my knee and the goring pain in both lungs. I focused on the

Hudson, less a river this far down than a tidal estuary that held huge volumes of Atlantic saltwater.

When I caught its briny scent, I pushed myself harder.

You're going to get there, I thought. *You're going to get there.*

My plan involved basic casting. Maneuver the Cerberus into position and blast him into the river. Nothing complicated. The salt and moving water would do the rest. I'd worry about the shadow NYPD later.

Incredibly, I still had the street to myself. The Cerberus must have stopped to engage the officers, tying up the reinforcements. Hell, I'd take it. But at that thought, a vehicle turned the corner and roared up behind me.

No, dammit. I struggled to find another gear, but I was spent.

"It's coming, Ethan!" someone shouted. "Hurry, get in!"

I turned as a battered green SUV pulled up beside me, its passenger window smashed. Behind the steering wheel, Gil was waving desperately for me to climb inside. I peered back. Still nothing, but what was he doing out here? He'd been safe in the building. Gil leaned over and opened the door for me.

"C'mon!" he shouted.

"Keep going," I panted. "Get out of here."

I tensed to shut the door, but hesitated. A glistening streak covered the passenger seat. More blood dotted the windshield. When I looked back at Gil, he continued to wave, but the eyes behind his glasses weren't right. They were too dark, the engorged pupils rimmed with slivers of smoldering light.

I lurched back from the door, fumbling to pull my cane into sword and staff.

Gil *had* been coming for me, but he hadn't made it. I pictured his mangled body being yanked from the vehicle while this thing climbed into his place, assuming his likeness. I was dealing with a shifter.

The creature's lips forked into a grin. "What's wrong ... *Everson?*"

Glass shattered and metal keened as the Gil likeness morphed back into a massive three-headed dog. I backpedaled toward the Hudson as the Cerberus shook off the ruined husk of the vehicle and pounced.

23

"*Respingere!*" I shouted.

The force from my shielded body knocked the Cerberus off course. But a paw, more lion's than canine's, raked me, leaving trenches of pain down the slats of my ribs. I reeled, an elbow pinned to my side. The Cerberus stalked around me. As if anticipating my plan, he placed himself between me and the Hudson.

"Who the fuck are you?" I growled.

"We could ask you the same," the middle head said. "You're out of your league, Everson Croft. You're standing between armies, and you don't even know it. Leave it alone."

The Doideag's words returned to me. *If ye should fail and war should come...*

But I was also thinking about the scrying spell. A couple times, Bear had noted an odd shine in Vince Cole's eyes, and I remembered his prodigious strength when he'd lifted Bear from the car.

That hadn't been Vince Cole.

"You're the one who drove Bear Goldburn to the body shop. Hacked out his kidneys."

"I drove him to the body shop, yes."

"So who did the hacking?"

"The one I serve."

"And who's that?"

The Cerberus barked a laugh. "What was it that killed the cat? Oh, yes. *Curiosity.*"

His eyes narrowed suddenly, and he lunged. I swung my sword, shouting the banishment Word. Light flashed from the inscribed rune as the blade cleaved the Cerberus's leading neck. He roared in agony, but a trailing head seized my leg. Pain speared the muscles of my thigh as I was lifted and flung. My shield blunted the impact against a building, but I landed hard, brain rattling in my skull.

Heavy pads pounded toward me as I pushed myself up. Though the streetscape had gone blurry, I could see the Cerberus incoming. His right head, the one whose neck I'd banish-cleaved, was flopping like a wet noodle.

I'd debilitated him.

I dug out my remaining salt and sent it flying. The Cerberus reared, squinting from the flames that broke across his faces. I ducked around and swung my blade, activating the banishment rune a second time as it disappeared into the left neck. I followed with a staff thrust to the shifter's chest. A force bolt from the opal end shoved him away before he could grab me.

When we faced off again, two of his heads were lolling. I wasn't in much better shape. A cut high on my brow was sending blood dribbling into my right eye; my ribs and right knee were throbbing; and my left thigh, where the Cerberus had grabbed me, was swelling to tire-like proportions.

I was also exhausted. The fact that Thelonious, my incubus spirit, was still too weak to claim me was little consolation. Only adrenaline was keeping me upright, and that wasn't going to last.

Just one head left to disable.

The Cerberus narrowed his angry, calculating eyes. The shifter recognized the danger, but he was also under orders to take me out. One of his limp heads struggled up weakly, then collapsed again.

"What's wrong?" I panted. "Necktile dysfunction?"

The goading was deliberate. I was trying to bring the creature into another careless charge. Once the final head was out of commission, I'd be able to complete my flight to the pier and finish him off.

But when the Cerberus launched at me this time, he lowered his head. I thrust my cocked sword anyway. The blade scraped off brow, clipping an ear. The flat of the Cerberus's head slammed into my shielded body, driving me from the edge of the sidewalk, legs staggering painfully, into a graffiti-covered building. His head met my chest again, this time pinning me against the stone wall at my back.

I squinted from the pressure and called more power to my shield. The Cerberus's rear legs dug in, upping the pounds per square inch. I grunted a Word. A repulsive force detonated from the shield, but it was too weak. The Cerberus barely faltered, and when his head bore down again, it pinned my sword arm.

This wasn't the plan, dammit.

Worse still, the other heads were recovering. One snarled and snapped at my staff arm, which I just managed to jerk out of the way. The other bounced up and down, using the momentum in its struggle to remain upright. I attempted another invocation, but I could barely summon the air, much less the force, and this one squibbed completely. All available power went to my shield now—which was starting to fail.

Gray spots eddied around my vision. My tongue turned thick in my mouth.

If I didn't do something fast, it would just be a question of whether I passed out before the Cerberus tore me apart or after.

With a grunted series of incantations, I reshaped my shield, pulling it inside my coat, and drove its energy as far into the ground as it would go. One of the Cerberus's recovering heads grabbed the arm of my coat. The sleeve tore away, leaving the rest of my coat intact, including the pocket that held my two remaining lightning grenades. Thank God for cheap stitching.

"*Attivare!*" I shouted.

The *crack* that followed was less a sound than an all-encompassing force. It blinded me and struck me deaf. I seemed to float rather than drop to the pavement, my body buzzing, the air raw with smoke and electricity.

I expected the Cerberus's teeth to seize and thrash me at any moment.

But as the street returned to hazy form, I saw my gamble had worked. The Cerberus was gone, probably limped off somewhere following the direct hit, and I was alive. My shield had channeled enough of the lightning's energy into the ground, sparing me the brunt. But I didn't need to see myself to know I was in bad shape. Pain burned through me as I rolled onto my side, both ears ringing.

Before I could summon healing magic, flashing lights arrived. The shadow NYPD.

I had managed to keep hold of my sword and staff, and I raised the blade weakly. The cruisers stopped a half block away, their red and blue lights arcing around the slummy stretch of Seventieth Street. A spotlight lit me up from above as a helicopter's rotary blades thumped through my partial deafness.

Back at the cruisers, a familiar figure was stalking toward me in a sidestep, both hands gripping her service pistol. I couldn't make out Vega's shouted commands, but they weren't hard to guess. She was making her arrest for the murder of Bear Goldburn. And this time, she would get it.

I cycled through my remaining resources before grunting a weak laugh. I had none.

As my vision steadied, it occurred to me Vega's weapon was aimed high. I struggled to turn my head. A dark figure moved in. The shifter? Hands grabbed me, but I was too weak to resist. Vega's voice rose in pitch, and her weapon cracked twice. The figure let out a cry, and I was falling again.

I landed with a thud.

A well-dressed couple jerked back in surprise, the man shielding the woman with an arm. Shadow Vega and the NYPD were gone. The sidewalk I was on featured a procession of lampposts that glowed against a clean building facade. I was back in the actual present. But it was all starting to blur.

"Call an ambulance!" the woman cried.

24

I looked over to find my wife sitting in a bedside chair, the window behind her glowing with sunlight. For a confused moment, I thought I was in her custody, but the pregnant swell of her stomach and the contours of our bedroom dissolved the notion.

"Hey," I rasped.

She looked up from her phone, her brow taut with concern.

"Hey, yourself." She came over and grasped my hand in both of hers. "How are you feeling?"

As I squeezed back, I performed a self-check. All the hurt places from last night were either painless or, like my left thigh, pulsating dully. The healing magic that moved through me suggested someone from the Order had been here.

I kissed her hand. "Much better."

"Here, drink some of this."

She lifted a large cup from our nightstand and held the straw to my lips. The water, enhanced with elixir, went down cold and soothing. When I nodded that I'd had enough she returned the cup and dried her hands on the thighs of her slacks.

"How did I end up here?" I asked.

"General notified me you were in their ER, and I notified the Order. We got you out of there as soon as we could."

My heart ached for her as I imagined the late-night call, the long drive to the hospital, the hours of waiting for me to awaken, wondering if I was going to be okay. And all while in her late third trimester.

"I'm really sorry about this," I said, gesturing to my supine body.

She leaned over and pressed her lips to mine. "Just shut up and tell me what happened."

"Which is it, shut up or tell you what happened?"

When she frowned, I snorted a weak laugh. I then told her everything, from my trip to the Discovery Society to being transported into the shadow present to fighting the Cerberus shifter to finally returning to the actual present on West Seventieth Street. The only part I left out was my encounter with her shadow. I didn't want her feeling guilty for something she'd had no control over. At one point, she touched the place where her shadow's bullet had seared my cheek, a thin scar now.

"What do you make of it all?" she asked when I finished.

"Well, for starters—and Hoffman's not going to like this— Bear Goldburn's killer definitely isn't Vince Cole. Bear wasn't even killed here. Everything the scrying spell showed me happened in the shadow present." That explained the heavily armed security I'd observed at the bar and thought was overkill. "The shifter took Bear to the body shop, where the shifter's master removed his kidneys."

"And his kidneys disappeared from his real body?"

"Apparently so. And I'm sure it has to do with the potion I found in his system. The same potion Robert Strock was carrying last night. I think he might be the 'master' in question. At the very least, it makes him a person of interest."

"Robert Strock died early this morning."

"What?" I pushed myself onto an elbow as she accessed the report on her phone.

"Yeah, his wife got up to use the bathroom, and when she came back to bed, she found him jaundiced and unresponsive. The first responders couldn't resuscitate him. He was declared dead at the hospital. But here's the part that's most interesting: 'Imaging showed he was absent his liver,'" she read.

"He was carrying the potion last night, just not in a bottle," I said, wanting to kick myself. "It was in his system. Someone else gave it to him."

"Any ideas who?"

"The two things the victims have in common are being among the city's most powerful men and holding fellowship positions at the Discovery Society. Everyone and their mother is going to be talking about the first, but my gut and magic are saying the second. And look at what's been taken. Kidneys and a liver."

"Purifying organs," she remarked.

"Suggesting this may not be a personal vendetta against the victims. The killer is after specific components from specific people. It also suggests they're not done. What's left among the purifying organs?" As part of her continuing education, Ricki had recently completed a course in forensic anatomy.

"The largest would be the lungs," she said. "Arguably a couple minor organs."

"So at least one more victim, possibly more. And the most likely targets are the remaining fellows, Sunita Sharma and Walter Mims. I think the potion in the victims' systems binds them to the fates of their shadow selves. Messy deaths over there, but complete mysteries here with no evidence or suspects."

"And if the perp is one of the fellows?"

I thought about Sunita's preternatural protection and Mims's consternated look when he spotted me at the meeting. "Could very well be, but they could also be carrying the potion inside them, like Strock. Or on the verge." I checked our bedside clock. It was a little after seven, meaning we had a shot at catching the two fellows at home. I lowered my legs off the side of the bed and sat up. "I need to see them," I said as the room wavered and steadied again. "Can the NYPD get their contact info and notify them they're in danger?"

"On it. I'll also put a watch on them. Guess who drew the case?"

"Hoffman?" I asked, taking my first tentative steps toward the closet.

"And you," she said from my elbow. "At the mayor's request. In fact, he wants you to call him as soon as possible."

Bear Goldburn and Robert Strock had been two of the cornerstones in Budge's recovery plans for the city. And now both were dead. I could only imagine the panicked meetings happening over the phone.

"The priority right now is denying the perp any more victims," I said. "I'll have to call the mayor from the road."

I had a shirt halfway off its hanger, when Ricki seized my wrist. Her intense eyes reminded me of her shadow. "I have a couple questions first," she said. "We're assuming the perp sent you to this alternate present, right? What's to stop them from sending you again?"

It was a great question. Unfortunately, I didn't have a great answer.

"I need to figure out how the perp managed it. It wasn't through the potion—if it'd been in my system, the hunting spell would have alerted me—which leaves remote magic of some kind. I'll prepare some potions before I head out again. I also have an idea for an enhanced weapon. If I *do* end up back there, I'll be ready."

I kissed her forehead, but her eyes remained grave.

"Who came from the Order?" I asked, changing the subject. "Arianna?"

"No, Gretchen."

I tuned into the currents of healing magic—traditional, but with odd fae-like swirls. And it was doing its job. I could barely feel the throbbing in my thigh now. Guilt twanged inside me. Maybe I'd been too hard on Gretchen.

"And guess who drove her to the hospital?"

With one leg inside my pants, I looked over. "No."

She nodded. "Bree-yark wanted to hang around until you'd recovered, but Gretchen insisted she needed to be taken home, and off they went."

"He *promised* he wouldn't talk to her."

"Oh, believe me, I gave him plenty of looks to let him know exactly how I felt. I think he was relieved to get out of there."

"Well, he'll be my first call this morning," I said. "I'm going to ask him to pick up a couple things for me."

"I'll get some coffee started while I call the department about the fellows."

When she left the room, I lowered myself to where she'd been keeping vigil and released a shaky breath. I'd kept it from her, but I was rattled to the core. She was right. There was nothing stopping the perp from casting me back to the shadow present, an even darker, more dangerous place than I'd let on.

A place where I'd nearly died.

But with the fear came a growing anger. By targeting me, the perp was threatening to make a widow of my wife, a fatherless child of my future daughter. And that thought pissed me off more than anything. When my hands ached, I realized I'd drawn them into fists. I pushed myself up again.

You want to duel, I thought at the perp. *Let's fucking duel.*

25

I had to force Ricki to take a nap while I worked in my lab. We were both spent, but her rest was more important, and I had a lot to do and not much time.

While beakers bubbled over burners, I ran another hunting spell on the potion that had been in Bear Goldburn's stomach. I siphoned a share of the essence into my cane and distributed the rest between a pair of amulets. I would be delivering one to Sunita Sharma and the other to Walter Mims. The NYPD had already contacted them, explained the danger, and told them to stay home. Cars were watching both places. So far, the two were complying.

With my potions needing another few minutes to reduce, I called Gretchen.

"What?" she answered.

"First, thanks for the healing last night. I feel a lot better."

"Well, it wasn't pleasant. You looked like something that got chewed up and shat out."

"Nice. Though I have to say, that's not far from what nearly happened."

Knowing her short attention span, I gave her the Cliff's Notes version of events. I'd apparently caught her in the middle of breakfast, because she smacked, slurped, and burped throughout my account.

"A Cerberus, huh?" she said, releasing a final belch.

"You're still helping on the case, right? I need to know a couple things. Mainly, how the perp shifted me to the shadow present. When you healed me, did you feel anything?"

"I felt a few things," she said coyly, "but it was completely necessary, I assure you. Anything energetic, though?" She cycled through her thinking noises. "Now that you mention it, there was a silver tint I thought odd. I just figured it was a residue from one of your spells. You've always been a slob in that department."

I tried to access it, but I couldn't feel anything. "Would you mind checking it out?"

"Sure," she said, surprising me to the point of suspicion. "I have a few errands to run, but I'll look for you as soon as I'm done. You said you needed to know a *couple* things. Is there a number two?"

"Yeah, do you know of any rituals that use livers, kidneys, and other purifying organs?"

"Hmm, not sure about rituals, but I once used them in a tasty quiche. Had to double up on the seasoning, though."

"I'm talking about human organs."

"Well, those came from an owl bear. I remember because it involved grating the beak for thickener. Boy, I really had to put my shoulder into that. Things are like rocks."

"Getting back to the ritual, is that something you could look into? I'd do it myself, but I'm desperately short on time."

Not only did I have to prepare for any future leaps into the shadow present, I needed to deny our perp any more organs, and that meant getting to the remaining two fellows, like an hour ago. As much as I was burning to find and hammer the killer, I needed to set up my defensive pieces first.

"I'll try to have some info when I come," Gretchen said, surprising me a second time. "Will Bree-yark be there?"

And there it was, the reason she was being so helpful.

"I'm not sure," I lied as a knock sounded downstairs.

Gretchen heard it too. "Is that Bree-yark?"

"I've gotta go. Thanks again for your help."

I ended the call and climbed down from the lab to answer the door. Tabitha, who didn't appear to have budged since the day before, squinted at me from her divan.

"What's a girl have to do to get a few calories around here?"

"I'll be happy to take your goat's milk out of the fridge, but you'll have to heat it up."

"God," she complained. "With this place wall-to-wall, you'd think *someone* would make themselves useful."

I answered the door to find Bree-yark carrying a brand new trench coat in the crook of his elbow and clutching a plastic shopping bag.

"Thanks a lot, man," I said, taking both items off him and jerking my head for him to enter.

He craned his stout neck as if to ensure the coast was clear before crossing the threshold. "Boy, am I happy to see you up and about!" he said, clapping my shoulder hard enough to knock me off balance. But his expression quickly turned stern. "You were supposed to call me when you headed out again."

"Sorry, I ran out of time. Barely made it to the Discovery Society myself."

I checked the receipts of the items he'd bought and pulled several twenties from my wallet. When he tried to refuse them, I tucked the folded bills into the breast pocket of his denim overalls. He started to pull them out, then appeared to think better of it. His pension from the goblin army barely got him through the month.

"Are you hungry?" I asked.

"Nah, I grabbed a pizza on the way over. Hey, Tabby!"

"Hi," she said, disconsolately. "Sorry, but that's all I have the energy for."

"Yeah, 'cause you've been cooped up inside this place too long," he said. "Everson and I are going on a couple house calls. Wanna come?"

I made a throat-slashing gesture—time was of the essence, and the last thing we needed was forty pounds of attitude weighing us down—but Bree-yark didn't catch on. He strode to the divan and stood over her.

"C'mon, I'll fix us a couple meals to go. That all right, Everson?"

Tabitha lifted her head. "Prepared meals, you say? Do we still have those tuna steaks?" she called past him.

"I think so," I said, and immediately regretted it.

"I suppose three or four spice-rubbed steaks with a balsamic drizzle wouldn't hurt," she moped.

Bree-yark ruffled the hair on her head, which she tolerated with flattened ears. "Attagirl!" he said. That told me just how much she liked him. For anyone else, the gesture would have meant certain death.

"And a half gallon of goat's milk warmed to one-twenty," she added.

As Bree-yark headed into the kitchen to get started, I made a mental note to pack a dropper bottle of knock-out potion.

"I'm assuming your wife told you?" Bree-yark said as he drove.

We were in his Hummer, his and Tabitha's lunches packed

and my new trench coat heavy with spell items. Tabitha had made herself comfortable in the back seat on a throw blanket that she'd had Bree-yark refold several times.

"About you and Gretchen showing up together last night?" I said.

"Look, it's not what you think. She came to my place to tell me you were in the hospital. She offered to ride with me—you know, use her magic so we'd get there faster. What was I supposed to do? I was freaking out."

His concern was moving, but I wasn't about to let him off the hook. "Where did you go after the hospital?"

"I took her home."

"And you just dropped her off, right?"

"Well, she might've invited me in for some pickled anchovies on rye. I was starving, Everson. And, well … it's my favorite snack."

As if Gretchen hadn't known that.

"How long did you stay?"

"An hour? Maybe two? We just talked," he added quickly. "But you know, it was kinda nice." His lips spread into a reflective smile. "She was actually interested in what I've been up to. And when I talked, she listened. That never happened when we were together. She's like another person."

Nope, I thought. *Same Gretchen, different game.*

"Bree-yark, you promised me you wouldn't talk to her."

"Yeah, well, what was the harm? Nothing came of it."

Not this time, but Gretchen's machinations were wearing him down. It wasn't a question of if, but when.

"Did you enjoy the hoagie?" he asked out of the blue.

"Huh? Oh, actually, I dropped it in the shadow present and it didn't make the trip back. Sorry about that."

"Well, there you go."

"There I go, what?"

"That was the deal. I promised not to talk to her if you promised to eat the hoagie."

I scoffed. "One, I had no control over that. And two, you didn't know I hadn't eaten the hoagie before you talked to her."

"A deal's still a deal."

Seeing his way free on a technicality, Bree-yark wasn't about to concede. He redoubled his grip on the steering wheel.

"Just think about Mae," I said. "Think about what that would do to her. Most importantly, think about what you'd be giving up. Honestly, compare a typical day with Gretchen to a typical day with Mae."

I watched his eyes dim then light up.

"See? There you go. I rest my case."

His eyes went dim again. "It's just…"

"Just what?"

"Gretchen said Enzo is about to propose."

"Yeah, I wouldn't believe that for a second."

"No, no, he took her to a jeweler after lunch yesterday to have her finger measured. She showed me the card and everything. She's really torn. She likes his company, but she's not sure he's the one. At the same time, she doesn't want to be alone."

"And how is that your problem?"

"Everson's right," Tabitha said from the back seat. "I'm no fan of Mae and that *thing* she calls her pet, but if I had to see Gretchen every day, I'd hang myself with my own tail. She's revolting. Even talking about her makes me nauseous."

Seeing he was outnumbered, Bree-yark grunted and became interested in the road.

Sunita's place was across the Hudson River in New Jersey. We pulled up in front of a modest house with red trim and a neat yard. Two unmarked surveillance vehicles were parked nearby. The NYPD knew we were coming but Sunita didn't. I pulled out my phone and called her.

"No answer," I said after the fifth ring.

Bree-yark and I got out and walked to the front door. I moved stiffly, thanks to a sawed-off shotgun holstered under my coat. The gun was from Bree-yark's collection and loaded with rock-salt shells that he'd purchased for me and I'd soaked in an enhancer. If the "master of many places" whisked me back to the shadow present again, his "shadow of many faces" wasn't going to be a happy shifter.

I rang the doorbell.

When no one came, my heart pounded.

"Maybe she's out back," Bree-yark offered.

The gate to the fenced backyard was latched. I released it with an invocation, and it opened onto a mini Eden. Footpaths tracked through lush gardens and around a pond. I crept forward, too anxious to appreciate any of it.

"Sunita?" I called.

Our path led to a set of steps climbing to a small deck. As I eyed the back door, I wondered if we were going to enter to find her on the floor, her face blue, hollow cavities where her lungs had been.

A splash sounded in the pond behind us, too large for a koi. I turned to find the water churning, waves lapping into the surrounding garden.

"What in thunder?" Bree-yark muttered, drawing a blade from his ankle sheath.

I didn't like it either. The once-still pond was acting like a meteor had dropped into it. I released my sword from my staff and drew the two apart. At the same moment, something almost as large as the pond thrust to the surface.

26

I stared, struggling to make sense of what I was seeing. The creature was brown and horny with multiple staring eyes. A dozen appendages, thick and segmented, writhed from a head that was also its body, churning the pond waters muddy.

"I've been to every corner of Faerie," Bree-yark said, stepping back, "and I've never—*argh!*"

An appendage lashed out, quick as a frog's tongue, and wrapped his leg. Before I could cleave it with my sword, it retracted. One moment Bree-yark was standing beside me, and in the next, he was over the pond, his work boots planted on either side of the creature's yawning mouth, which bristled with fangs.

"Everson!" he barked.

I invoked a shield around myself an instant before another appendage arrived and thumped against it.

"Hang tight!" I called, digging into a coat pocket.

But two more of the creature's tentacles were already wrapping Bree-yark. One immobilized his arms, pinning his blade to his side. The other circled his legs. Bree-yark grunted, straining to keep his feet from being pulled together and into the creature's mouth. Beyond its fangs, a purple tongue lurched back and forth.

"*Protezione!*" I shouted.

Bree-yark's legs faltered and his feet came together, but a wall of hardened air now spanned the creature's mouth. Denied its meal, the creature threw a thrashing tantrum that involved waving Bree-yark around. I clutched a vial of ice crystals, searching for an opening while trying to reassure Bree-yark help was coming.

There!

With a pair of Words, I dispersed the creature's muzzle and shot the vial into its mouth. As the vial slammed the back of its throat, I shouted, "*Ghiaccio!*"

The creature let out half a gagging noise before the released magic froze its convulsing throat muscles. The crystals worked quickly, growing frost over the creature's hide and films of ice over its many eyes. The tentacles went herky-jerky and then turned into rigid statues. I splashed into the pond as the entire creature began to tip. With hacks of my sword, I shattered the tentacles holding Bree-yark.

"Thank the—*gaaawds!*" he shouted.

Falling from the creature's grip, he broke through the sheet of ice spreading around us. I grabbed the back of his overalls and pulled him, sputtering, from the water. We landed in a flower bed and lay panting.

"What in the blazes was that?" he managed.

"No idea. But it could explain Sunita's disappearance."

At that moment, the back door to the house opened, and the missing woman stepped onto the deck in a bathrobe, her hair wrapped in a towel. She looked from us to the pond creature as she padded down the steps on bare feet.

"I am *so* sorry," she said.

Bree-yark glowered at her. "That monstrosity is *yours?*"

"An early experiment gone awry," the bioengineer said. "I didn't have the heart to destroy him, so I took him home, and he started growing. He's really protective of the house. I wish you'd told me you were coming."

"I tried to call, but you must have been in the shower," I said. "Sorry about your ... experiment." I gestured toward the frost-covered creature, half capsized in a thick layer of ice.

Sunita's story reminded me a lot of Tabitha. I hadn't been able to destroy her as a little one either. And as much as the full-grown cat got on my nerves, I knew the devastation I'd feel if I ever found her like this. But Sunita surprised me by waving a hand.

"No worries. His tissue was engineered to survive deep freezes. He'll be fine once he thaws, though it may take another week for the appendages to grow back."

"Great," Bree-yark muttered.

"You're a magic-user?" she said to me.

"I am," I admitted. "I'm also the reason you have police protection. Is there someplace we can talk?"

Twenty minutes later, we were sitting in her living room. Sunita was the one dressed now, while Bree-yark and I wore towel skirts as our clothes tumble-dried in the laundry room. Chilled from my ice attack, Bree-yark clutched a steaming mug of Darjeeling tea in both hands. Tabitha sat on the couch beside him. She was under no-talking orders, and her slitted eyes peered around critically.

"So you think Bear and Robert were killed because they're Discovery Society fellows?" Sunita asked after I'd given her the rundown.

"I do. Someone wanted their organs—for what purpose we

don't know yet. Does the Discovery Society have any rituals, anything that goes back to its beginnings? To do with gods, maybe, or patrons?"

She shook her head. "If anything we've become more scientific as an organization."

Remembering Walter Mims's dry lecture from the night before, I nodded and struck off my theory that a ritual had endowed their organs with special properties.

"Whoever did this has access to the club," I continued. "The perp slipped both victims a liquid. Might even have happened in the lounge, where I understand fellows and members mingle? The liquid bound them to alternate versions of themselves. Versions the perpetrator was able to attack with impunity."

"Good thing I don't drink," Sunita said with a hollow laugh.

She touched the protective pin on her shirt. I had guessed she was already somewhat versed, or at least accepting, of the esoteric, and that seemed to be bearing out so far. Her expression remained serious.

"The liquid isn't in you," I reassured her. "My hunting spell would have told me. But I want to give you something." I drew one of the two amulets I'd prepared from my satchel. "Until we catch the perpetrator, I want you to wear this at all times. The gem will glow if you come within fifteen feet of the liquid in question. It will also alert me. Check it before you eat or drink anything, okay?"

She nodded as she accepted the amulet and fastened it around her neck. Beyond her professional veneer, I caught a glimpse of the grief she must have been feeling over the death of Bear, her former lover. If she was the perp, she was doing a damned good acting job to portray that kind of nuance.

She recomposed herself as she sat back again. "Do you have any suspects?"

"I was actually about to ask if you'd noticed anything odd

lately," I said. "About the club, it's members? Anyone new hanging around?"

"I hate to name names," she said, "but I saw you sitting with Ludvig Lassgard at the meeting last night. His ancestry goes back to the club's founding. As he's always saying, exploration is in his blood. We've felt that should count for something, which is why we've kept him on as an associate, even though he can't really contribute to our mission. That may seem cruel, but it gives him access to the meetings and most of the club. He's a little strange, you may have noticed. I always considered him a harmless enthusiast, but twice in the last month, I caught him coming out of collection rooms he shouldn't have been in. He claimed he got turned around, but it was like he was looking for something."

"Any idea what?"

She shook her head. "Our collections are pretty extensive and more maps and artifacts arrive every few months. It could have been innocent," she hastened to add. "I just thought it unusual at the time, and since you asked..."

"No, I appreciate it. We'll follow up. You mentioned artifacts. Has there ever been a box like this in your collection?" I pulled out my phone and showed her the shot I'd taken in the landfill two days earlier.

She cocked an eyebrow. "A flip phone?"

"Yeah, it's the most complicated thing I can manage."

"You can say that again," Tabitha muttered, prompting a warning look from me.

But Sunita was engrossed now in studying the image. "It's pretty, but no," she said at last.

Still convinced the Hermes box was connected to the murders somehow, I'd been hoping for a conclusive link to the Discovery Society. But Sunita's mention of artifacts arriving regularly interested me.

"Who curates the collection?" I asked.

"That would be Walter. And he takes it very seriously."

I nodded. Walter Mims, our next stop. He'd be able to tell me more about the holdings. Maybe he would recognize the box.

"Has anything in the collection ever stood out to you?" I asked.

"Nothing specific, but—this is going to sound really out there," she interjected self-consciously.

"More 'out there' than that thing in your pond?" Bree-yark asked, peering warily out a window onto the backyard. The creature was still entrapped in ice, but the sun had melted the frost from its hide and several eyes were starting to blink.

"There's a basement in the building," she continued. "It's where Walter stores newly arrived artifacts. He takes us down there from time to time to show us pieces. I never like going. It always feels as if there's something shadowing us, something dark. The building is old. It was an orphanage before becoming the Discovery Society's headquarters." Remembering my trip to 1800s New York, that didn't surprise me; the city had been crawling with orphans.

"The orphanage would lock troubled children in these small isolation chambers in the basement, so I attributed the feeling to trapped memories or lingering spirits. Ever since I was a young girl, I've been sensitive to subtle energies. But it wasn't just me—the right hand of Ganesh would start vibrating when we were down there. God, listen to me," she laughed, touching the protection pin. "Nobel Prize-winning scientist. But now that you mention it, I suppose the feeling could have come from an artifact. The climate-controlled cases hold a dozen of them at any one time. Walter can show you."

"Isn't that who we're seeing next?" Bree-yark asked me.

"Yeah, I have an amulet for him too."

Sunita snorted. "Good luck getting him to wear it."

After the way he'd reacted to my mythology-and-lore credentials the night before, I'd been afraid of that.

"Just one more question before we grab our clothes and get out of your hair," I said. "Did Bear happen to mention anything in the last month about being watched or followed? Or just anything unusual?"

Sunita's gaze dropped and she sniffled. "To be honest, we stopped talking about six weeks ago. Some things happened that I won't get into, but he thought it was for the best. If there was anything unusual, he wouldn't have mentioned it to me. You might want to ask someone closer to him."

She seemed to be confirming the rumor of her and Bear's affair.

I was going to leave it there—we needed to get to Walter Mims—but since she'd given me an opening...

"Did you two meet through the club?"

"No, at a bioengineering conference."

"Huh. Did it have anything to do with his work at Ramsa Inc?"

"It was one of his passion projects. He'd become interested in a gene called 7Rb, obsessed with it really." Seeming to catch the fact she was talking to laypeople, she said, "That's a variant of what's commonly called the 'explorer gene.' It appeared in the human genome roughly twenty-five hundred years ago and shows up in a small percentage of the population. The variant acts as a super driver for exploration and innovation. Bear wanted to patent a therapy that could maximize its expression, give visionaries like him an edge. He was using himself as a test subject, even though his profile for the variant was already in the top thousandth of a percentile. But he confided in me that the trials were making him edgy and aggressive. I urged him to stop. He did, not long after. But he'd become so enamored with bioengineering by that point, he talked me into applying to become a fellow."

She opened her hands as though to say, *And here I am.*

It sounded as though he'd become enamored with her too, but that wasn't my business. I stood and straightened my towel skirt. "If you think of anything else that might be relevant, give me a call. And please, stay home. Don't let anyone in, even if you know them. We're working on this as fast as we can."

The Doideag's haunting verse came back to me:

If ye should fail and war should come, if seas should boil and lands should run...

Sunita's green eyes peered into mine as if picking up my troubled thoughts.

"This is bigger than just me and Walter, isn't it?" she said. "Or Bear and Robert?"

"I think the perp is using the organs for something that could prove catastrophic," I said. "If we let it happen."

Nodding decisively, she removed her Ganesh pin. "Then you should have this."

"No, no, I can't." I tried to back away, but the couch stopped me. "It's a family heirloom."

"I'll expect it back when you're done," she said, pinning it to my coat.

It was a touching gesture—if I could trust her.

I waited until we were back in Bree-yark's vehicle before unpinning the protection and burying it in a bag of neutralizing salt.

27

"Everson!" a boisterous voice said over the phone. "Long time, buddy."

We were just pulling away from Sunita's house, Walter Mims's address punched into Bree-yark's GPS, when my phone rang. I hadn't recognized the number, but the distinct voice belonged to Mayor Lowder. And it *had* been a while, about eight months, since we'd worked together. That was when infernal bags were detonating throughout the city, causing mass casualties and culminating in a demon attack at Yankee Stadium during game six of the American League Championship.

Strangely, that felt like the easier case right now.

"Hi, Mayor," I said. "I tried calling you earlier."

"It's Budge to you, and sorry about that. I've been in meetings all morning. The murders, first Goldburn and now Strock..." When he blew out his breath, I pictured him wiping his cowlick from his pudgy face. "Tragic, horrible. And it's really put the city in a tough spot. Our municipal bonds are taking a dump in trading right now. They're losing faith in us, Everson. I need some good news from you."

"Well, we're closer to understanding what's happening."

"Hold that thought. My secretary's trying to put Detective Hoffman through. You there, Detective?"

"Yeah," came Hoffman's raw voice.

"Go ahead, Everson," Budge said. "Tell us everything."

As Bree-yark drove back toward the city, and the smell of Tabitha's tuna lunch filled the Hummer, I broke down what I knew: how the perp was using the shadow present to attack the victims; and what I suspected: that the perp was targeting them for their organs and their connection to the Discovery Society.

Hoffman scoffed a couple times, but Budge was all ears. He'd learned a lot during the monster eradication campaign, though it also helped that his late wife had been a werewolf.

"Interesting," he remarked when I finished. "What do you think, Detective?"

"Great story, but our best lead is still Vince Cole, the attorney."

"Vince Cole?" I repeated. It was as if Hoffman had had putty in his ears for the last fifteen minutes. But according to Ricki, this was a pattern with her partner—favoring a suspect early and then stubbornly holding on, even as evidence mounted suggesting someone else was responsible. Given the immense pressure he was under, that instinct in Hoffman had probably kicked up another notch.

"Fine," I said. "What's his connection to Strock?"

"He worked with Strock in the past, on a libel case. Could have been a payment dispute."

"Cole's firm specializes in all-star clients," I said. "He's worked with just about every big name in the city."

"He worked with me once," Budge offered.

"What did you learn from the cell tower data on Cole's phone?" I asked.

"What were you even doing poking around the Discovery Society?" Hoffman asked irritably, confirming that the cell data lined up with Vince Cole's account of dropping Bear off that night. "You were supposed to be hunting Sven Roe and building golems."

"The Sup Squad is working on Sven, and the golems became unnecessary when my magic led me to the Discovery Society."

I was fudging the timeline a bit, but Hoffman didn't need to know that. He stammered before shouting, "Well, what do you want us to do? Raid this *shadow* place and round up all the owners of three-headed dogs?" The only reason he wasn't swearing was because the mayor was on the call.

"It's better than harassing an innocent man," I shot back.

"All right, all right," Budge stepped in. "The detective has a point, Everson. What's the plan? Where do we go from here?"

"What're you asking him for?" Hoffman growled. "I'm lead on this."

"And Everson's our special consultant," Budge said. "I want to hear what he has to say."

I pictured Hoffman's face growing redder around his grinding teeth.

"Well, the remaining fellows are under police watch," I said. "And I just delivered a special amulet to Sunita Sharma, one that will detect the potion the perp is using to bind his victims. I'm on my way to Walter Mims's to do the same. If the perp makes a move on either one, I'll get an alert. I also have an associate looking into how the perp might be using the organs. While she's doing that, I'd like to talk to Vince Cole."

"Why?" Hoffman barked.

"Because he was Goldburn's friend, and they were together the night of his murder. I have some questions."

"One, no one talks to him but me," Hoffman said. "I have a system. And two, he isn't talking."

"One, you don't know what to ask him. And two, just because he isn't talking to you doesn't mean he isn't talking."

"Oh, you want your shot, Sherlock?" Hoffman laughed. "Well, you go right ahead—he's in the Yellow Pages—but you're flying solo. Any lawsuits he slaps you with is on your dime, not the NYPD's."

"He does like to sue," Budge cautioned.

"Well, we'll see what happens," I said, not so sure anymore.

Budge sighed. "So, no persons of interest yet, huh?"

"Vince Cole," Hoffman repeated.

"Everson?" Budge said.

I remembered what Sunita had shared about Ludvig, but being strange and getting caught in a collection room didn't make him a serial killer. And I was afraid that when Hoffman recognized Cole as a dead end, he'd go after the next lukewarm lead like a shark in an inflatable kiddie pool. I decided to keep the suspicions about Ludvig to myself.

"No, but I have a hunch something in the Discovery Society collection is involved," I said. "Mims is its curator. I'll see what he can tell me."

"The papers smell blood," Budge said somberly. "Two are planning to run editorials tomorrow saying the progress of the last couple years was an illusion, that Murder City is back. If the story grows legs, this morning's sell-off is gonna be a whimper compared to the coming shitshow. And without that funding, we can kiss our redevelopment plans goodbye. We'll have to cut services, including police. Next thing you know, the tax base is fleeing, which means even less money. Then we really will be Murder City again. Christ, guys. I need something by the end of the day. Can you do that?" he pled.

I didn't want that future for the city or my family. It sounded too much like the shadow present. "We'll keep at it," I assured him.

Hoffman grumbled something incoherent.

"Gotta run, guys," the mayor said suddenly and clicked off.

I was about to end the call myself when Hoffman growled, "Croft."

I sighed. "Look, I'm not trying to be a pain in your ass. You drew a really bizarre pair of cases, and I'm doing everything I can to help. That's why you brought me in, right?"

"I just got a message that Mims left his place," he said.

"What?"

"Walked out. The officers on duty lost him in the subway. Thought you'd wanna know before heading over." Hoffman sounded as if the mayor's parting words had emptied his resolve, but my own was ramping up.

"Where was he last seen?"

"The Jefferson Street station."

"Okay, thanks."

"If you get something solid, let me know."

Hoffman may have wanted to stomp me for challenging him in front of the mayor, but he wasn't going to sever a lifeline. Before I could reply, he hung up.

"What's going on?" Bree-yark asked as I started to swear.

"Walter isn't at his apartment. He's gone AWOL."

"You think he's behind the murders?"

"Either that or he's being a dipshit."

With the phone pressed to my chin, I considered the mayor's plea and the Doideag's verses about a coming war. I also considered that I could be yanked into the shadow present at any moment.

"No more fucking around," I muttered.

"Oh, *you're* free to use that word when it suits you, I see," Tabitha said from the back seat.

I called Ricki, who had left the apartment for work shortly before me and Bree-yark.

"How's it going?" she answered.

"I need a favor."

A HALF HOUR LATER, the building superintendent was unlocking Walter Mims's door for me and a pair of NYPD officers. Ricki had arranged the "wellness check" on the pretext that Walter wasn't answering his phone and that the officers on duty might have been mistaken about seeing him leave.

We stepped into an untidy apartment whose living room had been transformed into an office, a large computer desk holding court, surrounded by several bookcases.

"Walter?" one of the officers called.

Leading with her sidearm, she and her partner disappeared into the back.

I nodded at the superintendent that we could take it from here, and he closed the door behind me. Legally, we were in a gray zone. Once the police ascertained Walter wasn't home, and there were no signs of foul play, we were required to leave.

Wasting no time, I activated my hunting spell while scanning the apartment on the physical and astral planes. Planetary models stood here and there while photos of colorful galaxies adorned the walls.

Nothing atypical, and my cane wasn't picking up anything.

"Place is empty," the officer said, reholstering her sidearm. "Let's go."

"Okay, just give me a sec," I said, ducking into the bathroom. "Nature calls."

"Croft, we're not supposed to—"

I snapped on the ventilation fan, cutting her off. I'd already sighted the brush sitting on the edge of the sink. Closer inspection revealed snagged strands of thin brown hair. *Got you, you son of a bitch.*

I was pulling several free when my phone rang. It was Ricki.

"I'm at the apartment," I said, speaking above the fan while trying not to be heard through the door. "Place is clean, but I've got some good material for a hunting spell. Shouldn't take too long to locate him."

"Don't bother," she said.

I stopped, a knot already forming in my gut. "Why not?"

"His body was just found."

28

By the time I arrived at Morningside Park, Hoffman was there, looking even more haggard than he'd sounded on the phone. He led me wearily past the police tape. In front of a park bench, a covered body lay flat on its back.

"First responders were trying to resuscitate him when I got here," Hoffman said. "Torso wasn't inflating."

"His lungs are gone," I said more than asked.

"Yup, and no cuts, like with the others." Standing unevenly on his ortho boot, he held up a photo. "This is how they found him."

I studied the image of Walter Mims sitting on the wrought-iron bench, neck craned back, the mouth below his inverted V mustache hanging open. His lips were deep blue, and his eyes stared from his crooked glasses in shock. Being suddenly without your lungs would do that, I thought grimly. Not a fate I would wish on anyone.

My cane wiggled, indicating Walter's body. At some point following last night's meeting, someone had slipped him the bonding potion and killed his shadow self. I glanced at the crowd gathered beyond the police perimeter.

"Was anyone with him?" I asked.

"Eyewitnesses say he came solo."

"Why would he leave the safety of his apartment and go to a random park?"

"To feed the birdies? The hell should I know?" Hoffman said irritably. "We're working on the warrant for his phone. Gonna see if he communicated with anyone before his death."

I was weighing different possibilities when Bree-yark called me. "Uh, Everson?"

I looked over to find him jerking his head toward a growing commotion. Gretchen was bumping and shouldering her way through the onlookers. She'd dolled up again, this time topping her outfit with an obscenely large sun hat. Oblivious to the crowd's complaints, she rose onto her tiptoes and peered around.

"There you are!" she called, spotting me.

"One sec," I said to Hoffman and ducked back under the police tape before Gretchen could barge into the crime scene.

I attempted to steer her from Bree-yark and Tabitha, but she used subtle enchantments to ensure we met right in front of them. "Oh, hi, Bree-yark," she said, affecting surprise. "Hello, Tiffany."

"It's *Tabitha,*" she hissed from her harness leash.

"What's up?" I asked Gretchen.

"I found the information you asked for on organ harvesting."

"Okay, great, but can we keep it down a little?" She was getting looks not only from the crowd now, but the investigative team. "In fact, let's go over here." I led her to the far side of a maple tree.

She checked to make sure Bree-yark followed before lowering her voice slightly. "In ancient Greece there was a movement among certain cult leaders to only use clean organs for their god offerings. They eliminated the brain and heart first, common sacrificial organs at the time. The cults believed they held humans' worst qualities: greed, lust, that sort of crap. Over time, other organs were struck out for this or that impurity—the stomach, for instance, because it was considered gluttonous. By the end, the puritanical cults deemed only three organs worthy of the gods."

"Let me guess—kidneys, liver, and lungs?" I peered back toward the crime scene.

"Yup, and they were offered in boiling blood, which represented the soul, the purest of the pure."

I nodded at her, impressed. She'd delivered a succinct explanation of exactly what I'd asked for. I couldn't remember that ever happening.

For Bree-yark's part, his expression remained stoic; he might have been thinking about our earlier talk. Tabitha was using him as a barrier so she wouldn't have to look at Gretchen's face. A few biting remarks emerged from behind Bree-yark's legs, but I was too fixated on the last thing Gretchen had said.

If there was blood yet to be harvested, the killer wasn't done. Though grisly, the idea also offered a sliver of hope. We could still stop the killer from completing what appeared to be a god offering.

"Was the Attican cult among them?" I asked.

"Now *that* I didn't find out," Gretchen said. "It's very possible, though. There were a number of puritanical cults active during that time. They worshipped gods across the entire pantheon, old and new."

"So maybe the Hermes cult, maybe not," I said, thinking out loud. "But why Discovery Society fellows? Why would they be targeted?"

Gretchen shrugged. "Anyone hungry? There's an oyster bar nearby that's supposed to be halfway decent."

I caught Bree-yark's ears perk up, but he quickly flattened them again.

"Hold on," I said as Gretchen started to turn. "You promised to check out that silver residue on me."

"Oh, right," she said unenthusiastically. Even putting on her best face for Bree-yark, she could only sustain her good will for so long. Arms folded, she cocked her head, eyes roving the length and breadth of my body.

"Ah, there it is," she said at last, then snorted. "Looks like you're festooned in tinsel."

"Did someone put it there?" I asked, struggling to come up with how or when that would have happened.

"The pattern's too random. It's almost like someone hit you with a blast of birdshot."

"Wait a minute," I said, thinking back. "When Bree-yark and I were in the landfill and the garbage animation had him by the leg, I didn't invoke a protection before dispersing the box's magic. There wasn't time. The release hit me in a scattershot, but because it didn't seem to do any damage, I dismissed it."

"Well, there you go," Gretchen said, losing complete interest.

"So that magic's the reason you're going into the shadow present?" Bree-yark asked me.

"More than likely."

I thought about my theory that the thieves' cult had developed the ability to cross in and out of the shadow present, focusing that magic into an object—possibly whatever was inside the box. Or even the box itself. The first time I'd crossed felt spontaneous, but the second time someone had not only sent me, but arranged for the police to be there to receive me. Once again, I tried to tap into the residue, but I couldn't feel it.

I turned to Gretchen. "Can you remove it?"

"Afraid not."

"You're not even going to try?" Bree-yark asked.

"Don't get your panties in a twist. My magic's telling me to leave it."

I eyed her suspiciously. "Are you sure that's not your stomach?"

"Pretty sure, but I'm getting cranky, which means I really do need to eat. And since you have Bree-yark on a leash even shorter than Tiffany's, it looks like I'll be asking Enzo to accompany me. Too-da-loo!"

In a flash of light, she disappeared.

"*Tiffany*," Tabitha spit, waddling from behind Bree-yark's legs. She squinted at Gretchen's just-vacated spot with murderous eyes. Bree-yark regarded the same spot gloomily before collecting himself.

"So you could still be sent back there?" he asked.

"Yeah, but at least I'll be ready." I patted my pockets of potions and the concealed shotgun, wishing I felt more confident than I did.

A sharp whistle sounded, and I looked to find Hoffman waving me back over.

"They're getting ready to bag him," he said when I arrived at the edge of the police tape. "Need anything off the body?" He shook several aspirin into his mouth and began crunching them.

I considered Walter's covered form. I could perform a scrying spell on the hairs, like I'd done with Bear's, but that would take time. His shadow had probably been similarly incapacitated by the shapeshifter, never getting a look at the killer's face.

"I'm good," I decided. "But can we agree this isn't the work of Vince Cole?"

The bruised bags of flesh around Hoffman's eyes bunched up as he ran his tongue around his teeth. "I'm willing to suspend that line of thinking till we find something better. What do you suggest?"

"Three murders, three Discovery Society fellows. I think it's time for a raid."

"Fine by me," he growled, "'cause I'm ready to break something."

29

With a blow from a battering ram, the front door to the Discovery Society splintered open, and the Sup Squad team poured inside. Hoffman and I followed, his sidearm drawn and my grip slick around my sword hilt. The last time I was here, I'd been sent to the shadow present. I was also ninety percent sure the killer had been here that night as well.

In the corridor of portraits, an iron-haired man was shouting and waving his hands as Sup Squad members ordered him to the ground at rifle point. I almost didn't recognize him without his hat and uniform, but the purple mole beside his nose was a giveaway.

"His name's Eldred," I said to Hoffman. "He's the doorman."

By the time we arrived, officers had patted him down, and he was sitting grumpily against the wall in an undershirt tucked into pressed gray slacks.

"What are you doing here?" Hoffman demanded. "Place is supposed to be closed."

"I have an apartment in the building," Eldred snapped back, making his mole bounce. "Did you know that door you just battered is hand carved? It goes back to the society's founding!"

"Like I give a shit," Hoffman snarled. "Anyone else live here besides you?"

When Eldred compressed his thin lips, I assumed the role of Good Cop and placed a restraining hand on Hoffman's arm. "Robert Strock was killed last night and Walter Mims earlier this morning," I said. "That's three fellows in the last week, and all under similar circumstances."

Eldred glanced over at me. Though he was trying to remain indignant, I could see that the news upset him.

"We're just trying to find and bring the killer to justice," I said.

"I'm the only one who lives here," he allowed. "But wait until the endowment hears about this."

"You can start by telling your *endowment* we have a no-knock warrant." Hoffman flapped the paper in front of his face. "If they have a fucking problem, they can take it up with the judge."

Though Hoffman was being needlessly rough, at least he'd recovered his spirit. We soon received the call that the five-story club was secure; Eldred was the only one here. Leaving him with an officer, we split up, each with our assignments. Mine was to go room-by-room, searching for any traces of the bonding potion.

I revisited the library and the meeting room, the last place I'd seen Strock and Mims alive. The staircase to the basement Sunita had mentioned was located in the back of a small storage room. I descended, flipping switches as I went, and stepped into an open area, the high ceiling helping temper my underground phobia. A pair of climate-controlled cases stood against a wall, holding several leather-bound books and exploration artifacts.

I looked them over before shifting to my wizard's senses.

Something stirred, making my skin prickle. It was a suggestion more than a presence, a shadow, but Sunita had been right to call it dark. It was also hungry. I tried to draw a sharper bead on it, but like an eye floater, every attempt only pushed it further away until I couldn't sense it anymore.

A bleed from the shadow realm?

Or from the past; it was hard to say. I spent another few minutes trying to find it before returning upstairs, relieved to be above ground again. Though the basement had been cool, my shirt clung damply to my back.

On the second floor, I arrived at the next location of interest: the club lounge. It was a cozy room with wood paneling and leather chairs. The Sup Squad had already pulled liquor bottles from cabinets and set them on the small bar.

As I passed my cane over the assemblage, it wiggled.

The hunting spell honed in on a mostly full bottle of single-malt scotch labeled *Discovery Select.*

I pictured Strock shooting the potion-laced drink before last night's meeting and Walter sipping it on ice after. Now both were dead. Sunita's teetotalling had likely spared her—for now, anyway. Before coming, we'd upped the police protection around her. She was the final living fellow, and I wanted to keep it that way.

"Bag this bottle as evidence," I told an officer.

As I stepped out, I nearly ran into Hoffman coming from another room holding a thick ledger.

"Mims's office," he said. "Can't get onto his computer yet, but it looks like he kept physical records of the club's inventory. I'll have it scanned for Vega so she can start going through it. Find anything?"

The shadow in the basement wouldn't mean anything to him, so I told him about the hit on the bottle in the lounge.

"Good, we'll check it for prints. The zoo crew's just arriving," he said, nodding at the staircase going down. "I'll get started on the interviews."

"I'll be there soon."

We had worked out the questions for the summoned members and staff ahead of time, and I trusted him to more or less follow my part of the script until I joined him.

I made a circuit of the remaining floors and collection rooms. None left the same impression I'd felt in the basement. At the end of the hallway on the top floor, I arrived at an open door to what must have been Eldred's apartment. As the club's lone resident, he had unfettered access to the collections as well as to the bottles in the lounge.

Leading with the hunting spell, I entered. The space was small, an efficiency really, featuring a solid brown area rug and sparse but immaculate furnishings. A pair of slippers sat in precise alignment beneath a bed whose covers had been tucked and folded. The bedside table held a sleeping mask and earplugs.

Control freak much?

I glanced over a wall-length bookcase holding several literary novels and a line of cookbooks. A few travel photos and artifacts adorned the shelves. Judging from his impressive record collection, Eldred's true passion was jazz. Probably how someone so tightly strung unwound in the evenings.

I snapped several pictures with my phone to look back over later.

Next I poked through a pair of unremarkable closets, then his bathroom. His cabinet held a few medicines, the only prescription bottle for something called Fludrocortisone. "Take twice a day with meals for low blood pressure," the label read. I snapped a photo, then closed the cabinet with a snort. Eldred struck me as anything *but* low blood pressure.

Spritzing his shower and sink with a homemade solution, I opened my wizard's senses. The solution was designed to react with even trace amounts of red blood cells, something that would have been in abundance if he'd cleaned up here after the shadow murders, but nada. Neither was my cane picking up the potion. I panned the apartment for any energetic anomalies before stepping out.

I still didn't like Eldred's access to everything, but at the very least it made him a good witness.

If he cooperates.

I returned to the library, where the arriving members and staff were filling out pre-interview paperwork. The actual interviews were being conducted in the meeting room in back. I knocked and entered to find Hoffman standing over Eldred, who was sitting with his arms folded.

"And I told you this was off record!" Hoffman shouted.

Color inflamed his cheeks, and his eyes were bulging from their bags.

I hurried over. "What's going on?"

Spiking his pen against his pad, Hoffman sat down with an explosive huff. "Eldred here is being a pain in the ass is what's happening. I've already explained that this is a voluntary process. Nothing he says can incriminate him or anyone else unless he chooses to say it on record."

"I won't be saying *anything* without the club's lawyers present," Eldred shot back.

"Why?" Hoffman challenged. "You hiding something?"

It looked as if Hoffman had met his match, but he was also on the verge of alienating our best potential witness, if he hadn't already.

"Whoa, all right," I said, sitting on Eldred's other side. "Let's all just take a few deep breaths here."

I took the paper Eldred had signed—damp and wrinkled from Hoffman seizing it at some point—and flattened it out. "Speaking as someone who's had plenty of dealings with the

NYPD, including being arrested and serving probation, this by itself protects you. A lawyer will tell you the same thing."

Eldred's eyes fell to the paper.

"I met you last night," I said, then chuckled. "I was actually that guy who showed up late. How long have you worked here?"

His shoulders retracted with importance. "Forty-two years."

"Wow, and you've lived here that whole time?"

"About half."

"Can I ask what brought you here?"

"The previous doorman was my father."

I'd managed to build a little rapport, but I could tell it was already wearing thin.

"You know, when I was up in the lounge, I noticed a bottle of scotch. Discovery Select? That's not one I'm familiar with. Is it connected to the club?"

I sensed that Eldred liked being a know-it-all, and his ready answer confirmed it.

"It was a label Strock created in *honor* of the Discovery Society. It hadn't gone public yet."

Probably why the perp chose it. They'd known Strock would drink and distribute it among the fellows. Though Hoffman still looked as if he'd bitten into a raw lemon, he kept quiet as he jotted down the info.

"We have a few questions about people coming in and out of the club," I said. "You're clearly in the best position to answer them, but if you'd rather not, we understand." I glanced over at Hoffman, who was looking back at me in disbelief. "I'm sure we can piece together that info from the staff," I finished.

Eldred scoffed. "They wouldn't know."

"Well, it won't hurt to ask them, right?"

"What kind of questions?" he asked, as if his time were important.

Hoffman allowed a grudging nod. My gamble had worked. We had him.

"For starters, do you keep a record of everyone who comes and goes?" I asked.

He held up the tablet from the night before. "It's all here. I check everyone in and out."

"Does anyone ever get in who shouldn't?"

"Our security is subtle but state of the art. We have rare collections to protect. Short of disabling the system and battering the door down"—He narrowed his eyes at Hoffman —"no one enters who shouldn't."

Hoffman cleared his throat. "Is it possible for anyone to come into the club and then hide till it closes?"

"No, it's not," Eldred stated.

"Have you ever seen a visitor or staff member somewhere in the club they shouldn't be?" I followed up.

"I have, as a matter of fact. And I don't mind telling you it was Ludvig Lassgard."

I pictured my happy, cross-eyed friend from the night before. The same person Sunita had named.

"What was he doing?" Hoffman asked.

"He was in a restricted room. The door was secured, but he claimed it was open and that he'd thought it was one of the public displays." Eldred scowled. "He plays the fool, but Ludvig knows exactly what he's doing. I've watched him. He's cleverer than he lets on. Did you know we had two pieces go missing last month?"

I straightened. "From the collection? What were they?"

"I'm not sure. I happened to overhear Walter talking about it. I brought up my suspicions about Ludvig, but Walter wanted to ensure it wasn't a stocking error before implicating anyone, especially his protégé."

Could explain why he was being so stern with Ludvig last night, I thought.

"Can you give us a minute?" I said to Eldred, standing and angling my head for Hoffman to follow. Grunting, he pushed himself from his chair and limped over to the far corner of the meeting room.

"Is Lassgard coming?" I whispered.

"Supposed to be. We contacted everyone who was listed as staff or a member."

"The other fellow, Sharma, said the same thing about him sketching around the collection rooms."

"Probably pawning antiques on the side," Hoffman said. "That's the club's problem. I'm trying to catch a killer here."

"Right, but what if one of the items compelled him. Remember the infernal bags last year? That all started with a necklace some guy found in the ruins of the Financial District. Cursed items pop up every so often, compelling people to kill, often people with no histories of criminality or violence."

"Well, how do we know *he* wasn't the one compelled?"

He squinted past me at Eldred, who'd picked up the form he had signed and was reading it over. I could tell by Hoffman's expression, he was doing the Vince Cole thing again, holding stubbornly to his favorite suspect.

"I don't like him," he muttered.

"Well, I can't say I'm a huge fan either, but we have more people to talk to, and Ludvig should be at the top of that list."

Hoffman's phone rang, and he dug it out of a pocket. "Hoffman," he answered, then listened for several seconds. "No shit?" He moved the phone from his mouth. "We just got the data back on Mims's phone," he told me. "Someone called and talked to him right before he left his apartment and—" He moved the phone back to his mouth. "Him, huh? Okay, sounds good. Yeah, we'll take it from there."

"*Who?*" I mouthed, the suspense killing me.

As he continued to talk, Hoffman scribbled on his pad and turned it around for me to see. His eyebrows went up in a gesture of concession.

Ludvig Lassgard, it read.

30

I was still looking at what Hoffman had written, that Ludvig was the last to call Walter before he was killed, when my own phone began to ring.

"Hello?" I answered distractedly.

"Professor Croft," came a prim voice.

For a moment I debated whether to fake a bad connection and end the call, but I cleared my throat. "Hi, Professor Snodgrass."

"Yes, I'm calling because—well, first, how are you doing?"

The last time he'd seen me, my office had just blown up and I was half cooked, not that he'd shown any concern. The present show sounded forced, as if his wife had scolded and shamed him into it the night before.

"Better," I replied.

"Yes, well, I apologize for reacting the way I did. I suppose it was the shock of—"

"Not to be rude," I cut in, "but I'm in the middle of something pretty important."

I looked over at Hoffman who was still on his phone,

discussing Ludvig. I heard him say something about picking him up.

"Yes, fine, this will only take a minute," Snodgrass said, sounding relieved to be past the niceties. "First, in light of yesterday's events, I went ahead and canceled your remaining classes this week."

"Appreciated," I said, surprising myself by meaning it.

"You didn't appear in any shape to teach, and I felt you could use the time to recover. It's just for this week, though."

Okay, now I was growing wary. "That was ... thoughtful of you."

"But what I really wanted to talk to you about was your lesson plans."

God. He was not going to let that go. I very nearly ended the call, but his next words stopped me cold.

"What I could read of them looked remarkably ... well, adequate. Organized, concise, supported by academic literature. To the extent mythology can be considered academic, but we won't revisit that debate here. I do appreciate—that is to say, I'm *glad* to see you took the new requirement seriously."

"My lesson plans?" I asked.

"Yes, while inspecting your office with an engineer I found them amid the debris. They were damaged, of course, but—"

"You found my lesson plans?"

"The only thing is, well, I hate to ask, but can you send me an unsullied version by Friday's deadline? I'll need it for the official file."

I was too dumbfounded to react to his very Snodgrassian request.

I had never written any lesson plans. But I'd asked "Sven Roe" to.

I thought back to the security footage of the young man

stooped before my office, bringing his pack around to his front. I was convinced he'd rendered the exploding sigil, but had he been sliding the lesson plans under my door? That didn't explain away the fire circle he'd drawn a day earlier, though, or his insistence that I teach him magic. He was still a piece of the puzzle somehow.

My magic nodded in agreement.

"You didn't throw them out, did you?" I all but shouted.

"Your tattered plans? No… I have them here in my office."

"Okay, hold onto them," I breathed. "I don't have another copy, and I, ah, I'm going to need them to make a new one."

"One of several duties a graduate assistant could have performed for you," he reminded me, sounding especially smug—no doubt from my apparent sudden about-face in the compliance department. But I wasn't thinking about his stupid requirement. I now had something tangible to hunt Sven.

"I'll get over there as soon as I can," I said.

I ended the call at the same time Detective Hoffman ended his.

"Lassgard was just picked up," he said. "We're getting the search warrants, but I want to head down to 1PP to see if we can get him talking. You already know him, so I want you there too. You did pretty good with what's-his-name." He jerked his thumb toward Eldred who was still at the table, then broke into a broad smile that lumped up his face. "I have a good feeling about this, Everson."

I did too, so why was my magic urging me to find Sven instead?

"I'm afraid you're going to have to start without me."

Hoffman's smile shrank. "What the hell for?"

"That call I got was a potential lead on Sven Roe."

"Guy who blew your door off the hinges? Screw him. If he's involved, we'll squeeze the info from Lassgard."

"Look, I happen to agree with that reasoning, but…" There

was nothing to do but level with him, even as the flesh around his eyes trembled angrily. "Well, my magic's telling me otherwise."

"Your *magic*," he spat.

"The same magic that led us here," I reminded him.

Glancing back at Eldred, Hoffman grumbled a few choice words before whistling a member of the Sup Squad over. "Take him where he needs to go," he said of me.

"Thanks, I'll call you as soon as I have something."

Before I could turn, he grabbed the shoulder of my coat and aimed a thick finger at my face. "You heard the mayor, we only have till tonight. You leave me hanging, and I'll take your ass down with me."

"Noted," I said.

Snodgrass wasn't in his office when I arrived at Midtown College, but he'd left the plans in a folder with the department secretary. I hustled it to the faculty restroom on the second floor and sealed the door with a locking spell.

Let's see what you left me, Sven...

The four pages inside were both fire and water damaged and barely holding on by a staple. They were the lesson plans for my class all right, but why would he have labored over them if he'd planned on killing me the next morning? Another of his games, like debating me in class or going by a pseudonym that turned out to be a rearrangement of my own name? Whatever the reason, he'd clearly put thought into the plans, which was a godsend. Mental efforts imprinted almost as well as emotions.

I wasted no time building a casting circle and uttering the appropriate chants. Within minutes, wispy essence was curling from the pages into the opal end of my cane. The cane stiffened and kicked hard in my grip, as if hooking a fish. I pulled back until I had a clear direction and grinned.

Got you.

The hunting spell led me through Midtown until I was looking up at an iconic landmark. From the strength of the spell, I'd known Sven was close—so close that I dismissed my Sup Squad driver and jogged after the spell on foot—but I hadn't been expecting the iconic entrance to Grand Central Terminal.

I passed under the Pershing Square Viaduct, entered the Terminal, and accessed the main concourse. From there, I followed the spell down a few ramps until it pulled me into a side stairwell. My chest started to tighten and my breaths to speed up—my longstanding phobia of going underground. The sounds of commuters and trains faded, and before long, I was in a restricted area of the station.

I crept down a steel staircase and through dust-covered machine rooms with giant rotary converters that once powered the old trains. Spots that could have been blood dotted the floor every few feet.

At a rusty metal door on which a faded "61" had been stamped, I realized where I was. The fabled Track 61, a hidden line that once spirited U.S. presidents from Grand Central to an elevator below the Waldorf Astoria Hotel. Defunct for almost a century, it made for a great hiding place.

I inspected the riveted frame. On the floor, I caught the edge of a familiar sigil. Angular like the one Claudius had found in the aftermath of the explosion at my office, this one was intact and humming.

So Sven did set the trap yesterday.

After sliding my lesson plans under?

It didn't make sense, but my priority right now was to find Sven.

I drained off the energy of the sigil and tested the door. It was locked, but a few grains of dragon sand in the keyhole remedied that. The melted bolt plopped to the floor as I eased the door open and pushed light from the shield enclosing me. The space beyond was bisected by a single track, a network of metal beams and pillars supporting the tunnel.

My spell tugged toward a lone box car in the center of Track 61.

I resisted the impulse to enclose the car in a sphere and pull out the available oxygen, rendering its occupant unconscious. If the door was warded, the car would be too, and that collision of magic could have ugly consequences. Right now Sven held the defensive advantage. Better to make him come to me.

"Sven Roe?" I called. "It's Professor Croft."

The words echoed briefly, the stuffy air down here quickly smothering them. Inside the box car, something scuffed.

"I'm alone," I said. "I just want to talk to you."

A moan grew into words: "Go away..."

Dark flames whooshed up on either side of the car and took humanoid forms.

Fire golems. Great.

And the two were armed with steel cables. I moved back as the lead golem lashed his cable, producing a whipcrack inches from my face. His buddy followed suit, his own crack leaving an imprint of flames in front of my retracted pelvis.

Sorry, guys, but Ricki may want another kid.

With a shout, I enclosed the lead golem in a sphere, while pulling a vial of ice crystals from a coat pocket. I'd gone to the ice well a couple times lately, but I was two for two, and if it wasn't broke...

"Ghiaccio!"

A subzero cone blasted from the tube and engulfed the second golem in a plume of steam. Still shaky from last night's beating, I struggled to maintain the two invocations while expelling oxygen from the sphere around the first golem. Sweat poured down the sides of my face and around my clenched jaw.

Shit, can't do it.

With a gasp, I released the sphere, sending out a burst of flames. My ice attack wasn't faring much better. The golem was bracing against the blast with folded arms, the fire at his core turning brighter as it pulled in more magic. I tossed away the exhausted vial and sidestepped, placing several pillars between us. The golems resumed their attack, their fiery cables sparking and clanging against metal.

I'd put down the landfill animation by dispelling the source of the magic, the metal box.

Probably in the box car, I thought, *but Red and Hot here aren't letting me get any closer.*

Every time I stepped around, the golems did the same, blocking my path to the car and lashing their cables to keep me away.

I drew the sword from my cane. The light from the golems swam around the blade's second symbol, the one for fire. The rune was potent enough that I'd only developed the capacity to really control it in the last couple months. But would it be powerful enough to absorb two fire animations?

One of the golems charged, giving me a chance to find out.

I grimaced against the bite of steel across my shielded back and drove my sword into his gut. Fire wrapped the blade. Aligned to the rune, I spoke its word. For a dizzying moment, I was back in the rock quarry holding the efreet, a primal white flame, the heart of all flames, flickering in her eyes. A sharp whoosh brought me back, and I blinked to find the golem twisting and diminishing into the rune.

It's working, I thought through gritted teeth.

More of the golem disappeared, until he was a messy whirlwind of flames.

But as my blade went from red to a molten orange, my hope faltered. The handle was becoming uncomfortably warm. That hadn't happened before. Wherever the fire was going, it wasn't going there fast enough, and the backed-up energy was gathering in the blade. A blade whose metal was reaching its limits.

Swinging my sword at the other golem, I shouted, *"Disfare!"*

The gathered fire released with such violence that I staggered back and the engulfed golem dropped his cables. His contours wavered as the magic struggled to sustain his form. A couple times the golem disappeared altogether. At last, he succumbed for good, the torrent of fire sweeping him into nothing.

"Hallelujah," I sighed.

I closed the rune and stood panting in the blistering space. Worried the animating magic would recover before I did, I limped to the back of the box car. At the top of three steps, a rear door stood ajar.

Draining another warding sigil, I inched the door open, ready to spring back. But no more flames erupted. Across the dark interior, a ragged breath rose and fell. I grew out the light from my staff until a lump took shape in the far corner, a figure curled on his side in a dirty sleeping bag. Even in the light, he looked like a shadow.

"Sven?"

"Go awaaay..." he moaned again.

He pushed a hand out, as if he were fighting something in a dream. The movement made him grimace and he clutched his shoulder. The protective animations may have been game for a fight, but he was in no condition himself, shifter or not.

But I was becoming more and more certain he *wasn't* the shifter.

I dispersed my shield to lessen the chances of triggering any remaining sigils and made my way toward him. The backpack I'd seen him carrying the day before lay near the foot of his sleeping bag, a couple soup cans spilling from its open mouth. When I squatted beside him, I smelled blood.

"Sven," I repeated. "It's Professor Croft."

Forgetting his pain from only a moment earlier, he attempted to shove me away with the same arm before contorting suddenly and dropping back into semiconsciousness. The kid was badly hurt.

Regretting I hadn't brought gloves, I inspected the shoulder of his gray shirt, black with blood, until I located a hole in the fabric. I ripped it open, laying bare a swatch of pale skin that turned gory around a gunshot wound. He mumbled feverishly as I peered under his shoulder. An exit wound had made an even bigger mess in back. Judging from the amount of blood-caking, the injury was hours old, and the droplets I'd seen en route indicated it had happened elsewhere.

"What in the world have you been up to, Sven?" I whispered.

Soft light swelled from my cane's opal as I started into a healing incantation.

He'd managed to make it down here without being seen, suggesting he'd been shot last night or early this morning, but his condition had worsened with blood loss and probably the start of infection.

I stopped suddenly and stared at him.

I was remembering the dark figure who'd grabbed me last night in the shadow present. Vega had fired at him twice, the figure crying out before dropping me again in the actual present.

"Holy hell," I said. "That was you."

Sven Roe had brought me back.

31

With layers of healing light swaddling him, Sven's breaths deepened with his sleep.

I lifted one of his eyelids to make absolutely sure he wasn't the shifter before sitting back on my heels. I'd performed enough healings in my time that for the past twenty minutes my mind had been free to ponder. But I was still no closer to understanding who he was, why he'd planted a fire sigil under my office door yesterday morning, and then rescued me from the shadow present last night.

Reaching over, I pulled his pack toward me, spilling the remaining soup cans. Inside the main compartment, I found a spare shirt, a toiletry bag, matchbooks, a portable music player, and a handful of scavenged things: among them, a bag of condiment packets. It was as if he'd packed hastily for a trip and then improvised once he'd gotten there.

In the small pockets, I found a notebook and writing utensils, one of them the silver-flecked grease pencil he'd used to draw the casting circle he'd left me. I opened the notebook to discover practice drawings of other circle renderings. He'd penned little notes here and there, as I might have done.

But how in the hell was he powering them?

As the pages progressed, I noticed the patterns suddenly go from round to more angular, like those on the Hermes box.

He has it, I thought with certainty.

I stood and searched the rest of the car but found only mundane odds and ends. Outside, I crawled beneath the car and peered into various compartments. I was finishing up when the obvious struck me. Back inside, I unzipped Sven's sleeping bag, and there it was, clamped between his knees—the small box. It was still in the salt bag, explaining why the citywide wards hadn't detected it again and alerted me.

I started to reach for it, then stopped.

I thought about the powerful guardian animations I'd encountered, first in the landfill, then here. Those hadn't come from Sven, but the Hermes box. For whatever reason, it wanted to be with him, not me.

But for good or ill?

The best answers would come from the kid himself, but that was going to be a while. My healing magic was having to pull triple duty—repair bone and tissue, restore a very depleted blood supply, and fight an infection.

Maybe I could get some help with the last two. Surprised to find a bar of signal on my phone, I called Ricki.

"I located Sven," I said, crossing to the far side of the box car.

"You did? Is he in custody?"

"Not exactly. We're under Grand Central Terminal. He suffered a gunshot wound and is in bad shape."

"Who shot him?"

"It's, ah, sort of a long story, but it happened in the shadow present. He's the reason I made it back. He grabbed and transported me somehow. He also has the box I recovered from the landfill." I'd zipped Sven's sleeping bag up again, but I could still make out the small lump between his knees.

"He was the one who stole it back from our apartment?"

"I won't know that until I can talk to him, and that's where I need some help. A couple years ago, you called your EMT friend when you needed blood. We met him in a garage really close to here, in fact."

She had been shot by a gang boss at Ferguson Towers. I'd removed the bullet and commenced a healing spell, but she'd insisted on continuing before she had fully recovered, nearly passing out. That had been our second case together, and the first time I realized I had more than professional feelings for her.

"Larry," she said. "He and his wife were at our wedding," she added thinly.

"Oh, yeah, that's right. Well, do you think he'd be willing to treat someone off the books?"

"Why off the books? If you're worried about the NYPD, I can take care of that."

So much had just happened, I'd nearly forgotten about the police efforts to find him.

"Because he's hiding down here," I said, glancing around the dark box car. "And I don't think it's just from the NYPD."

"All right, where are you exactly?"

"An old line under Grand Central."

"That explains the connection. Is there a place you can bring him safely?"

I peered out the car's window. Even if I found my way back up, I'd be carrying Sven into one of the busiest train stations in the country. As my eyes traced the tracks into the darkness, an idea hit me.

"Can you call the Waldorf Astoria and ask if their elevator to Track 61 still works?"

MIRACULOUSLY, the hotel had restored the elevator two months earlier with plans to begin offering tours of the historical oddity. After a hike down the tracks that involved shooing away rats and a wandering soul eater, I stood before a large metal door, cradling Sven, still in his sleeping bag. Machinery clanked and rattled somewhere overhead. Before long, the door opened to reveal a hefty gray-haired man wearing blue scrubs.

"This our guy?" Larry asked from behind a wheelchair.

"I really appreciate you doing this," I said, carrying Sven past a mechanic and into a large cargo space. The elevator had been built to carry presidential limos.

"Well, when Ricki asks a favor..." Larry paused to help me set Sven in the chair. "...she doesn't really let you say no, does she?"

"True enough," I chuckled, shaking out my aching arms.

Once Larry buckled Sven in place, he wasted no time inserting an IV cannula into his arm and attaching a bag of blood and a bag of saline. As the bags began to fill their drip chambers, the mechanic sent the elevator up. I'd carefully placed the Hermes box in Sven's pack, leaving the soup cans in the car, and I adjusted it on my back now. Larry used the slow, rattling ascent to check Sven's vitals.

"How is he?" The strength of concern in my voice surprised me. But Sven's youth coupled with the fact he'd pulled me from the shadow present made me responsible for him.

"Pressure's a little low, but the fluids will fix that. You seem to have a knack for stabilizing gunshot victims."

"Well, you learn from experience," I hedged. Larry didn't know about my magic.

When the elevator stopped, the mechanic had us transfer to a personnel elevator. After a couple floors, he handed us off to a hotel official, who showed us to a room being watched by plain-clothes officers.

I didn't know the rules on bragging about your spouse, so I didn't say anything, but Ricki had delivered on everything.

Larry wheeled Sven into the room, and the two of us lifted him onto a sumptuous bed. While I removed his sleeping bag and arranged the covers, Larry transferred the fluid bags to a bedside pole and hooked Sven up to a monitor. He administered an antibiotic shot to his shoulder and cleaned the wounds.

"Not nearly as bad as I was expecting," he remarked.

As he sutured the healing wounds closed, he said, "Oh, hey, forgot to ask Ricki. How'd you like that thingy we got you for your wedding?"

"Oh, it was ... great," I replied, my face already warming. I had no idea what he was talking about. "Much appreciated."

"Use it?"

"Yeah, a few times now."

He turned to me, his brow creased. "How's that possible?"

Before things could go from socially awkward to disastrous, Sven stirred and opened his eyes. Larry tied off the suture and clipped it. "He's all yours," he whispered. "If you need me, I'll be outside."

I waited for him to close the door before approaching the bed.

Sharpness was returning to Sven's dark eyes. He peered at me, then around the room. I could all but read his thoughts, especially when he began feeling around his legs, the sudden movement jiggling the fluid bags overhead.

"It's in here," I said, raising his pack.

Sven stopped searching for the box, but wariness remained in his eyes. I placed his pack on a chair close enough to calm him. Hopefully, the box too. I didn't need it throwing up any more guardians.

Sven stared at it for several moments, long enough for the bags to go still again, before licking his bottom lip and returning his gaze to mine. I caught the craving—needing something but wishing he didn't. When I shifted my senses to the astral realm, I could see the threads now that bound him to the box.

He cleared his throat, bringing me back.

"Hi, Professor."

32

"Hi, Sven," I said. "But that's not your name, is it? And you're not really my student."

I doubted he was nineteen either, but that wasn't high on my concern-list at the moment. Though his eyes remained fixed on mine, I could tell his mind was darting around in search of an answer.

"No," he finally admitted.

"Then let's start there. What's your real name?"

"I'd rather not say."

"Why not?"

"Because I've been using Sven Roe. For the sake of consistency I'd like to keep using it, at least until this is over."

"Until what's over?"

He glanced toward his pack. "I'm not sure."

"How did the box come into your possession?"

"I found it."

"At the Discovery Society?"

"No, but you shouldn't go there."

"Why not?"

"You just shouldn't."

He was being evasive, and I thought I knew why.

"The police search has been called off," I told him.

"But I'm in your custody, right?" he said, confirming he'd caught wind of the hunt.

"You're in my *care*. You're not under arrest, though, no. Whether it stays that way is up to you."

Understanding the deal, he nodded. "I stole the box, last month. From a mansion in Tribeca. It was in the owner's private collection."

"So you're a cat burglar?"

He let out a dry laugh. "No, Prof. I'd never stolen anything before in my life. I mean, beyond the odd pack of gum when I was a kid. Wish it had stayed that way. Guess I should start at the beginning?"

"Please do."

"About a year ago, I found an old rune book in Benson's Books on Ninth. It spoke to me. Not literally. It spoke to me like mythology does. In fact, I was there hunting for a rare book on Sumerian myths."

I almost asked him if it was the one by Fleming, but I didn't want to interrupt.

"Anyway, I got the rune book—*paid* for it—and started practicing. The runes were pretty basic. Bending light, jiggling small objects, that sort of thing. Parlor tricks that I could sort of do, but not great. The big leap happened with the final rune, Vagueness. Once I got that one to work, I could walk all around the apartment without my mom noticing. She even called me for dinner a couple times when I was standing right next to her. It also helped with some problems I'd been having."

"Bullies?" I asked, noticing the lateral crook in his nose.

"Street gangs. I had the rune tattooed on my thigh in silver ink. Cost half my savings, but it was worth it. Whenever I saw the Skulls or Boyz coming, I could invoke it and walk right past them." His eyes shone at the memory. "It was like having an invisibility cloak. I started taking longer walks around the city. Seven, eight, ten miles at a time. I even went out at night, got into historic places I wasn't supposed to. That's how I fell in love with New York, as messed up as it is."

He and I had some things in common, but I didn't want him getting too comfortable yet.

"Did you use the vagueness rune to steal the box?" I asked.

The excitement left his eyes. "That rune and a couple others, yeah. I can't even really explain how it happened. I was taking one of my walks, and I found myself in front of a mansion on Reade Street. Nothing about it stood out from the others, but I couldn't stop staring. When I finally continued, it felt like a voice was calling me back."

The Hermes box, I thought.

"That night, I dreamt I broke into the mansion. It was incredibly vivid—from which runes I used, to my path through the house, to entering a walk-in vault and retrieving a little metal chest." He glanced toward his pack again. "The next morning I thought, 'Huh, weird dream.' But it stayed with me, only it was more like, I don't know, an *obsession*. I couldn't stop thinking about it. Every day the pressure around it built and built until it felt like if I didn't do what the dream showed me, I'd go insane."

He was describing an enchantment, no doubt given off by whatever was inside the box.

"So one night, I did it," Sven said simply. "I stole it. The trunk was exactly where it had been in the dream. By the time the adrenaline hangover went away, the obsession was gone. Still, I had no idea what I was supposed to do with the chest. I tried to open it a few times, but the lid wouldn't budge."

"You don't know what's inside?" I asked, concealing my disappointment.

"No, so I started rendering the symbols on the lid, testing their power."

I nodded, remembering how the drawings in his notebook had changed.

"Nothing really happened except that over time I came to understand their features."

That was the enchantment bonding him more strongly to the item, infusing him with arcane knowledge.

"I began adding some of the features to my existing runes, and whoa! I could create fire. The rune ignited half my bed that first time before I beat it out with a pillow. And with the rune I'd been using to move small objects, I could suddenly generate huge forces, even scarier in some ways than the fire. But when I added the features to my vagueness rune..." Excitement returned to his eyes. "I found myself in another reality, another version of the city. The same place, but really different."

He'd evidently become imbued with the magic that had coated me in the landfill, enabling my own journey to that other version of the city.

"And excuse me for swearing, Professor, but that's when shit got serious. The vivid dreams came back, only now they were about a big war."

"A big war?" I echoed, remembering what the Doideag had prophesied.

"And not just any war. The Titanomachy."

The Titanomachy was the battle between the Titans, led by Cronus, and the Greek gods of Olympus, led by Cronus's son, Zeus. The original clash of the Titans, it pitted the older generation of gods against the younger in the highest-stakes battle in Greek mythology, for control of the entire Universe.

"At least that's what I think it was," he said. "I could see lightning bolts, the Hecatonchires were chucking stones with their hundred hands, cyclopes were running past. There was smoke everywhere and earth-shaking explosions and the shadows of giant, grappling gods. It was crazy. Also really scary."

"What were you doing in the dream?"

"I was *fighting* in the freaking thing."

"And the obsession you described after the first dream...?" I asked carefully.

Sven gave a solemn nod. "It came back. Not as insistent. Yet. But it's there."

I trained my gaze on his pack. What in the hell was the Hermes box doing to him?

"Twice I tried to ditch it in the other reality," he said, following my gaze. "And twice it found its way back to me."

I remembered the first hit on the box the week before, when I'd gone to an alley and found nothing. The second time, Sven must have tossed it in a dumpster, which explained how it ended up in the landfill. Though I'd packed the box in salt and placed it in my casting circle, the threads to Sven remained. Which meant I'd been wrong about someone stealing the box from my lab; the box had *stolen* itself.

But Sven had just confirmed something else.

"When you said you found yourself in a different reality," I said. "You're talking about this one, aren't you?"

His dusky appearance was the first clue. I'd noticed it the other day in my classroom. Beneath the fluorescent lights he'd still appeared to be in partial shade, but at the time I hadn't given it a lot of thought. It also explained why I hadn't detected his magic. Its source was on the other plane.

And then there was his account of the city. Though still dodgy, Manhattan wasn't so dangerous that you couldn't take a walk alone in broad daylight. People did it all the time. But not in the shadow present.

Sven nodded. "Yeah. And this place is... It's just..." His eyes glistened as he looked around the room. "It's amazing."

"I can only imagine," I said gently.

It must have been like someone who'd been colorblind seeing clearly for the first time. And that was to say nothing of experiencing a version of the city that was considerably nicer than the one he'd grown up in.

"Anyway..." He wiped his eyes. "I learned about you from a search at the New York Public Library. The one here," he clarified. "There were articles about your role in the mayor's monster-eradication program, and they said you were a professor at Midtown College. I wanted to check you out, so I audited your course—which I enjoyed, by the way, even if we see tricksters differently. When you brought up the grad assistance thing, I saw it as a chance to get your help. But first I needed you to take me seriously."

"The fire circle you left on my desk," I said.

He gave me a guilty look. "It was a spur-of-the-moment thing."

"Was the one you drew under my office door spur-of-the-moment too?" My voice turned hard as I replayed the explosion that had thrown me into a wall, incinerated my favorite coat, and ripped into skin.

Sven looked down at his hands. "I can't explain that. I was delivering your lesson plans. You weren't there, so I slid them under the door. And the next thing I knew, I was drawing the rune. It wasn't one I'd rendered before—a combo of force and fire. I even used tanzanite. I knew it might hurt you, but ... it felt *necessary*."

"Like the compulsion of your stealing dream?"

"Sort of, but different. Like I needed to do it in order to convince you of something important."

I thought about the aftermath, tracking the tanzanite to the Gowdie sisters, where I received the Doideag's prophecy.

"Well, just talk to me next time," I said. "I'm not sure I'll survive another round of convincing."

"Don't worry," he said, his chuckle scared-sounding. "When I saw the police were after me, I knew I'd messed up. Knew I'd lost you as a potential source of help. I returned to my city, never planning to come back here."

"Why didn't you look for my shadow?"

A cloud passed over his already dim face. "You don't, um, exist over there."

"I don't?" Even though we were talking about a probable version of myself, a knot tightened in my gut.

He shook his head. "I don't think any magic-users do. Not ones like you, anyway."

That explained why no one from the Order had contacted him. It did raise questions about what had happened to the magical community in the shadow present, but that was more a curiosity right now than a concern.

"How did you find me last night?" I asked.

"Right place, right time. I was out walking—thinking about you, actually. I was freaking out over the rune I planted, debating whether to go back and check on you. I hadn't even gone home yet. I heard a bunch of commotion, went over to see what was happening, and there you were, on the sidewalk with the police incoming. I grabbed you to take you back, but I had to switch my focus from the vagueness rune to the transport version, which always negates the first. That's when the pig saw and shot me."

"I appreciate the assist," I said, even as my voice turned taut. "Just keep in mind that the woman you call a 'pig' was doing her job. She thought you were a threat." Had I just stood up for shadow Vega?

Sven gave me a strange look before shrugging it off. "Well, she'd seen me, so I couldn't go back there. But the police were hunting me here too. Wanted in two realities," he said in disbelief. "Bet that's never happened before."

"You'd be surprised," I muttered.

"I used the vagueness rune to make my way down to Track 61. It's where I'd go when I stayed here overnight. But I was hurting too much to draw a healing rune." He winced at the memory and peeked at his sutured wound, which was already scarring. "I climbed into my bag, and that's all I remember until I woke up here. I know I freaked when I first saw you, but I'm super glad you're all right."

He made a *whew* gesture across his brow.

I nodded, but I was thinking about how he'd found me in the shadow present. I doubted it was by accident. Like with the sigil under my door, he'd been compelled. Was the Hermes box trying to draw me into its web too?

"You told me to avoid the Discovery Society," I said. "Why?"

"Remember how I described being transfixed on the mansion on Reade Street? Well, it was just the opposite with the Discovery Society. The first time I walked past, a voice urged me to keep going. Better yet, avoid it all together. And it felt like something was watching me through a window. I got out of there as fast as I could, my vagueness rune at full power, but for the next few blocks I was sure I was being followed."

"By whom?" I asked, anticipating a description of the perp.

But Sven was shaking his head. "It was more a feeling than anything—heart pounding, senses at high alert. There were a couple people I suspected, but they either got into a cab or turned down another street." He blew out a shaky breath. "All I can say is something bad's happening inside that place."

I experienced a strange sense of déjà vu, not only with what Sunita had said about a dark presence, but what I'd experienced myself in the club's basement.

"And you're talking about the one in your reality, right?" I asked.

"Yeah."

"What's it like over there?"

"I didn't know anything about it until a classmate of mine brought it up once. She said it used to be a meeting place for explorers and scientists, but they all got sacked, and the club went super-secret. No one's really sure what goes on in there, but she said people started hearing chanting at night. She's into wild conspiracy theories, so I brushed it off. But after my experience, I'm not so sure."

I considered the info. Our raid on the club here had turned up evidence of the potion, but I wondered what a raid on the shadow version would have revealed. If Sven's friend was to be believed, Goldburn, Strock, and Mims were probably no longer members of the explorer-club-turned-cult, much less fellows. The NYPD would have deemed them random victims in a version of the city where random murders were commonplace, especially without a wizard consultant on the force.

Which made Vega's attempted arrest of me remarkable. We weren't talking about an anonymous tip. The perp would have been influential for the police to have responded in force as they did.

Fear the master of many places, the Doideag had said.

I left that to marinate and reviewed everything else Sven had told me. As I did, I felt the information I'd assembled in the last couple days shift around like puzzle pieces, several of them clicking together.

A change must have come over my face because Sven said, "What is it?"

I nodded at his pack. "I think I know what's inside the box."

33

"You do?" Sven asked, pushing himself up in the bed.

Though his color was hard to gauge, he looked stronger. A portion of both fluid bags had already dripped into him, and the glow of my healing magic was thinning, indicating it was past the heavy-lifting phase.

"The symbols on the box, the ones you grafted onto your runes, go back to a cult devoted to Hermes," I said.

"Really?" It came out a stunned whisper, and understandably. I'd just told him that the runic magic he'd been practicing connected to a mythology he'd been fascinated with since childhood.

"They were a thieves' guild, in fact."

Sven nodded and recovered his voice. "Hermes was a patron of thieves."

"As well as of borders, which likely explains the ability to transit between your reality and mine."

"But the other manifestations don't necessarily follow," he said.

"They do if you consider what's inside the box. Have you ever heard of the Emerald Tablet?"

"It was one of the early *Hermetica* translations."

"The most important *Hermetica* translation," I stressed. "It became the foundation for alchemy in the West."

"As above, so below," he recited. "Makes sense, then. Transforming pure energy into fire and force. But the texts appeared later, during the Hellenistic Period. Why would an ancient Greek cult build a chest to protect something that hadn't even been written yet?" Though he was verging on argumentative again, the kid was sharp. Had he been an actual student, he would've made a great assistant.

"You're right to ask that. The known texts were based on earlier ones. There's a tale left out of the main Greek myths that says Hermes stole pieces of universal knowledge from his aunts and uncles, the major gods of Olympus, and put them on a sacred tablet. It was named, appropriately enough, the Tablet of Hermes. And it was from this tablet that the later texts sprung, including the famous Emerald Tablet. They're what gave humankind science, philosophy, medicine, alchemy. I'm starting to think the devotees in question were the Attican cult."

Sven's eyes widened. "The tablet is in that box?"

"At least a fragment of it," I said. "If so, it holds Hermes's essence."

"I've been carrying the original Hermes around this whole time?" he practically shouted.

"Yes and no. It's too deep to get into right now, but the short version is this. Mythology uses one name for gods like Hermes, but there are actually several variants, depending on the cult who worshipped him. The collective belief in a god creates the template; cultic rites and worship carried out over time shape the god into specific beings. So, yes, you've been carrying a *version* of Hermes in your pack."

As Sven stared at the pack, the monitor on the bedside table showed the uptick in his heart rate.

"What does he want with me?" he asked.

I had a couple theories, but I didn't want to scare him. Sven might've been gifted, but he was still a kid.

"I'm going to call some associates," I said. "I want them to take a look at the nature of the bonding."

Claudius arrived first, stumbling from a portal before he turned sharply.

"Back!" he snapped, kicking a chirping ball of fur that had rolled out after him. "Back inside!"

He signed the portal closed before more of the critters could spill out. After shaking hairs from the hem of his robe, he angled his blue-tinted shades around the room. I expected some explanation for the fur balls, but when he spotted me, he only muttered something about pet dander and sneezed.

"Thanks for coming," I said.

"It's always a pleasure." He wiped his nose. "And your young charge?"

"Over there." I gestured to the bed. Sven was sitting up now, eating a hamburger I'd ordered from room service.

Claudius tucked his curtains of black hair behind his ears in order to see better. "Ah, yes, yes."

I made their introductions, then watched carefully to see whether Claudius remembered what I'd told him over the phone. But he got right to work, inspecting the salt-packed box I'd pulled from Sven's pack and placed beside him on the bed. In his heyday, Claudius had been an expert in complex bindings.

Light flashed, and now Gretchen was standing in front of me.

"Where is he?" she said without preamble.

"There." I gestured to the bed again. "Can you check his soul while Claudius finishes inspecting the bindings?"

She looked around and lowered her voice. "I meant Bree-yark."

"I said he *might* be here later."

Which wasn't true. When I'd left the park with Hoffman earlier, Bree-yark had taken Tabitha back to my apartment, where he planned to spend the rest of the day. I hadn't felt right dangling him out there as Gretchen bait, but she'd acted indifferent when I called and asked for her help. Now, not only was she here, but she'd changed outfits since the park, opting for a pink cloche hat this time.

"His soul's fine," she said.

"Are you sure? You barely glanced at him."

"Well," Claudius said, straightening from his stoop, "this is certainly one for the books." He shuffled over. "Oh, hello, Gretchen! What a delight!" He gave her hand a long kiss, causing Gretchen to straighten proudly.

"At least *he* knows how to greet a woman," she said to me.

I looked between them, the two most powerful members the Order could spare. "What did you find, Claudius?" I asked impatiently.

He released her hand at last and rubbed his chin. "The box has him bound fairly tightly. I *could* attempt to undo it, but here's the dilemma. If I fail, it could do irreparable harm. And if I succeed, he won't be able to access the magic to return."

"He'd be stuck here?"

"I'm afraid so. The thing with the two realms is this: If you exist in one but not the other, you travel back and forth as you are. Provided you have the ability." He gestured to Sven and me as examples. "However, if you exist in both, you shift from one *form* to the other. Do you follow me?"

"I hadn't realized that," I said. "But what does it have to do with the binding?"

Claudius started to answer, then stopped and screwed up his face. "Hmm, it seems I lost my train of thought, but the fact of the matter remains. If I did manage to free him, he wouldn't be able to return home."

I looked over at Sven, who was still eating. He may have preferred this version of the city, but he'd spoken of a mother in the shadow one.

"Let's hold off then." I turned to Gretchen. "And you're sure his soul's all right?"

"Yes, Gretchen, what do you think?" Claudius asked solicitously.

Without Bree-yark here to impress, I could tell she'd been readying a flippant answer, but flattered by Claudius's attention, she gave Sven a second look. "Sure. If the box doesn't keep wrapping him like fishing line. Much more, and he'll be soul-strangled, and soul deaths are agonizing."

I patted my hand toward the floor for her to keep it down, but that's what I'd been afraid of. "Is it trying to hurt him?" I whispered.

"I don't think so," Claudius interjected. "It just appears to be clinging to him desperately."

A knock sounded, and an officer escorted Mae Johnson inside. As usual, she'd brought Buster in his pet carrier.

"What's *she* doing here?" Gretchen snapped, not bothering to lower her voice.

I stepped forward to receive Mae, showing her into the room as the officer backed out again. I introduced her to everyone, including Gretchen, even though their meeting the morning before had nearly come to blows. Mae appeared to have moved past it, though, and she smiled graciously. Claudius, overcome by the presence of another woman, went through the same prostrations he had with Gretchen.

"All righty, then," I said, separating his lips from Mae's hand before Gretchen could voice her growing outrage. I steered Mae toward the bed. "I asked her here to take a look at the binding."

"Why?" Gretchen said. "She's just a big—"

"*Nether-whisperer,*" I cut in. "And the citywide wards picked up nether qualities in the box. If we can't release the bonds, maybe she can coax them into loosening their hold. It's worth a shot."

"I'm always happy to help, hon," Mae said.

She exclaimed over Sven's handsomeness when I introduced them. The shadows of his face deepened, which I realized was a blush. After some more pleasantries, she set down her carrier and took the box onto her lap.

"Sven and I were talking about the Titanomachy earlier," I said, waving Claudius and Gretchen over. I wanted everyone to hear what I'd been piecing together. "That was the mythological battle between the Titans and the gods of Olympus. When Zeus's side won, he cast his father, Cronus, and his allies into Tartarus. It's like a Hades below Hades. In many versions of the myths, that's where Cronus's story ends. But like the Hermes cult, there were Cronus cults too. And what was Cronus?"

Claudius pursed his lips in thought while Gretchen rolled her eyes.

"A god of time," Sven said, wiping his mouth with a cloth napkin. "He later became synonymous with Father Time, which is why he's always shown with a scythe. Cronus used one to castrate his father, Uranus."

I snapped my fingers. "Exactly. I think an artifact from a Cronus cult made its way to the Discovery Society. That artifact bonded to someone, and now that someone is using potions and *time* structures—the shadow and actual presents—to extract organs for a ritual. A ritual intended to free Cronus from Tartarus."

"Oh, my," Claudius said, looking from me to Gretchen worriedly.

"That someone also has help, a shapeshifter who can assume any form, including Cerberus, suggesting it may have roots in the Greek mythos too. Fortunately, I think it's confined to the shadow present."

Fear the *shadow* of many faces, I'd been told. But I wasn't sure the same held true for the perp: a master of *many places*.

I pointed to the box Mae was whispering over. "All of this activity awakened the Hermes essence, and the Tablet put out a call. That call attracted perhaps the only person in the shadow city who practiced magic of a kind the Tablet could use." I raised my finger to indicate Sven, who stared back for a second before nodding importantly.

"The bonding enhanced your runic abilities," I said. "It also enabled you to cross into the actual present, where I believe you were meant to find help." I gestured to indicate all of us present. The explanation also fit with the Doideag's questions:

Can a children's love restore lost time? The cult's worship for Cronus, a god of time.

Can the fleet of foot avert the crime? A reference to Hermes, who was often depicted with winged feet.

One was trying to bring Cronus back; the other was intent on stopping him.

But Gretchen reared back, nearly losing her cloche hat. "This has nothing to do with *me*."

"Oh, yes, it does," I said. "Because if the ritual is as powerful as I think it is, not only will Cronus be freed from Tartarus, he's going to want to cleanse the world and start over."

"I believe Professor Croft is right," Sven said. "Cronus presided over the Golden Age. According to the myths, there was no need for laws because his human creations were perfect. They behaved and worshipped him without question. There's no way he's going to stand for what we've become."

Mae *hmph*ed in agreement, a sound Buster tried to mimic.

"But it's all happening in that stupid shadow present," Gretchen shot back.

"That may be where it begins," I said. "But once Cronus replaces humankind with another worshipping race over there, that worship will grow his power. Eventually he'll want to take back what he considers his rightful domain—the entire Universe, our in-living-color part included. As a god of time, he'll be able to transit from the shadow realm. The war that follows will be cataclysmic."

I was thinking of Sven's dream now as well as the Doideag's prophecy.

"Far better if we keep him from emerging from Tartarus in the first place," I said. "And that means finding the killer before he claims the blood of the final victim, and recovering the Cronus artifact."

Mae gave the box a final pat and set it back beside Sven. "I believe I talked it into lightening up some."

Gretchen scoffed, but when Claudius took a closer look, he said, "By Jove, she has," and stared at Mae with newfound reverence. "I would love to learn about your, ah, methods. Perhaps some night over dinner?"

"Goodness, I'm afraid I don't stay up that late."

"Well, um, I'm sure we could arrange something—"

Gretchen huffed loudly. "It won't last," she said of the tempered box. "It's still going to strangle him."

Sven looked over at me. "Strangle me?"

"No, no," I said quickly, stepping in front of Gretchen. "It's desperate, but it's not going to strangle you."

I felt more confident saying that now, knowing Mae could

soften the bonding. Once the Cronus threat was averted, I was counting on the Hermes Tablet to release him from its hold altogether. But before I could say as much, my phone rang. I excused myself and stepped away from the others.

"How is he?" Ricki asked.

"Much better. Sitting up now and eating. Thanks again for arranging this."

"Good. I've been going over the Discovery Society records Hoffman sent me, and I found a pair of items listed in last month's inventory that are missing from this one's. The first was a journal from a 1909 Arctic expedition."

"Huh." Not what I'd been expecting. "And the other one?"

"A compass from another expedition, to the North Pole, it looks like."

That lined up with Eldred's account of overhearing Walter Mims mention two stolen items, but neither one fit my theory at all.

"Anything else?" I asked with flagging hope.

"I'll give the records another pass, but those were the only two discrepancies I found. Mims marked them, in fact."

My phone beeped, and I checked the caller.

"Hey, could you hold on for a minute?" I said. "Hoffman's calling, and I promised him an update."

I switched over. "Hey."

"Lassgard confessed," he said.

Adrenaline shot through me. "To the murders?"

"Not yet, but he might as well have. To stealing from the collection rooms."

"Really," I said suspiciously. With the kind of pressure Hoffman was under, I could see him strong-arming a fragile Ludvig into admitting something he hadn't done.

"Yeah, yeah, I know what you're thinking. But the team found a vault hidden in the back of his closet. They blew it open, and it was packed with old explorer crap. A couple still had tags from the club: a journal and compass."

"Any older artifacts?" I asked. "Like something you'd find in an archeological dig?"

"The team didn't report anything like that, but if he's got it, he'll tell me." Hoffman let out a gruff chuckle. "The kid's scared shitless. He's singing up a storm."

"Did he say why he called Walter Mims?"

"Don't worry. I'm working up to that."

"Wait for me," I said. "I'm heading there now."

I switched back to Ricki and filled her in on the development.

"Do you think it's him?" she asked.

"It looks bad, but if Ludvig can travel to the shadow present, I don't think he'd stash the stolen goods here versus there. Sort of defeats the purpose. But I want to get over there before Hoffman screws this up."

"Smart. Can I be doing anything?"

My thoughts went to the Discovery Society. Even if the major activity was happening in the shadow present, what clues might an entity operating between realities leave? What had been out of place?

"Actually, yeah," I said after a moment. "I'm going to send you a photo I took at the club."

I attached the image to a text and sent it to her, already feeling a little stupid.

"A medicine bottle?" she said.

"The doorman at the Discovery Society is taking it. Can you read the info on the label all right?"

"Yes, but what am I supposed to do with it?"

"It's a hunch, I admit, but I want to know why his doctor prescribed it. Is that going to take a warrant?" I'd had enough contact with Eldred to know he wouldn't give up the info voluntarily, especially since it had nothing to do with the investigation.

"I can get the information through a written request, but I'll need to explain why it's relevant."

"How creative are you willing to get?"

She sighed. "If I wasn't married to you..."

"I know, I know, I'd be in trouble."

"I'll see what I can do."

34

Claudius and Gretchen remained with Sven—Gretchen only because she still thought Bree-yark was coming—while a police cruiser took Mae and Buster home and another drove me downtown.

Hoffman was waiting outside the interview room when I arrived. I didn't think the man could look any more rundown, but the bruised bags under his eyes had grown their own bags. He was also starting to stink. His lips contorted into a mean smile as he jerked his thumb toward the one-way mirror.

"I was about to go back in without you, but look—the long wait softened him up even more." He snorted a laugh. "Would you get a load of that sap?"

Beyond the mirror, Ludvig sat at a small metal table, his curtains of blond hair shaking as he sobbed into his cuffed hands. He let out what at first sounded like one of his giggles, but it tailed off into a pitiful whine.

"Let's go," I said, not enjoying the show nearly as much as Hoffman.

He led the way in, limping on his ortho boot, and we took the chairs opposite Ludvig.

"Cheer up," Hoffman said. "I brought you a friend."

Ludvig peered up and then wiped his crossed eyes with the sides of his hands. "Ev—Everson?" he stammered.

"Yeah, it's me," I said. "I'm helping out with the investigation. Care to tell me what's going on?"

"It's true," he said. "I—I took them, but it wasn't stealing. Or if it was, I was stealing them back. All of the things in my vault belonged to my great grandfather, Jesper Lassgard. When he died, the Discovery Society claimed them. My mother fought for them, but he never deeded them, and the Society had better lawyers. The items belong with the Lassgard family." His eyes straightened with determination.

"So you were never interested in membership?" I said. "You just wanted access?"

He nodded, sobbing once before controlling himself again. "I copied Walter's master key. Over time, I located all of my great grandfather's things in the collections. Then it was a matter of replacing them with counterfeits. I succeeded until the final two. Walter told me he was about to move them to a warehouse, along with an entire polar collection, so I took the journal and compass that night. But before I could replace them, he noticed them missing."

I remembered what Eldred had said: *He's cleverer than he lets on.*

"And that's why you played the fool," I said. "So no one would think you capable of that level of deception." I suspected the foolery also included him soliciting sponsorship for a wizard. He'd fooled *me,* that was for sure.

"Yes, but I never meant to get Walter into trouble."

"He was in trouble?" Hoffman grunted. "What for?"

"The missing items. The collection belongs to the endowment, but it was Walter's responsibility. Some suspected me—I know Eldred did—but Walter only asked me one time if I knew anything about the missing items, and I told him no. He was prepared to bear the consequences, and I—I couldn't allow that. He had nothing to do with the Society seizing them. Even though the sponsorship was a con on my part, he was always very tolerant of me. He answered my strange questions. And now he's—"

He began sobbing into his hands again. Hoffman gave me a tired look that told me he didn't believe the show for a second. But for me, it added up.

"Tell us why you called Walter earlier today," I said.

Ludvig nodded and wiped his eyes on his shirt collar this time.

"I was going to come clean," he said, "at least about those two items. I—I was going to offer to return them and ask—well, plead—that he not report me, that he say they were found in a stock room, no harm done. He would be off the hook, and I would promise never to set foot in the club again."

That explained why Walter had left his apartment despite the police warning.

"Is that why you killed him?" Hoffman asked. "'Cause he wouldn't play along."

Ludvig shook his head emphatically. "By the time I got to our meeting place, the police were there. At first I thought he'd called them, that it was a sting, so I left. I only found out later he'd been killed."

"And we're supposed to swallow that shit?" Hoffman said.

"Did you ever take anything else from the collection?" I asked, talking over Hoffman. "Anything that wasn't your great grandfather's?"

"No, just his maps, journals, and some instruments and gear."

"Why are three fellows of the Council dead?" Hoffman asked bluntly.

"I have no idea at all. If I did, I would tell you."

"Sure you would," Hoffman said.

I signaled for a recess, and Hoffman and I went back out into the hall.

"I believe him," I said.

"That's why you're not a detective," he snarled. "C'mon, his place is hot with stolen shit from the club, and you said it yourself—one of those things was probably cursed. Sent him on a killing spree. We've got our guy."

"The items don't fit what we're looking for," I said. "And 'our guy' wouldn't have surrendered to the police so easily. He needs the blood from his final victim."

A door opened, and Ricki walked in carrying a folded piece of paper.

"How's it going with Lassgard?" she asked.

"Better if your husband wasn't being such a tool," Hoffman said.

"He got you this far, didn't he?"

While Hoffman grumbled, she opened the piece of paper.

"The info on the Fludrocortisone," she said, as I stepped around to peer over her shoulder.

"It's a low blood pressure med, but it's also prescribed in cases of orthostatic intolerance. The doctor admitted it's a fallback when the problem can't be diagnosed." She looked up at me. "Eldred was having blackouts."

My heart skipped. "When did they start?"

"Last month. He told the doctor he'd hear buzzing and then have about two minutes to lie down before he passed out. The episodes ranged anywhere from twenty minutes to a couple hours. It started suddenly with no triggers that he could think of. All of his scans and EEGs came back fine."

I turned to Hoffman. "Is the Sup Squad still at the Discovery Society?"

"Should be," he grunted.

"Tell them to detain Eldred."

He looked from me to the interview room and back. "What the hell for?"

The explanation fit with something Claudius had said at the Waldorf: If you existed in one realm but not the other, you traveled back and forth as you were. If you existed in both, you shifted from one *form* to the other.

"Because Eldred's shadow is the killer," I said.

WHILE HOFFMAN CALLED the Sup Squad, I explained my thinking to Ricki.

"The Cronus artifact I had in mind never arrived here. It arrived *there*, in the shadow present. Eldred's shadow found it, and it compelled him. Just like the Hermes Tablet compelled Sven. The difference is that Sven doesn't exist here, so he's able to travel between the two realms. Eldred does, so his shadow has to occupy his form."

"Explaining his sudden blackouts," she said, nodding.

"I think the shadow Eldred had the artifact for a while. The shapeshifter is probably its guardian, much like the animations are for the Hermes box. He used the artifact and shifter to assume power there, transforming the Discovery Society from a scientific organization into a cult to Cronus." I was going off what Sven's classmate had told him.

"Eldred became the 'master of many places,'" I continued. "'Many places' signifying the nature of the club. When the faith in Cronus reached a certain pitch, he was ordered to perform a powerful ritual that involved harvesting pure organs and blood." My words were coming faster as I tried to keep pace with my avalanching thoughts. "But, clean or not, the shadow organs weren't going to be potent enough—he needed the real articles. So he brewed a potion that would bind the fellows to their shadows, possessed the actual Eldred to slip the potion to them here, extracted the organs back there, and voila. He has the organs without leaving any evidence of his crimes in our reality."

"But what was it about the fellows?" she asked. "Why harvest from them and not easier marks?"

"I think it relates to something Sunita told me. She said Bear was obsessed with a gene called 7Rb, a variant of what's known as the 'explorer gene.' He was funding research into it. The gene only exists in a small percentage of people, and in addition to exploration, it's believed to spur innovation, one of the most important assets in Bear's industry. He wanted to develop a therapy that could maximize the gene's expression. Sunita said his profile for the gene was off the charts. Given Robert Strock's and Walter Mims's pedigrees and achievements, I wouldn't be surprised if the same were true of their 7Rb expressions."

"And you think they were singled out for that?"

My magic had been nodding along with me the whole time, and it wasn't stopping.

"That particular variant didn't appear until about twenty-five hundred years ago, which also happened to be the height of ancient Greek culture. You won't find this in any of the scientific journals, but I think the variant is an artifact of intense worship to one of the gods of travel, quite possibly Hermes. If so, its offering would give the Cronus essence a boost of god vitality. He was Hermes's grandfather after all."

Hoffman lowered his phone and stepped toward us. "They found Eldred."

"Good, we should put him in one of the warded cells in the Basement," I said. "That should keep his shadow from..." I tailed off when I saw Hoffman shaking his head.

"He was swinging from a belt in his apartment."

I stared at him. "Eldred killed himself?"

"Well, he wasn't trying to grow another inch."

"What does it mean?" Ricki asked me.

An icy hand gripped my heart. "It means his shadow has completed his work here. He's bonded the final victim."

Snapping my eyes closed, I tuned into the amulet I'd given Sunita. It wasn't signaling a hit on the potion, thank God, but I pulled out my phone and called her anyway, my pulse thumping in my ear.

"Hello, Everson," she answered.

"Are you still wearing the amulet?"

"Yes, I'm looking at it right now. Is everything all right?"

I was panting, but I couldn't help it. "It's not glowing?"

"No, it's been dim since you gave it to me."

"And you feel all right?"

"Fine, except that you're starting to scare me."

"I'm sorry." I exhaled, scrambling to think. "The club members. Do any of them have explorer pedigrees?"

"Most are researchers. Well, except for Ludvig—his great grandfather was the famous expeditioner—but he's not officially a member."

I turned slowly toward the one-way mirror. Ludvig was still at the table, staring soberly at his cuffed hands.

"Why?" Sunita asked.

Ludvig looked up as I entered the interview room.

Exploration is in my blood, I heard him saying when we'd met the night before.

My own blood roared in my head as I stepped toward him. He followed the tip of my cane down to his stomach, his expression going from confused to concerned. I tapped into what remained of the hunting spell on the bonding potion.

"Attivare," I whispered.

The cane wiggled.

35

"What's going on?" Ludvig asked.

"Yeah, and feel free to clue me in too," Hoffman snarled, limping in behind me. "I'm only lead here."

My cane wiggled again. "The potion's inside him," I said.

Ludvig looked between my cane and my face. "P-Potion?"

"Did you have a drink at the Discovery Society after last night's meeting?" I asked him.

"No, I left."

"What about once you were home?"

"Just the usual. A couple glasses of water, warm milk before bed. Oh, and a bit of *Discovery Select*. A bottle arrived at my apartment yesterday, a gift from the club. After seeing the scene at the park with the police this morning, I—I needed something to calm myself. I took two shots. Maybe three." He licked his lips nervously. "Why? What's going on?"

"I need you to drink this," I said, pulling a vial from a coat pocket. I spoke an incantation, causing the clear liquid inside to bubble as I handed it to him. "It's a potion to negate the one inside you."

"O-okay," he stammered, shooting it in one tilt.

I waited, but my cane continued to wiggle. Having already taken effect, the bonding potion was glued fast to his system.

"Give us a minute," I said, swearing silently.

I turned to Hoffman, and we walked back toward Ricki, who'd remained in the doorway.

"Eldred has Ludvig's shadow version," I said in a lowered voice. "He's the final victim. Eldred is going to drain him for his offering, if he hasn't already started. When that happens, this Ludvig will die from blood loss. Not only that, but Eldred will release a major Greek god from an underworld prison."

Hoffman's face lumped up as he tried to make sense of what I was saying, but Ricki understood the urgency.

"What do you need to do?" she asked.

"I need to go there," I said. "Fast."

Concern lines creased her brow, but she knew it was my job. "Do you have everything you need?"

I patted my coat pockets and then the holstered shotgun I'd been carrying all day—security in case the killer yanked me back to the shadow present again. It hadn't happened, but the upshot was I was prepared now. I had a good idea where he'd be performing the ritual, too, but I needed to be sure.

"Just about," I said. "I'm going to cast a hunting spell on Ludvig's hair. While I'm doing that, can you call Claudius?"

"And tell him what?" she asked.

"That I'm going to need a ride."

I'd just finished the hunting spell when Claudius emerged through a portal outside the interview room with Sven in tow. His curtains of hair were in disarray, but it appeared to have been one of Claudius's more benign transits, with nothing clinging to or chasing him. He closed the portal and pressed his fingers into his stomach.

"Darn it, I can already feel things slowing down."

I stepped over to Sven, who was glancing around the corridor. "How are you feeling?"

"Much better, thanks," he said, hiking up his pack and massaging his healed shoulder. "It's just a little tender."

When he spotted Ricki, he jerked back a step.

"It's all right," I said. "She's cool here. Sven, this is my wife, Detective Vega. And this is Sven Roe—until he tells us otherwise."

Sven looked between us in surprise before gathering himself and coming forward. Ricki greeted him with a handshake, glancing over at me in a way that said, *I trust you'll explain his reaction later.*

I nodded quickly.

"All right," I said. "Claudius is going to take me and Sven to the Discovery Society. From there, Sven will transport me to the shadow realm. After I stop the ritual and recover the object, he'll bring me back."

"That easy, huh?" Ricki said. "Can't you take anyone else?"

I stepped over to her. "I'd bring backup if I could, believe me, but the tablet only endowed Sven and me with the ability to cross."

"Do you think Eldred's expecting you?"

"I *know* he's expecting me," I replied honestly, taking another inventory of my coat by feel. "But I've been at this game longer than he has." Finishing my pat-down, I kissed her firmly. "He's not going to win."

She fixed my eyes with hers. "Be careful."

I held the sides of her stomach, then turned to Claudius. "You ready?"

He was grimacing as if trying to force-start his peristaltic motion, but he straightened quickly and waved Sven and me over.

"I have a route in mind," he said. "Best if we link arms, I think."

"The less complicated, the better," I stressed.

"Yes, yes."

I took the middle position, his bony elbow hooked in my right arm and Sven's elbow in my left. As Claudius signed into the air, I took a final look around. Hoffman was leaning against a wall, his face set in a frown, but he shifted his crossed arms enough to give me a thumbs-up. Beside him, Ricki watched intently. She nodded that she believed in me. I winked and nodded back.

Finally, I caught Ludvig through the one-way mirror. Maybe it was an effect of the fluorescent lights, but his skin looked as if it was starting to blanch. Was his shadow being blood-drained at that moment?

"Here we go!" Claudius called. "Hold on!"

THE PORTAL that sucked us inside sounded like a 747 turbine and lifted me from my feet. I hugged Claudius's and Sven's arms against my sides as chaotic forces assailed us, trying to wrench us apart. I lost my hold on one, then the other, my body flipping around like a mailbox caught in a tornado.

In the next moment, horns were blaring, and I was spinning on my back. Tires squealed a few feet to my right. To my left, a cabbie was leaning out his window, shouting at me to move. Collecting my cane, I pushed myself up from the street and stumbled backwards. I tripped and landed seat-down on a sidewalk. A short distance away, Claudius and Sven were recovering from their own spills, Claudius hopping on one foot to reclaim a lost slipper.

"My apologies," he called over a shoulder, straightening his blue-tinted shades. "The realm was a lot more temperamental than I remember."

I went to check on Sven, who was rising stiffly. He nodded that he was all right and opened his pack to check on the Hermes box. I did the same with the spell items in my coat. Miraculously, they were all present and intact.

"The good thing," Claudius said as he rejoined us with both slippers, "is that the turbulence seems to have gotten things moving again." He smiled and patted his stomach, then noticed the plaque for the Discovery Society on the townhouse at Sven's back. "Ah, and I see we've made it."

"Yeah, thanks," I said thinly.

"Well, if that's all for now, I should log a couple more hours of phone time before my date with Elsie." He squinted in sudden bafflement. "Or was Edna tonight and Elsie tomorrow?" He shook his head. "Well, in either case…"

Oblivious to the crowd around us, he signed a portal into being and disappeared through it. I gestured for Sven to follow me, and we hurried from the stunned onlookers and into the alley behind the club.

"I don't know why we can't do this inside," Sven said.

"Because I don't know what's going to be waiting for us over there."

"I can *help*," he insisted. "I'm a vessel for Hermes."

"You are helping."

"I mean in the club."

"I know what you mean, but what if something happened to you? I'd be trapped there." I would also never forgive myself, but I was talking to a teenager. "Stick to the plan, all right? Get me there and then wait. When I'm done, I'll come to you. Right here," I emphasized, pointing at our spot behind the dumpster. "Well, here when we get there," I amended.

He sighed, but I held his gaze until he nodded. "All right," he agreed.

"I wouldn't have gotten to this point without you," I said. "Are you ready?"

A determined look came over his face, and he embraced me. I patted his back before realizing he was transporting us. My stomach dipped, and the scene changed from late afternoon to a smoky dusk.

Sven stepped back, a shadow being back in his shadow element. I peered up. A board covered the second-story window I'd broken through the night before. As I'd hoped, the security bars hadn't been replaced. A gap remained, large enough to squeeze through. But first, the hunting spell.

I was piggy-backing off Eldred's bonding potion, betting that it would enable me to use Ludvig's hair in the actual present to hunt his shadow here. When my cane jerked in my grip, I was relieved to see I'd bet right. The cane steadied and angled downward, telling me I'd been right about something else: the ritual was happening in the basement. I activated a stealth potion and downed it in three quick gulps.

"Good luck," Sven said.

"If you get into any trouble, go back. There's a package store on West Seventieth called Morton's that exists in both our realities. If I don't see you here, or if for some reason I can't come out this way, I'll head to the store. When you think it's safe, pick me up there."

He nodded.

I squeezed his good shoulder and, with a force invocation, launched myself onto the window ledge.

36

I touched the end of my cane to the boarded window and whispered a Word. Having taken a couple trips the shadow present now, I knew to compensate for the weaker energy. Nails groaned and popped loose, releasing the board. Before it could pancake into the room, I caught it with another invocation and lowered it gently.

The door I'd blown through in my escape looked as if it had been removed. Fortunately, the window was to one side of the rectangle of light from the corridor and hidden in darkness. By the time I squeezed through the broken security bars, my stealth potion had taken effect, and I landed inside without so much as a thump. I poked my head back out. Sven wasn't in sight, telling me he'd activated his vagueness rune. I flashed a thumbs-up to tell him so far, so good and replaced the board over the window.

My cane wiggled, still indicating Ludvig was in the basement.

With my back to a wall, I listened into the corridor. I'd never been the ultimate strategist—part of the reason I hadn't given up trying to recruit the Blue Wolf—but I felt I had a good grasp of the situation.

Eldred wasn't a magic-user, but he could concoct potions, probably with the help of the powerful artifact he wielded. He would also have zealous devotees. Those were my assumptions. More certain was his influence over the NYPD and that he retained the services of a powerful shapeshifter. So, experienced or not, Eldred was dangerous. Even more so since my invocations weren't as strong here.

Down the corridor, someone cleared his throat. I stiffened, but no footsteps approached.

Sentry, I thought.

Pulling a second potion from my pocket, I activated it and drank it down. The potion bubbled in my stomach, trying to take effect, but I suppressed it. The many-many potion was for just in case.

I peeked around the corner. A tall man stood twenty feet away, his butt against the wall. Farther down, beyond the staircase, stood a second man. They were armed with walkie-talkies and holstered firearms, but neither item looked police-issue. These were Society devotees. I'd half expected hooded robes and creepy amulets, but the two were dressed as if they'd just come from church, which made them seem creepier somehow.

I waited for the closer man to turn away before slipping out. From there, I crept toward him.

And past him.

Even with the stealth potion, I didn't release my breath until I'd accessed the stairs and was halfway down. The walls were fire-damaged from the storm I'd unleashed the night before. The carpeting had since been removed, exposing old wood that, without the potion, would have creaked beneath my weight.

I emerged onto the ground floor, where more devotees were stationed along the hall of portraits. I slipped past them like a specter. Engaging these guys would only slow me down and sound a major alarm. Like the single-minded tug of my cane, my goal remained getting to the basement.

I moved more quickly now, becoming increasingly conscious of the passing seconds. How much longer did Ludvig have? Or, God forbid, was the ritual already complete? The passing portraits weren't of famous explorers and researchers anymore, I noticed, but staring men and women. Their plaques bore no names, just the same eerie title: *Moró*. Greek for *baby*.

The flag had changed as well, to a black banner with a criss-crossing of scythes.

"SOCIETY OF CRONUS," it read.

Farther down the corridor, the portraits grew larger and the titles took on military ranks. It culminated in an entire section for the leadership. The Society's president, listed simply as "Eldred," looked much as he did in the actual present, except that his combed-back hair was jet black and the mole beside his nose had ballooned, its weight pulling down the lower lid of his right eye.

Four portraits beneath showed the rest of the cabinet. His number two, a balding man with a long face, was the only one smiling. Crescents gleamed around his irises.

Beware the shadow of many faces.

For better or worse, my assumptions were bearing out so far.

The door to the library was closed and locked. I retrieved my vial of dragon sand, shook out two granules, and placed them in the keyhole. I looked down the corridor before whispering, *"Fuoco."*

The granules superheated until a transparent finger of white fire jetted from the keyhole. It was the visual subtlety I'd wanted, but I hadn't factored in the corridor's acoustics. The flame's steady hiss reverberated from the walls, drawing the closest devotee's attention. The portly man hiked up his pants and began to amble toward me.

Shit.

The flame had disappeared back inside the keyhole, but smoke was beginning to curl out, and I could hear the metal bubbling in the door's locking mechanism. The man had his walkie-talkie in hand, ready for action, while his other hand gripped his holstered pistol.

The thing with stealth potions was they made you inconspicuous more than invisible. Once a person knew where to look, the gig was up.

Aiming my cane at the runner along the floor, I whispered, "*Vigore.*"

The force shoved the rug into a small hillock, which the man met with his next step. He stumbled and went down swearing. Another devotee hurried over to help him. I used the distraction to open the door, slip inside the library, and seal the door with a locking spell.

Outside, I could hear one of them saying, "I knew this was a tripping hazard waiting to happen."

The lights were out in the library. I listened into the darkness before casting up a crackling ball. As its illumination spread, I shouldn't have been as surprised as I was to see that the library had become a temple. Gone were the bookcases and taxidermy mounts. In their places stood rows of wooden pews and a large altar that featured the same crisscross of scythes on the flag, only these were dripping.

Yeah, that seems normal.

My ears rang with the ominous silence as I peered around to orient myself. If the NYPD were here, they were likely covering the outside of the building. The same wouldn't be true of the shifter.

I sheathed my cane through my belt and pulled the sawed-off shotgun from its holster. I'd been carrying it under my coat for so long, it felt strange to have nothing banging my ribs. The hunting spell led me across the temple, toward a door I recognized as the storage room with stairs to the basement.

I tested the door and found it barred solidly from the inside. From beyond and below, I caught a faint sound. A cry was tailing off into sobs that made both my arms break out in gooseflesh.

Ludvig's still alive.

Though my pulse quickened, stealth remained the name of the game. Using a weak force invocation like an echo locator, I sent it under the door and into the space beyond. The lock was a bar dropped into a pair of brackets.

Behind me, the door to the temple shook violently. Two shots sounded. My locking spell fractured, sending the energy rushing back into me. Heart banging, I snuffed out the ball of light just as the door flew open.

A quasi military force stormed inside, covering the room with their rifles. Night vision oculars glinted as they spread apart, barrels panning back and forth. Sup Squad? I sidestepped toward the altar, fishing for another stealth potion. The time factor coupled with my casting had burned through enough of the first dose for its effects to begin thinning. If I didn't conceal myself, it would only be a matter of time before—

"Freeze!" one of them barked.

The massive armored man rushed toward me, two members flanking him, while the remaining six continued searching the temple for accomplices. I summoned a form-fitting shield even though it would serve little better than cardboard against their high-powered rifles—or this guy's bulky fists, for that matter.

He stopped ten feet in front of me, rifle angled down at my forehead. "Drop your weapons!"

I knelt carefully, placed my shotgun and cane on the ground, and knee-walked back from them, arms raised.

"Hands on your head!" he shouted, looming over me.

One of the flanking men lunged in and swept the gun and

cane aside with a booted foot. The other began patting me down, but when he discovered how loaded my coat was, he pulled the entire thing off before searching my pants. When he finished, he zip-tied my hands behind my back.

"We have him," the big man radioed.

Though the situation looked dire, I'd known this might happen. I released my hold over the many-many potion I'd drunk upstairs and felt it come alive in my system like a carbonated drink. And then fizz out.

Are you freaking kidding me?

The lights in the temple snapped on, and the shadow of my wife entered.

37

"Yeah, that's him," Shadow Vega said, holstering her sidearm. "Good work."

The large man backed away as she strode forward, his and his teammates' rifles covering me from three angles. But I was watching Vega. She was still carrying that hard, beaten-down look that made my heart ache. She stopped in front of me, fists on her hips, the lines around her dark eyes narrowing.

"Everson Croft," she said coldly.

Ricki Vega, I thought, *my lovely wife.*

But I kept my mouth shut and focused on kickstarting the many-many potion.

"You're under arrest for the murders of Bear Goldburn, Robert Strock, and Walter Mims." Though her lower lip wrinkled, I knew she was as disappointed with herself as she was disgusted by me. She'd had me the night before, and I'd gotten away, gone on to murder two more as far as she knew.

"All clear!" the men called.

They returned from back rooms, a pair taking positions in the temple while the rest joined the group around me. Their eyes were hidden by their helmet visors, but their jaws were matching blocks of contempt. The huge guy who'd first spotted me looked ready to stomp me with his size fifteen boots.

But there was an odd glint in Vega's eyes. It could have been that I was still semi-spectral from the stealth potion, but I believed it was something else. I didn't know my backstory here—how my shadow had died, or if he'd even existed in the first place—but Vega would have investigated it, and she was trying to make sense of something.

"Want us to tenderize him before throwing him in the wagon?" the large man asked.

"No, I've got him," Vega said, the hardness returning to her face. "Collect his things, but be careful. He was carrying explosives last night."

As she reached for my arm, I said, "You didn't check the basement."

She stopped. "What did you say?"

I jerked my head toward the door behind me. "Your men searched every room in here. Why not the basement?" I was trying to buy time, more for Ludvig than myself—he hadn't sounded as if he had many screams left. If I could convince her to breach the door, Eldred would have to suspend the ritual.

But Vega responded by pulling me roughly to my feet.

"You were ordered not to, weren't you?" I said. "Told it was off limits? You have to be wondering why. Could it be that Eldred murdered those three men, and he's killing a fourth down there as we speak?"

"Shut it," she snapped.

The semicircle of men parted as she tugged me toward the temple door.

"The basement," I repeated in a lowered voice. "Go look, and you'll see what I'm talking about. He gave you my name because I was getting too close. He called you here last night and again tonight so I couldn't stop him. Why else would I have come back? Look around at this place for crissake. He's killing people for sacrificial organs."

Vega tightened her grip on my arm, but had it faltered?

"Look, I know this isn't what you signed up for." The words came spontaneously, from a sudden need to connect with her. I was remembering Ricki's story about her father, a youth counselor who'd been killed trying to broker peace between warring gangs. When the entire 43rd Precinct showed up to his service, hats off, she knew at seventeen she wanted to be a cop. Gambling that some version of the story held true in this reality, I said, "I know it's not what your father inspired—"

The stock end of a rifle cracked into my side, and I staggered to the floor. When I squinted up, the huge guy was looming over me.

"My wife told you to shut it," he growled.

The throbbing became an afterthought as I stared between him and Vega. His wife?

"Jag—" she started to say, but the many-many potion chose that moment to activate. Like a pack of Mentos dropped into a bucket of Diet Coke, it frothed violently inside me. Vega and her husband jumped back as two likenesses of me ballooned from my sides and assumed independent form.

"The fuck?" Jag muttered, moving his rifle barrel across the three of us.

Two more likenesses popped from the existing ones, and then two more from them. In the span of seconds there were more than a dozen of us. But the duplicating was just getting started. In another moment, a mass of Everson Crofts blocked Vega and her husband from my view.

About freaking time.

As the temple filled with more of my likenesses, I gained my feet and squeezed my way through them and away from the Sup

Squad. Shown to me by Gretchen just last month, the many-many potion was part manifestation, part enchantment. The likenesses weren't designed to attack, just confuse and take up space. Great for arrests-in-progress. And they were duplicating extra fast now.

A shot sounded, but most Squad members were engaging them with punches and rifle blows. I tapped into three of the manifestations, and they met me at the door to the storage room. One was carrying my coat, the other my cane and shotgun. A third circled behind me and snapped the zip tie binding my wrists.

"Thanks, boys."

I claimed my coat, donning it and pulling out a tube of sleeping potion.

Being manhandled was fun and all, but because I can't have you guys following me...

I activated the potion and aimed it into the temple. As vapors began issuing from the tube, I summoned a force and swung the pink torrent that erupted back and forth, covering everyone and everything. Beyond the manifestations, I could hear members of the Sup Squad thudding to the floor.

I caught myself hoping Vega's landing wasn't too hard.

I dropped the empty tube and held my breath as the sleeping vapors eddied around me. Reclaiming my cane and shotgun, I turned back to the door. Through a combination of invocations, I directed a force beneath the door, bounced it off a wall of hardened air, and slammed it into the bottom of the lever bar. As the bar hopped from its brackets, I yanked the door open and sealed it behind me.

Let's go, I thought, heart pumping in my tightening chest, shield crackling around me.

I descended the stairs and emerged into what should have been the basement. I slowed, my shield's light glowing over massive stalactites and stalagmites, pale mist swirling through the damp air. I was in a cavern.

More precisely, I was in a version of Cronus's underworld prison, Tartarus, which was bleeding into the shadow present and probably had been for some time. Following the ritual, it would be fully present, along with the god himself. Tartarus would return, but Cronus would remain.

Where was the ritual happening?

I drove my light out, only for the glare from the mist to reduce my visibility. Spectral faces appeared, confirming something I'd suspected about the space, and then melded back into the drifting fog.

I withdrew my light and with a steadying breath blocked out everything except the hunting spell. Within several steps, a figure appeared in a hollow. He was trussed up in a standing position, wrists bound behind him, his lean body angled forward. Hanks of light-colored hair hung over his face.

"*Ludvig,*" I whispered.

I lifted his lolling head. The collar of his shirt was blood-soaked. A deep wound across his neck opened like an evil grin. Dammit. I looked down. No blood on the ground, suggesting it had been collected in a receptacle and spirited off to join the other victims' $7Rb$-rich organs for the ritualistic offering.

His hair shook, startling me.

"Ludvig?"

A low gargle became words: "Help me..."

"Hold still, man. I'm right here."

The opal in my cane glowed as I uttered words of healing. I had to at least start the process, stabilize him. It would cost precious time, but I couldn't leave him here to die. I lifted his head and passed my cane over his wound. When he grimaced, I remembered the debilitating potion Bear had been given, how, in his memory, I'd been unable to move a muscle. So either the potion was waning or something else was happening.

"You're going to be all right," I assured him, raising his eyelid with a thumb before lowering his head back down.

"Don't leave me..."

"I'm not going anywhere, man."

Backing up several steps, I slid my cane through my belt. Ludvig's head came up. He stared from my shotgun to me, revealing the shining crescents around his irises. I squeezed the trigger. The shifter screamed as the blast of enhanced rock salt tore through him and erupted out his back in shadowy flames.

Costing me precious time had been the whole point.

"You almost had me," I grunted, pumping the action. "Almost."

The next blast sent the shifter to the ground, where he began contorting into grotesque shapes. The flames licked over features that were human one moment and bestial the next. Screams became barks which turned into serpentine hisses.

The attack was having an effect on the environment too. Around us, the cavern was faltering, exposing a basement like the one I'd explored in the actual present.

The far side was taken up by a stainless steel work area with a large refrigerator and instrument cabinets. Eldred stood at a mortician's table in a black apron and gloves. His subject was shadow Ludvig, the real one this time.

Ludvig was shirtless and on his back, a metal tube running from his neck to a vat on a large burner. I didn't have to look inside the vat to know it held Bear's kidneys, Strock's liver, Walter's lungs, and was filling with Ludvig's blood. Above the chugging of a small pump, I could hear the blood trickling in. An archaic casting circle surrounded the steaming receptacle.

Not exactly what I'd been picturing, but a ritual offering was a ritual offering.

I sent a final shell into the burning shifter, the salt scattering him into smoke, but there was no time to celebrate. Eldred's back remained to me as I moved toward him. He was whistling a tune, just as he'd been when he extracted Bear's kidneys in Wilson's Body Shop. Headphones covered his ears, which brought to mind the albums I'd seen in his apartment. But I didn't like this show of vulnerability.

Either the guy's delusionally overconfident, or he's got an ace up his sleeve.

I reholstered the shotgun and drew my cane into sword and staff.

"Entrapolarle," I whispered.

The air around Eldred hardened, but only momentarily. A sharp force cleaved my magic, causing me to draw a hissing breath. That's when I spotted the small scythe resting on a tray beside him. It was the artifact that had come to the Discovery Society in the shadow present, the one that had bonded shadow Eldred and ultimately compelled him to kill. Its blade gleamed in the harsh light of the work area, casting a protective field.

"Eldred!" I shouted.

He paused and straightened. Pulling his headphones down around his neck, he turned partway toward me.

"Ah, Everson," he said, returning to work on the tube in Ludvig's jugular. "I thought you might show up."

The seal on the tube was loose—I could hear the sputter of leaking air—which was slowing the blood-draining. Ludvig looked catatonic and deathly pale, but he was still breathing. If I could get close enough, I could start a healing spell. The protective field from the scythe bent around them, though, glinting occasionally.

"What are you doing?" I said.

"Completing my offering to Cronus."

"Why?" I growled. "So he can wipe you and everyone off the face of the Earth?"

"The moment Prometheus created his version of humans, we were lost. Laws became necessary to control them, then more laws. And when the order broke down, all our *exalted* species could manage was complete and utter chaos. You've seen our version of the city. Yours is only a crisis away from the same. Much better to start over, return to the way things were. A single race of obedient humans."

"And you're okay with being purged?"

"It's the only way," he said, as if the answer were self-evident.

Cronus may have been speaking through him, but I suspected that Eldred the control freak had been a ready vessel.

"Truth be told, you alarmed me last night at the club," he said. "I'd no idea how you knew to go there, but when I saw your name on the list, the mayor's beloved wizard, I figured it could only be for one reason. I brought you here and thought that was that." He was confirming he'd supplied my name to the police and then pulled me into the shadow realm where they were waiting. When they failed to apprehend me, he released the shifter.

"I didn't count on you having help," he chuckled, referring to Sven pulling me back out. "But that's all behind us now. It was never personal, Everson. Like you, I was assigned a task, one I'm also duty bound to fulfill."

"Duty bound? You murdered three people, and you're killing a fourth."

"I'm honoring them."

"Really."

"Think about who these men are, Everson, what their blood represents. They come from lines of mapmakers, discoverers, and creators. They take unknowns and turn them into knowns. In so doing, they bring *order* to the world, something I value greatly. Indeed, I love these men. I love what they represent. Lacking their gifts, I was happy to serve them for as long as I did. But even these luminaries with their god-blessed blood couldn't forestall the descent into disorder and chaos. Until now—as honored offerings to Cronus."

As Eldred stepped back, I noticed that the sound of leaking air had stopped. The blood trickling from Ludvig into the vat became a steady pour. The casting circle glowed deep red and the gathering steam turned dark. The cavern features, disrupted by the shifter's demise, hardened again.

Eldred peeled off his gloves and lifted the small scythe reverently from the tray.

"This kind of legacy," he said, staring at the blade, "these men could never have achieved in life."

When a low rumble shook the basement, Eldred turned toward me. The growing mole I'd seen in his portrait had become a pendulous tumor mapped with purple veins and covering half his face. A smile grew beneath it.

"He's coming," he said.

38

"Beautiful, isn't it?" Eldred said.

I didn't know whether he meant the scythe's blade, which he'd resumed staring at, or Cronus's impending arrival. The basement cavern rumbled again, making his tumor jiggle.

Not long ago, I would have thrown everything I had at the protective field around Eldred and the scythe, hoping something, *anything,* would bring it down. In fact, a part of me still wanted to do just that, but I would only exhaust myself. And trusting my magic meant believing it had provided me everything I needed.

While Eldred had been talking, I'd been taking stock, gathering all the shadowy energy I could.

I thought about what Sunita Sharma had told me regarding the building's history. Troubled orphans locked away in the basement. The god seed in the 7Rb gene variant may have attracted the Scythe of Cronus to the club, but it was the energy down here that had enabled its ancient power to take hold. Cronus was a swallower of children after all—his own, the eventual gods of Olympus. And I didn't doubt his most zealous cults had made sacrifices to him in kind.

The spectral faces I'd seen, which continued to drift around the cavern, all belonged to children. Not spirits, but embodiments of the intense fear and loneliness their seclusion had imprinted on the space.

The Cronus energy was feeding off that. It was the same hunger I sensed earlier in the day while checking out the actual basement. I hadn't been able to pinpoint the source because it was a bleed from the shadow realm, but it belonged to Cronus.

It was also a weakness.

Eldred's ritual was filling the god with new energy, but I could still deny him the old. I activated the first rune on my blade, the one for banishment. The energy I'd been gathering hummed around my mental prism. I waited for the rune's light to go pure white before releasing it.

"Disfare!"

The light detonated in all directions, tearing through the drifting apparitions and scattering them. They twisted and writhed, struggling to hold their forms, but the light was relentless, driving them against walls and into corners, where they had nowhere to go. One by one, the imprinted energies burst from existence.

Be at peace, I thought as they dwindled to nothing.

Eldred's eyes shot up from the scythe as the protective field around him buckled.

Lunging, I drove my sword forward. The still-glowing blade pierced the weakened field and sent it shattering to the ground like sheet glass. Around us, the cavern thinned from view and the rumbling receded.

"What are you doing?" Eldred demanded.

He hustled over to the steaming vat and, raising the scythe above it, began chanting in ancient Greek, trying to hasten the ritual. Before the disorganized energy could stabilize, I planted a shoe against the vat's side and shoved. It toppled from the burner, spilling blood and organs over the basement floor.

"What are you doing?" Eldred screamed this time. "Stop!"

While he struggled to push the macabre contents back inside the vat, I hurried to the mortician's table. By growing my aura out, I killed the pump. I then drew the drain tube from Ludvig's neck, trying to ignore the way his crossed eyes stared upward, deathlike. With a spurt of blood, the tube came free. I hovered my staff's opal over the hole, chanting words of healing. Faint light plugged the wound like cotton.

But that was all I had time for.

I spun and brought my sword up. It met the flash of the descending scythe with an air-ringing clang. But the scythe was no longer the small artifact Eldred had been handling just moments ago. The blade had grown along with the handle such that the weapon Eldred gripped in both fists was now taller than him.

His eyes glinted zealously. "You won't win."

"Funny, I said the same thing about you before coming. And since we can't both be right..."

I blocked his next blow, which came in from the side, and thrust my staff. He grunted as the invoked force that emerged from the wood blasted him across the room. I chased him down, closing the distance as he landed on his back in a skid. Though he was a small man, and he wielded the scythe awkwardly, I'd felt the power in both blows. I didn't want to absorb any more if I didn't have to.

"Entrapolarle," I called.

With no protective shielding to interfere now, the air around his head warped, hardening into an airtight sphere. Returning my sword inside my staff, I arrived above him as he was pushing himself upright. When he saw me, he struggled to raise the scythe into striking position. I grabbed the handle.

"Why don't you let go of that before you hurt yourself?" I said.

From inside the sphere, he released a soundless scream, then struggled like a man possessed. His eyes bugged and his tumor shook as he fought to wrench the scythe from my one-handed grasp. He kicked at me several times, but his legs came well short of the mark. Blood streamed from his mouth where he must have bitten his tongue.

I could have squeezed the sphere into a small ball and ended it, but he was a vessel, much like Sven. Anyway, his efforts were only succeeding in exhausting his oxygen. Even with the weaker energy here, I could keep the sphere airtight for as long as it took, which was only a matter of seconds now.

There we go.

His legs buckled, and he dropped to his knees. But by some fanatical reserve, he was still gripping the scythe, his fingernails caked with the blood offering he'd tried to shove back into the vat.

I touched my cane to his chest and released a minor force. His back slapped to the floor, head banging against concrete, and the scythe was mine. I could feel prodigious power humming the length of it, disorganized though that power was at the moment. The scythe needed to be destroyed here and now.

I was striding toward the vat, already digging in my pocket for my most important potion, when someone shouted, "Stop!"

I looked over and swore.

Shadow Vega had entered the basement and was approaching in her characteristic sidestep, service weapon aimed with both hands. Not enough time had passed for her to recover from the sleeping potion, meaning she'd escaped the temple room, only returning again when the mist had cleared.

Backup must have helped her take the door down, but she'd entered alone, no doubt against her superiors' wishes.

"Drop the weapon," she ordered.

She was glancing around as she advanced, her professional eyes absorbing the scene. The cavern underworld may have thinned to almost nothing, but there was still plenty to look at: the toppled vat, the spilled organs and running blood, the mortician's table, where Ludvig lay supine. Eldred was also out on his back—and I'd been walking away from him with a giant scythe over my shoulder.

"I know how this must look," I said.

"Yeah, fucked up," she snarled. "Like that stunt you pulled upstairs."

But she was moving her weapon between me and Eldred now. That was progress.

"This is where he was storing the organs of his victims," I said, nodding at the fridge. "And that's Ludvig Lassgard, victim number four. It was a ritual sacrifice. The gloves he used are in that bin. There should be evidence all over them."

"I still need you to drop the weapon and surrender," she said firmly. "The investigation will sort everything out."

"No it won't, and you know that."

Though her eyes appeared hard on the surface, I recognized the emotions swimming underneath: a mixture of defiance and despair. She'd joined the NYPD for noble reasons, only for her unit to be treated like a goon squad for the powerful. I didn't know the extent of Eldred's power here, but he and his Society clearly had pull with the police, either directly or through higher-ups in the city.

Vega was opening her mouth when the entire basement rocked. She staggered back, and I stumbled for my own footing, eventually going down.

Around me, the basement was becoming the cavern again. I

may have cleared the space of the orphan energy, but the ritual had sent up enough of its own potency for the Cronus entity to resume his arrival. Regardless, the scythe was the focus element, and the objective remained the same. Destroy it.

"What's going on?" Vega shouted.

"Stay put!" I shouted back.

I gained my feet as the shaking fell to tremors. I tried not to look at the mess around the vat as I righted it and pulled a tube from my pocket. Uttering the activation word, I spiked it into the large container. The tube shattered, and the iron gray liquid inside grew, steaming and bubbling, until it filled the entire vat. Thin green currents of enchantment-busting magic swam through the thick medium.

I plunged the scythe inside, blade first.

Now for the catalyst. As I drew my sword, shots cracked.

For an instant, I thought they were meant for me, but I looked over to find Vega aiming her weapon into the darkness, backing away from something. High above the floor, a serpentine head lunged, hissing, from the void. Another followed, and then ten more. A massive hydra lumbered into view.

Great, the ritual also restored the shifter, I thought, recognizing the eyes.

"Come to me!" I shouted at Vega, but the call was lost to her next series of shots.

I manifested a wall of hardened air between her and the hydra, then turned back to my work. The scythe stood on its head inside the bubbling vat, but the potion would need intense heat to destroy an object this powerful. I activated the second rune on my blade. As flames licked up, I pushed, directing the fire into the vat.

The heat excited the green currents, and they swarmed the scythe.

Behind me, the weak invocation walling off the hydra failed.

I looked over as one of the serpentine heads seized Vega's shoulder through the spilling sparks and flung her. She landed against a cavern wall and rolled to the floor.

"Ricki!" I shouted.

The hydra had started toward me, but I'd shown my hand. Its two dozen eyes narrowed maliciously through the gloom before rotating its heads toward Vega, who was still down and helpless.

I upped the power through the fire rune. "C'mon, dammit."

But the gathered energy wasn't strong enough, and the magic in the scythe was fighting back, resisting the efforts to break it down. The hydra began stalking toward Vega.

Shit, I thought, breaking off the fiery expulsion.

I slotted my sword and pulled out the shotgun. As I ran toward the hydra, I pumped the action, expelling the spent shell, and aimed high. Salt and flames tore through the hydra's dozen heads. Shrieking, it reared back its necks. Arriving in front of Vega, I sent a shell into the monster, sending it back another step. I pumped and fired twice more before checking on Vega. She was out, but breathing.

I eyed the recovering hydra as I pushed fresh shells into the gun. The attack wasn't having the same effect as earlier. The flames were too fleeting. This was a more powerful version of the shifter than the one I'd scattered.

"When you're out of *salt,*" one of the heads hissed, "I'll still be here."

I glanced over at Eldred—only he wasn't where I'd dropped him. He'd staggered to the vat and was pulling the dripping scythe free. I rotated the gun toward him and fired, but the field taking hold around him scattered the blast. The field looked weak enough to take down, but not from my distance.

"Go on," the hydra dared, half its heads peering at Eldred,

"and I'll rip her apart." The remaining heads looked down at Vega.

She was a shadow, a probability. Whatever happened to her here would have no bearing on my actual wife. Even so, she was a shadow of the woman I loved more than anything, and I couldn't separate the two.

I raised my weapon at the hydra's grinning faces.

At the same moment, something kicked in a coat pocket.

Huh?

When it kicked again, I pulled out a bag of gray salt. I tore the shaking bag open with my teeth, spilling its contents. Something gold flashed among the salt crystals: a hand holding the end of a tusk. The protective pin Sunita had given me. It jittered over the ground, seeming to react to the shifter's presence.

"Attivare!" I shouted.

I was acting on magical instinct, not sure what to expect. Certainly not what followed. A shadow of the four-armed elephant god Ganesh sprang from the pin and squared his growing body toward the hydra. The shifter's smiles shrank as it backed away. Ganesh charged. With an ear-splitting bugle, he drove a tusk through the hydra's chest. Necks and arms became entangled and serpentine jaws snapped.

The two fell to the ground, the cavern now shaking with their battle.

I picked up the pin and quickly attached it to Vega's jacket before wheeling back toward Eldred. He'd raised the scythe over the spilled offerings, trying to resume the ritual. With Vega protected now, I sprinted toward him. He looked up as my sword came down. It flashed off the field, sending it into a wobble. I jumped back from his clumsy swing, but I could feel the scythe's returning power.

"Do you like jazz, Everson?" he asked in a crazed voice.

I grunted into my next swing. The impact shook his shield

again, but once more I was having to move away to avoid a counterstrike.

"I do, and it's strange," he panted. "Jazz would seem the antithesis of order, yes?"

Once more, we traded swings, but his field was strengthening. My blow barely affected it this time.

"But that's what I enjoy," he went on. "The suspense, the *fear* of uncertainty and chaos, only to arrive at the same satisfying conclusion as your more structured genres. The same can be said of tonight. It may not have gone exactly as planned, and yet Cronus will be restored."

I ducked as the scythe whistled overhead, his last line pinging around the two questions the Doideag had posed:

> *Can a children's love restore lost time?*
> *Can the fleet of foot avert the crime?*

Fleet of foot, I thought.

I searched for the silvery magic I'd been peppered with in the landfill. This time I found it, and I knew why. It was responding to the Hermes Tablet, which was in Sven's possession right outside. Focusing into the magic, I infused it with energy. Immediately, my limbs began to lighten and my heart rate picked up.

Eldred's next swing seemed to arrive in slower motion. I stepped aside and came back in, this time landing two sword strikes. The next time I managed four, then six.

Eldred backpedaled, wide-eyed, as his protection faltered. His tumor was lurching all over the place, pulling his facial features in grotesque directions. For an instant, the air distorted sharply around me, as if Eldred were trying to send me back to the actual present, but the Hermes magic negated it.

"The thing with jazz," I said, grunting into still more swings, "is that some of it's just crap."

My next blow shattered the protection, the released energy knocking me back several paces. Eldred wheeled toward the mortician's table and raised the scythe high above Ludvig's neck. "Accept this potent life offering!" he shrieked to his god.

Too distant to block him, I thrust my staff. *"Vigore!"*

The released force shoved the table back. The descending scythe caught the metal edge and deflected at an odd angle. Eldred dropped to the floor, the bloodied scythe clanging from his grasp.

His neck hung to one side, partially severed by his own stroke.

Behind me, Ganesh was stomping the downed hydra with his massive feet. Under different circumstances, I would have loved a ringside seat, but I still had a scythe to destroy.

I plunged it into the vat once more and drove elemental fire into the potion. The enchantment-busting magic took up where it left off, crowding the scythe. As before, the scythe fought back. It was pulling in all of the available energy—the ritual, the offerings, the god seed in the 7Rb variant, even Eldred's expelling shadow spirit.

I tapped into my own reserves, down to marrow and molecule, pushing it all through the fire rune. My blade went molten, and a shimmering white line grew along its length. The handle turned hot, unbearably so. The sweat pouring from my body evaporated into plumes. My palms began to blister.

But still I gripped, still I upped the heat.

Wage, young mage, till your final breath...

Whether it was an effect of the exertion and torrid heat, I suddenly perceived a massive, wavering shadow looming opposite me. It reached down as if to claim the scythe. I gave a final gut-churning push, and the threads of magic that had been swarming the scythe disappeared inside it. The weapon trembled.

I broke off the fire and, backpedaling, shouted, *"Protezione!"*

A wall of hardened air rose around the vat an instant before the scythe erupted, sending the boiling potion everywhere. I landed hard on my back, hands throbbing, steam coming off me. By the time I sat up, the large shadow figure was gone, the basement was back, and the Scythe of Cronus was no more.

I looked over as the elephant god shrank back inside the pin. The hydra had vanished along with everything else.

Vega was still down, but she'd suffered no further harm. I rose on unsteady legs, feeling as if I could sleep for a week. I stepped over Eldred's partly decapitated body to check on Ludvig. My healing magic had shrunk the hole in his neck, and his breathing was even. With medical attention, he would recover.

I was staggering toward Vega when a shadowy figure appeared in front of me.

I stiffened and drew my sword back before allowing it to sag to my side. "What are you doing here? I told you to wait outside."

But even as I scolded Sven, I was damned glad to see him.

"I was compelled by Hermes," he said, hooking his thumb at his pack. He looked around at the carnage. "Holy shit."

"Yeah," I agreed. "It's done, though."

"Ready to go back?" he asked.

"Just about."

I completed my journey to Vega and knelt beside her. Her shoulder was torn up and she'd suffered a solid blow to the head. With my final vestiges of magic, I covered both in healing light, then watched as the tension in her brow softened and her eyes stopped shifting behind her lids. She'd be all right too.

Grunted commands sounded from the temple room above us.

"Officer down!" I called.

I removed the pin from Vega's lapel and tucked a strand of hair behind her ear. Boots sounded on the steps as I returned to Sven.

"Let's go," I said.

39

The burns on my hands healed over the next couple days, but recovering from my exhaustion took longer. Overwhelming the Scythe of Cronus had taken even more energy than I'd realized, and it was all I could do to get out of bed.

Snodgrass balked at the extra week off, but a call from Ricki to his wife brought him around quickly. In fact, he ended up subbing my courses, deciphering what he could from the burnt and water-damaged lesson plans Sven had written.

I would've given anything to have been there.

I received a number of calls during my convalescence. The first was from Mayor "Budge" Lowder. Political animal or not, he always gave credit where due. At the same time, he was never particularly sentimental.

"Did you see the bond markets this morning?" he effused. "New York municipals are soaring!" Not only had he been able to announce the killer's death, he was also in talks with Bear Goldburn's replacement at Ramsa Inc. to go forward with the chip plant in Brooklyn, and he was negotiating with another major developer to take over the projects the late Robert Strock had been slated to complete.

"My favorite wizard," he finished with a contented sigh. "I knew I could count on you. So, when can I get you in front of the cameras? How about a weekend presser? I want the city to know who to thank."

Having learned my lesson from his eradication campaign, I said, "Actually, better they don't."

I also received a call from Vince Cole, the lawyer. He thanked me for bringing his friend's killer to justice. He also wanted me to know he was dropping his lawsuit against the NYPD. But he surprised me with his next question.

"What can I do for *you?*"

My answer was to explain Ludvig's situation. With his shadow safe and the potion out of his system, he was recovering. But because he'd confessed to the thefts of his great grandfather's possessions, he remained in custody. Cole agreed to take his case pro bono and assured me that not only would he get him released, but that by the time they were done, every last item would be legally his.

Not long after, Bear's wife called, tearful, but grateful. In the course of our conversation, I learned that she'd been concerned over his sudden aggression. Vince had noticed too. Believing drugs involved, they'd been planning an intervention—that's why they'd been communicating behind his back. Neither one had known about the trials to enhance his explorer gene.

The woman who had, Sunita Sharma, visited me the next day, and I was able to return her Ganesh pin. She listened, stunned, as I described how the elephant god had sprung forth to confront and ultimately stomp the shifter, sparing shadow Vega and allowing me to focus on Eldred. When she replaced the pin on the shoulder of her sari, I believe she did so with newfound reverence for the heirloom.

Several friends visited, including Mae and Bree-yark— though separately, I noticed. Tony, back from his cousins' now that the apartment was deemed safe, popped in and out of my room throughout the week. He'd discovered *Mad Libs*, the choose-a-noun, choose-a-color game, and we laughed through an entire book together.

"Can this count toward my summer reading?" he asked.

"You'll have to check with your mom, but I'm thinking probably not?"

Undeterred, he flipped the page and we started on the next one.

Claudius showed up too. By his surprised reaction, I suspected he'd meant to transport somewhere else, but he played it off well. He fished a couple Werther's Originals from a pocket, and we enjoyed them together, him sucking and slurping contentedly, before he had to leave for wherever he'd intended to go.

"Oh!" he said, popping his head from the closing portal. "I'm supposed to tell you someone from the Order is coming tomorrow..."

I finally wrote my review for Gowdie's. Giving the antique store four stars took an inordinate amount of willpower, and praising it, modestly or not, more still. But a deal was a deal, especially with swamp hags. In the end, I described their store as "enchanting" and the sisters as "colorful," but I made sure to mention their aversion to haggling. The city didn't need any more Doug the Shrubs.

I happened to be alone in the apartment the following day when a knock sounded on the door. Remembering Claudius's parting message, I expected Gretchen. I was surprised to find one of the most powerful magic-users in the world standing on my threshold instead. She was dressed in slacks and a fern-green blouse, her long white hair braided neatly.

"Arianna," I stammered.

"Hello, Everson," she said in her strong, maternal voice.

She had been very close with my mother. In fact, she was the one who had delivered me in the Refuge. We hugged, and I showed her into the apartment.

"How are you feeling?" she asked.

"Still tired, but improving every day."

"Well, let's see what we can do about that."

With a few softly spoken words, she sent an invigorating charge through me. When the sensation settled, I felt like I'd just awakened from a power nap. My nerves hummed, rested and alert.

"Thanks," I said, testing my legs. "Hey, would you mind taking a walk? I know you just got here, but I've been cooped up inside all week."

Tabitha stirred enough on the divan to murmur, "You haven't suffered alone."

Arianna smiled. "Say no more. I know the feeling," she added, perhaps referring to her time in the Harkless Rift.

We descended to the street and strolled through the West Village. It had rained earlier, and the air over the damp sidewalks smelled fresh. My legs bounced in a way they hadn't in many days. Though Arianna said nothing, I suspected she'd restored at least part of the year of youth I'd bargained off to the hag sisters.

"You must be wondering why I never came," she said.

"It did cross my mind," I admitted.

"Our work in the interplanar realms has been eye-opening, Everson. At first, we believed the damage Chaos inflicted to have been limited, and that's where we've focused our efforts. But the interplanar layers aren't static. They're always in flux. And with each shift, more breaches are exposed. Some resulted from that seminal event, but others are much older. Tens or even hundreds of thousands of years, in some cases. They explain why certain events occur cyclically. Some breaches we can close and others, we've learned, we cannot. We're updating our maps to note the cycles. What this all means is that in addition to our work on the tears, we must remain in constant motion ourselves, shifting senior members to the episodic breaches we can't close to repel anything coming through."

"Are you saying you won't be able to help down here?" I asked in concern. I always felt like a kid in Arianna's presence, which wasn't so strange when you considered she had a few centuries on me.

"We'll help when and where we can. But given the state of things, you should never expect it. Always remember, the same magic that moves through us moves through you." She looked at me meaningfully. "You've proven yourself more than capable, Everson. Just look at the events of last week."

Sure, I'd listened to my magic, but I'd also gotten caught up in the flurry of events and moving pieces. I knew what she was saying, though. The ability was there. It was a matter of continuing to develop it through practice.

"Has this ever happened before?" I asked. "An entity threatening from a shadow present."

"Not like this, no. Though the layer between the actual and the probable is thin, the ability to bridge the two was only developed one time, in one age, and then it was lost. Until the item reappeared."

There was the Hermes Tablet and the Scythe of Cronus, so why was she using the singular?

"I'm not referring to either," Arianna said, picking up the question. "I mean the container. The box was the work of superior magic, craftsmanship, and intense worship, while the Hermes Tablet, as well as the Scythe of Cronus, were manifestations of the realms being worshipped—gifts from the gods, as it were. Do you remember what I told you about your mother's emo ball after it was destroyed?"

I pulled the glass orb from my pocket. The glowing mist inside shifted, filling me with her love.

"This is an object, but because my mother created it in a thought realm, it still exists there as pure Form. If it were to break again, another could be created from that Form." The emo ball dimmed slightly as I understood what Arianna was telling me. "The same's true of the Scythe of Cronus?"

"And the Hermes Tablet," she confirmed. "They're objects—powerful objects—but they came from Forms that still exist in their original realms."

Which meant the Scythe of Cronus could reappear. I remembered the giant shadow that had appeared opposite me the moment before the scythe's destruction. In that moment, I'd felt its prodigious hunger and hatred for humans.

My hand trembled as I replaced the emo ball in my pocket.

"The Hermes Tablet came into being at the height of Attican worship for the god," she explained. "When the Atticans became persecuted, they sealed the Tablet inside the box and hid it in the shadow realm, planning to recover it when the danger passed. But they were executed. Robbers found it some centuries later. Aggressive attempts to open the box led to death, and it was especially reactive to magical presences." As she said this, I recalled my battle with the guardians in the landfill and at Track 61. "The box was lost and found and bought and sold many times," she continued, "finally ending up in a private collection in the shadow version of this city, where it called to Sven. I see this all from what you've reported as well as from the residue that still clings to you."

"Does the Scythe of Cronus have a similar story?" I asked.

"No. It simply manifested."

"How?"

"It's hard to say without the object, which you were right to destroy, but we believe Cronus has an ally, another god probably.

This god not only forged the scythe from its original Form, but also the shifter guardian, whose preferred shapes were the monstrous children of Typhon and Echidna."

"We may be dealing with a potion-maker too," I said, thinking of the bonding and debilitation potions Eldred had used.

"The Order is assigning you this case, Everson. Your best resource may be the Hermes Tablet. Its essence is determined to prevent Cronus's return. But don't compel it to speak, and certainly don't attempt to force the lid. What's inside can no longer be looked upon with mortal eyes. Let it talk to you, when and where it chooses. Remember, you're dealing with a god essence, and they're often capricious. Few more than Hermes."

I'd been surprised the Order hadn't taken the box, as they'd done with other powerful objects in the past, but they had their reasons. I thought about the Tablet's attachment to Sven. Though it had relaxed its hold following the destruction of the scythe, I was still concerned for the young man.

"Is it safe with Sven and he with it?"

"It's chosen him," she said. "This we mustn't question. And through him, it's also chosen you. While the Tablet is in his possession, I expect you to guide and watch over him."

It sounded as if I'd be getting a student in Sven after all, which was fine. He'd grown on me.

"I did some reading this past week," I said. "With the decline of Greek civilization and the rise of Rome, the god Hermes became Mercury, of course. But what I hadn't known was that with the later rise of Catholicism, Mercury was briefly identified with Saint Michael, the line from which my magic comes."

Arianna nodded sagely. "The protective symbols on the box repelled you, as they were designed to, but the tablet inside sensed a kindred spirit, perhaps because both of your parents had strong lines to the First Saint Michael."

"You don't think this is over," I said more than asked.

"The forces of Cronus have been thwarted, but whatever is to come straddles the shadow realm. I can't see clearly enough to say one way or the other."

With the future uncertain, the Doideag's prophecy suddenly felt heavy in my mind.

"A soothsayer predicted a lot of what happened," I said. "But she also said that if war came, I should, quote, 'allies gather eleven and one, and be not afraid of thine own blood.' Any idea what that means?"

"Did your magic lead you to this *soothsayer?*" she asked, knowing full well I was referring to a hideous Doideag.

"I think so."

"Then I would first note the 'if' in her prophecy. This suggests it may never come to pass. And if it does, you have a solution in the subsequent words, one that will become evident when the time arrives."

"She also said 'come night's fall, accept your death.'"

As I spoke the line, it felt especially dire. I thought of my wife and Tony and our future daughter.

Arianna stopped and placed her vein-lined hands on my shoulders.

"Everson, even in your gravest hour, your magic will never mislead you."

Her eyes glimmered with something. Hope? Sadness? But I nodded. They were the words I needed to hear.

"I'll remember that."

40

The mayor's Concert on the South Lawn went forward that weekend, and Bree-yark drove Ricki, Tony, and me to Central Park. It was a sunny Saturday in mid-June, not too hot, with a pleasant breeze blowing through the trees. Several thousand people turned out, most of them concentrated around the new bandshell, where a rock group was jamming.

We chose a place on the far edge of the lawn to spare Bree-yark's sensitive ears. Tony spotted a kids' soccer game and ran over to join in. As Ricki and I spread out a blanket, it seemed impossible we'd battled a goblin brigade here just a couple years earlier and barely escaped a napalm drop.

"Oh, look," she said. "It's Mae."

Bree-yark started and followed her pointed finger. Sure enough, Mae Johnson was crossing the lawn toward us with her pet carrier in one hand and a large wicker basket in the other.

"You ambushed me," Bree-yark said.

"It's just a picnic, no pressure." I clapped his back. "Why don't you go give her a hand?"

His eyes brightened in alarm, but the squalling of a guitar solo replaced the panic with ear-flattening irritation. Grumbling that he should have known what we were up to, he hustled over to meet her.

"Think he'll forgive us?" Ricki asked.

"Depends on how many times he passes out."

She peered past me. "Well, would you look at that?" she said with a strange smile. "It's my partner."

When I turned to find Hoffman ambling over, I knew I'd been ambushed. He appeared considerably better than the last time I'd seen him. In fact, he had an almost calm look about him, thanks in part to his attire. He was wearing a fishing T-shirt, baggy cargo shorts, and a flipflop opposite his ortho boot.

"Hey, guys." He nodded at Ricki before fixing his gaze on me. The bags under his eyes had retreated back into his face, leaving only faint smudges. "I realized I, um, never thanked you for your help on the case."

My wife had apparently realized that too. She stood to one side with her arms crossed, watching to ensure her detective partner did the deed properly. Hoffman glanced over as he extended his hand. When I accepted his shake, his emotions seemed to take over. He pulled me into an awkward hug.

"I'm not good at these things, Croft," he whispered harshly. "But you did save my ass."

"It was a bit of a winding road," I managed inside his strong embrace, "but we got there eventually."

He chortled and jerked me hard against him. "I owe you, buddy."

Something told me he'd forget the promise the next time we butted heads, but I'd take it for now. I patted his broad back.

"Hey, I want you to meet my family," he said as we separated.

A middle-aged woman with dark hair and two boys had hung back, and he waved them forward now. The boys looked about ten and eight, their thick builds and curly brown hair marking them as Hoffman's brood.

"This is my wife, Kay," he said of the surprisingly pretty woman. "And my boys, Joey and Anthony."

"A pleasure to meet you," Kay said in a strong New York accent as she handed me a gift-wrapped bottle.

The boys took my hand shyly, the older one tucking a football under his opposite arm. When Hoffman chuckled and ruffled his hair, I could see how proud he was to be a father. I also understood the fear I'd seen on his face when he'd pulled me aside in Bear's apartment. He'd needed to keep his job not only for his sake, but theirs. I was especially pleased now that I'd been able to help.

"Why don't you guys join us?" I said, looking over at where Bree-yark was meeting Mae and taking her large basket. "There's plenty of food."

"Aw, we'd love to," Hoffman said, "but we've got a party to get to at her parents' place."

"It's their fiftieth wedding anniversary," Kay explained, taking her husband's hand.

"And I'm in charge of the grill," he added importantly.

"Well, wish them a happy anniversary for us," I said, Ricki echoing the sentiment.

When the Hoffmans were out of earshot, I said, "Thanks for looking out for me."

"What do you mean?" She nudged me. "That came straight from Hoffman's heart."

"Sure it did."

I unwrapped the gift and snorted. It was a bottle of *Discovery Select*. Hoffman grinned over a shoulder and shot me a finger pistol. I wasn't going to touch the scotch, but I'd find a spot for the bottle in my library. Something to remember our case by. I watched him and his family disappear beyond the crowd.

"They actually look like a functioning unit," I remarked.

"Thanks to Kay," she said. "Hoff lucked out with her big time."

"Speaking of families..." I turned to her. "I've had a lot of time to think this past week. Even though the box disappearing from the loft ended up being a false alarm, I talked to the building's owner yesterday. Turns out there's a basement efficiency he's taken a couple stabs at fixing up, but at this point he's willing to sell. I could use it for casting and storing anything that seems even borderline iffy. Who knows, it might even help with my phobia," I added.

She smiled. "Whatever you decide is best, I'll support."

Given the concern she'd shown, I'd expected her to be staunchly in favor of the move. "Really?"

"I may not always understand Everson, the magic-user..." She rose onto her tiptoes to kiss me. "But I trust Everson, the man."

"Then I'll talk with the owner again Monday, see how low I can get him. We're going to have a little girl who'll be able to shoot up and down that ladder before we know it. Best if we have something set up well in advance."

"See?" she said, telling me I'd given the right answer.

Bree-yark returned with Mae's basket. He still looked distraught, but Mae was chatting away, and by the time the food had been passed around and we were all settled on our blankets, he looked semi-relaxed. Until we heard a familiar voice...

"Yoo-hoo!"

You're kidding me, I thought with a groan.

I looked over to see Gretchen prancing toward us, this time in blue capri pants and a striped shirt. She'd pinned an actual sailor's hat atop her tied-back hair, and an airy red scarf fluttered around her neck.

"What are the odds of running into you here?" she panted happily as she arrived. "Well, Enzo and I are finally off on our travels. In fact, we're on our way to the pier now." She nodded at her boyfriend, who was standing in another suit and broad-rimmed fedora, his arms loaded with suitcases.

"Our boat leaves in thirty minutes."

"And your route just happened to take you through Central Park?" I asked dryly.

"Unless of course someone thinks I shouldn't go," she continued, ignoring me. "In fact, *now* would be the time to tell me."

She looked pointedly at Bree-yark, who was glancing between her and Enzo. But like me, he seemed to be noticing something off about Gretchen's boyfriend. Standing in full sun, his proportions didn't seem quite right. And why was she always keeping him at a distance?

When the wind picked up, I angled my cane and released a force invocation just strong enough to send the fedora toppling from his head. A monstrous face with a jutting jaw appeared, causing Gretchen to turn with a start. She snapped her fingers, restoring the hat to his head, but Bree-yark had already seen enough.

"Enzo's a ... shaved bugbear?" he asked.

"Why, of course not!" Gretchen replied with a nervous laugh. "Where did you ever get that silly notion? He's an amazing, adventurous man, who—"

I displaced his hat a second time, causing the bugbear to go lumbering after it. Suitcases trailed behind him, many of them coming open. All were empty.

With a cry of frustration, Gretchen replaced the hat again and strengthened the enchantment she'd been using to control the fae creature. He stopped and knelt, recovering the luggage like a proper gentleman. But it was too late. Bree-yark was snorting laughter, and I was doing my best not to join him.

Gretchen wheeled on us, eyes wide. I feared the worst, but

more mortified than outraged, she snapped her fingers and, in twin flashes, disappeared along with her bugbear prop. She didn't even bother with the luggage.

"I suspect that will be the end of that," I said.

"I don't know what just happened," Mae remarked, wiping her hands off and turning to Bree-yark, "but one thing's become clear. Either you're not ready to make an honest woman of me, or you're too scared to ask. So I'm going to make this as easy as possible. *Yes.* Now all you have to do is supply the question."

Bree-yark looked over at me, eyes bright with panic.

I nodded fervently and made a bandage-ripping gesture across my arm.

He turned back to her. "Will you m-marry me?" he stammered.

Laughing, she shook his ear and kissed his cheek. "I just told you."

Bree-yark released a surprised chortle, the brightness in his eyes softening to a diffuse in-love-ness. Standing, he bowed low before Mae, then helped her to her feet, in full control of himself once more.

"If you'll excuse us," he said, "my fiancée and I are going to take a walk. We have a future to discuss."

"Congratulations, you two," Ricki called.

"I think he'll forgive us," I decided, as he escorted her away.

Ricki was agreeing when my phone vibrated. It was a text from Trevor of the Sup Squad.

> I know we're done with the Sven business but I got a message from the tech who was working on his facial recognition match. Nothing came up, but he got a few close hits based on morphology. Thought I'd send one along. Congrats on cracking the triple homicide. Hope to work with you again soon.

An image was uploading, but it was going to take a few minutes on my primitive device.

There hadn't been any matches because Sven had never existed here, something I'd yet to explain to Trevor. I was snapping the phone closed when a prickling rush of magic told me someone was watching. Off to the right, I spotted a shadowy figure hanging out near the edge of the trees.

"Well, speak of the devil."

"Is that Sven?" Ricki asked.

"Yeah, I left him a message at our spot telling him we'd be here." I waved him over, but he shook his head and waved for me to come to him instead.

"He's not still afraid of me, is he?" she asked.

I'd finally told Ricki about encountering her shadow, how she'd tried to apprehend me for the murders and discharged her weapon at Sven. She'd only asked a couple questions before dropping it. She said she needed to get used to the idea of a living, breathing version of herself existing elsewhere. I didn't mention her shadow's marital status. Probably because I would *never* get used to that.

"No, I think this is something else," I said. "Will you be all right for a couple minutes?"

"I will if you drag Mae's basket over here." She patted her belly. "We're ready for seconds."

I did as she asked, kissed her, and was about to join Sven when I remembered something I'd been meaning to ask.

"Oh, hey, what did Larry and his wife get us for our wedding?"

"The private box for the Mets game on Memorial Day," she said. "Why?"

I snapped my fingers. Damn. "Because I told him we'd used their gift 'a few times.'"

Ricki shook her head as I left and jogged over to where Sven was waiting. Despite the warm weather, he was wearing gray jeans and a long-sleeve hoodie shirt, the straps of his pack hugging his narrow shoulders.

"Hey, buddy," I said as I arrived in front of him. "I was wondering when I'd see you again. Why don't you join us?"

"Nah, I'm good." But he was blinking his dark eyes nervously. "I promised I'd tell you my real name when this was over."

"Okay."

"It's Alec DeFazio, and I'm actually fifteen."

"I guessed the fifteen part, but it's good to meet you, Alec DeFazio."

I shook his hand, then hesitated. DeFazio. I knew that name.

In a flash, I was back at Gowdie's Antique Store, the hag sisters circling me as they rattled off my failed relationships. Jennifer DeFazio had been one of them, a girl I'd dated in college before she decided I wasn't attentive enough.

My flip phone hummed, alerting me that the image of the close match had finished uploading. I opened it to find my faculty photo staring back at me.

I raised my stunned eyes to Alec.

"I'm your son," he said.

SHADOW DEEP
PROF CROFT BOOK 10

Discovering the shadow realm was only the beginning.

I've taken on my first ever apprentice. A mage of my bloodline, Alec is as headstrong as he is powerful, his magic bolstered by a shifty trickster god.

If that weren't enough, I've been recruited into an NYPD task force on missing persons. Cases in the city are exploding, a little girl among the most recently disappeared. As a soon-to-be father, this one cuts close to the heart.

But just as I uncover a bizarre lead, I'm yanked back to the shadow realm—a darker, more dangerous New York—where a nefarious entity has targeted Alec in order to get to me. Hunted and on the run, our one ally may be Detective Vega. Only she's not my wife there, and I'm on her department's shoot-to-kill list.

As disappearances in my city climb and dangers in the shadow realm deepen, I'm a wizard caught between realities.

And I'm getting desperate...

AVAILABLE NOW!

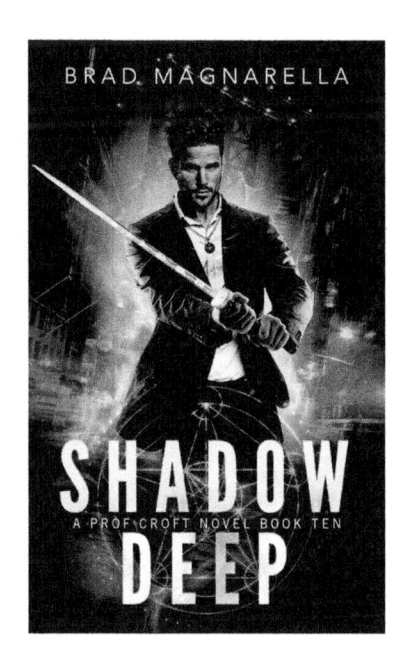

Shadow Deep
(Prof Croft, Book 10)

AUTHOR'S NOTES

If you saw that final moment coming, I salute you, because I didn't. At least not when I first sat down to *Shadow Duel*. At some point during their graduate assistantship meeting, I heard Sven make the surprising declaration to Croft, and I knew I'd just written the ending.

Yet further proof that characters live much more interesting lives than their authors.

My research for this installment was mostly internet-based. That usually includes a perusal of the spell list on Roll20, various mythology sites, as well as interesting New York City locations. This time, I focused on the Explorers Club, an actual institution on East 70th Street, which is much as it's described in the book (minus the shadow doorman and bonding potions, of course), and Track 61, where Sven hides out.

Fun fact: Track 61 was famously used by Franklin Delano Roosevelt in 1944, when he gave an address at the Waldorf Astoria. Contrary to a popular myth, the car where Croft finds Sven is not FDR's car, but lowly Baggage Car 002, which transported crane rigging throughout Grand Central before being abandoned. It housed a ghoul family for a short time before becoming Sven's hideout.

As I write this, I have several ideas for the subsequent books—which may or may not survive first contact with the characters. See above. Though I can't help but think Croft will encounter shadow Vega again. There's a story there, and with our Vega on light duty, now seems a good time to explore it.

I have several people to thank for their help in bringing *Shadow Duel* into the world.

Thank you to the team at Damonza.com for designing another stellar cover. Kudos to my beta and advanced readers, including Beverly Collie, Mark Denman, Linda Ash, Erin Halbmaier, Susie Johnson, and Bob Singer, who provided valuable feedback during the writing process. And thanks to Sharlene Magnarella and Donna Rich for taking on the painstaking task of final proofing. Naturally, any errors that remain are this author's alone.

I also want to give a shout out to James Patrick Cronin, who brings all the books in the Croftverse to life through his gifted narration on the audio editions. Those books, including samples, can be found at Audible.com.

Prof Croft 9 was written in Guanajuato, Mexico. Thanks to the owners and staff at my preferred work spots for tolerating this laptop-toting gringo and serving up excellent coffee: Café Tal, Vivo Café, and Cueva Café.

And none of this would be possible without the Strange Brigade, my dedicated fan group whose enthusiasm serves as motivation jet fuel, book after book.

Last but not least, thank you, fearless reader, for taking another ride with the Prof.

Till the next one...

Best Wishes,

Brad Magnarella

P.S. Be sure to check out my website to learn more about the Croftverse, download a pair of free prequels, and find out what's coming! That's all at bradmagnarella.com

CROFTVERSE CATALOGUE

PROF CROFT PREQUELS
Book of Souls

Siren Call

MAIN SERIES
Demon Moon

Blood Deal

Purge City

Death Mage

Black Luck

Power Game

Druid Bond

Night Rune

Shadow Duel

Shadow Deep

Godly Wars

Angel Doom

SPIN-OFFS
Croft & Tabby

Croft & Wesson

BLUE WOLF
Blue Curse

Blue Shadow

Blue Howl

Blue Venom

Blue Blood

Blue Storm

SPIN-OFF

Legion Files

For the entire chronology go to bradmagnarella.com

ABOUT THE AUTHOR

Brad Magnarella writes urban fantasy for the same reason most read it...

To explore worlds where magic crackles from fingertips, vampires and shifters walk city streets, cats talk (some excessively), and good prevails against all odds. It's shamelessly fun.

His two main series, Prof Croft and Blue Wolf, make up the growing Croftverse, with over a quarter-million books sold to date and an Independent Audiobook Award nomination.

Hopelessly nomadic, Brad can be found in a rented room overseas or hiking America's backcountry.

Or just go to www.bradmagnarella.com

Printed in Great Britain
by Amazon